IRREPLACEABLE

A NOVEL BY

CHARLES PINNING

DAUBENTON PRESS

PARIS

Daubenton Edition Populaire
Daubenton Press
1 Rue Mirage
75005 Paris, France

All inquiries and correspondence please contact:
info@daubentonpress.com

Cover design: Félicité Lartigue

Edition Populaire and colophon are registered trademarks of Daubenton Press

First Daubenton Edition Populaire [trade paperback edition] 2013

ISBN-13: 978-0615853949
ISBN-10: 0615853943

TO

MARY PONTE PINNING AND JOHN H. PINNING

MY MOTHER AND FATHER

CONTENTS

PART ONE

Irreplaceable

"Where is my family?"

Marzipan Renaud, *The Innocents*

PART ONE

PROLOGUE

◆

A mother's advice to her son.

IN HER LAST DAYS, I TOLD MY MOTHER HOW
SORRY I was that I'd never given her the grandchild I knew
she'd always longed for.

"Don't worry about that," she said, her voice calm but so
final. "Things have a way of working out—just not the way
we think they will."

"I haven't disappointed you?"

The hand that first held mine took it once more.

"How could you? You've had your writing...your
photography. You have made me so proud."

"But my personal life, Mama. It's been such a shambles."

"Don't say that. Everybody's personal life has problems."

"But Mama, Lila dying. I'm not sure I've ever recovered.
Geoffrey Hayes says that ever after I've been a 'wreckuva
guy.'"

"Geoffrey Hayes is a drunk. He's the wreck."

"What about my wives? What the hell was I thinking
about?"

"Saving them. You've always married strays. The last one I
didn't understand. She just never wanted to sit down and
have a cup of tea with me. Well, she was a teenager."

"She wasn't a teenager, Mama."

"Well, she wasn't a woman either."

"She was too young, I'll admit that. It was my fault. I should've just dated her. I didn't have to marry her."

"She trapped you. Men are sitting ducks when a woman wants them."

"You just said she wasn't a woman."

"Hey, don't pick on me! I'm an old lady. Whatever happened to that movie star you liked?"

"Aleda Collie? Nothing happened to her. She's a movie star, that's what happened to her."

"You two used to like each other, didn't you? I liked her in that TV show, what was it, she was a detective."

"*The Dish and the Spoon.*"

"That was it. I think you should look her up. She would be good for you. Listen to your old mother."

"I'll think about it, Mama."

"Don't think about it. Do it!"

A few days later my mother quietly slipped away, and in the weeks that followed, in the sifting down of memories, the shifting feelings, I pondered our last conversations including her desire that I get in touch with Aleda. It was an idea I'd toyed with over the years, but each time I came to the same conclusion: it wouldn't work.

First there was the geographic impossibility. Aleda lived on the other side of the continent. Second, and most importantly, she was out of my league. I didn't have enough money to play with her.

"Nice fantasy, Mama. But even dead, you can see this bird won't fly."

That was a bad thing to say. The truth was, I didn't have concrete feelings about death.

I poured myself a glass of wine and stood still in my quiet house. I closed my eyes and made the sad admission to myself: "I am alone."

Then the phone rang.

It was Aleda Collie.

CHAPTER 1

♦

Mrs. Gardner's Party. Swanson and Aleda reunite. RISD
Museum robbed.

A VENETIAN PALAZZO LIT ENTIRELY BY
CANDLELIGHT. Candelabra in every room, candlelight
reaching up four stories. An open courtyard in the center
filled with trees and flowers and fountains and birds singing.

From the second floor Tapestry Room surge the fresh and
reckless tonalities of Debussy, performed by fifty members of
the Boston Philharmonic.

A birdcage elevator whirls down from the private residence
on the fourth floor. Fires blaze in hooded fireplaces big
enough to walk into. Galleries, cloisters, halls, passageways,
swarming with guests in evening clothes; shimmery gowns,
black tie, white tie, cutaways and everywhere paintings,
sculpture, antiquities, rare books—Art.

In a room with walls covered in red brocade hangs one of
the world's most famous paintings: Titian's *Rape of Europa*.
Jupiter, disguised as a white bull carries off the Phoenician
princess, Europa, against a bruised and bloody sky, while
onlookers from the shore and angels with arrows are helpless
to intervene.

A man excitedly flips wooden panels hung like shutters.
Attached to the panels are framed drawings and paintings.

"She hasn't just collected old masters. Look here: Degas! A bunch of them!"

"And there's a Manet downstairs, a man wearing a top hat," says an exceptionally handsome woman, auburn hair swept back. She is, in fact, the very woman whose presence has brought me here tonight and my eyes brim up.

"Yes, yes," responds the man, "and a Matisse downstairs, too. But, by God I love Degas! The man has a way with the horse. I ride the hunt, myself."

"I find the horseman quite attractive," she says. "The coat, the breeches, the boots...the crop. Are you familiar with the work of Doctor Freud?"

Falling snow can be seen through the windows.

In the second floor Dutch Room, the walls covered in green brocade, Isabella Stewart Gardner herself and Bernard Berenson, her art broker, stand in front of Rembrandt's only seascape, the imposing five foot high *Storm on the Sea of Galilee*. Crammed together in a tempest-tossed boat, Jesus tries to calm his terrified disciples.

Gardner glimmers in a violet dress that displays to maximum effect her shapely figure, the fine modeling of her shoulders and back. Two enormous diamonds sparkle in her hair.

"Where would I be without you, Bernard? You who found these two friends for me," and she gestures to Rembrandt's *Storm* and its neighbor, another Rembrandt, *A Lady and Gentleman in Black*.

Berenson puffs contentedly on his cigar, his face a dainty valentine decorated with a luxuriant mustache and pointed beard. He coughs, a small cough.

"But remember Bernard, it was I who found the Vermeer,"

and Gardner's gaze crosses the room to a smaller, but no less valuable painting of a young woman playing a clavichord. *The Concert* has all of Vermeer's characteristic precision, slanting light and shadows.

Berenson releases a cloud of smoke. "I wonder where all of this will be in a hundred years?" he muses.

"It will be as we see it tonight," bristles Gardner. "When I die, this will become a museum to enchant the public. I have stipulated that nothing will be added nor subtracted. Not even moved."

An ancient Chinese "Big Nipple" gong sounds and the palace falls silent, all two hundred guests freezing in mid-gesture, mid-conversation as Gardner makes her final pronouncement:

"Nothing here will ever change!"

"CUT! Print it! That's a take."

Lights bang up illuminating the cavernous drill hall of the Cranston Street Armory, as January 1915 comes to a halt, replaced by October 2010. Actors swarm off the set, a gigantic doll house-like cutaway of Fenway Court, today known as the Isabella Stewart Gardner Museum, and crew scurry through the rooms dousing the candles, packing away the food and beverages.

Aleda is talking to the director and I step back to stay clear of the commotion, but where I can still keep an eye on her.

I have to smile. "Here I am," I murmur, finishing the thought silently: waiting for Aleda again, thirty-four years later.

Running a hand through my hair, pinching my upper lip I can vaguely smell the Alberto VO5. At fifty-three, my greying hair is dryer and needed something. I decided my height needed something too. Even though I wear orthotics, boosting my five-nine to almost five-ten, I'd snipped the heels off a pair of extra running shoe inserts and stuck those into the shoes too, for an extra quarter-inch. My recollection is that, in bare feet, Aleda and I are the same height.

A pair of blue-grey corduroys, an ancient black and white herringbone Harris Tweed sports coat, the lining ripped up, but nobody can see that...hand knitted grey and black scarf...Looking good. Distinguished, I hope. Yet jaunty.

She's nodding her head, smiling, breaks off...she's coming toward me now, removing an elaborate peacock feather hairpin, shaking loose her famous hair. I remember when she gave me a smoldering look from my portable black and white TV and told me she used L'Oreal Preference hair coloring *"Because, I'm worth it."*

Our eyes meet, the pace quickens, we are moving toward each other....

"Swanson," she purrs, as though it's she who's been waiting for me her entire life. Southern gals know how to make a guy feel like he's the only guy in the world. It's a femininity this Yankee boy has come to increasingly appreciate. Northern ladies are often too dry and sharp-edged for my taste.

"Aleda." Her name floats out of my mouth like an iridescent bubble and we embrace.

"How did it look?" she asks excitedly.

"Almost as beautiful as you."

"You're a dangerous man, Swanson."

God that smile. She turns it on like a light. Same smile right off the cover of a 1976 *Glamour* magazine.

"It was a dream, Aleda. A sumptuous evening hosted by

Isabella Stewart Gardner in 1915. And your scene with that
guy in front of the Degas—is it Degas or Degases? Funny,
funny, funny."

"The humor played? I wanted to toss in a little funny/sexy.
I think funny and sexy are important. Don't you?" That
smile again, relaxing down into a mischievous grin. Aleda
was always best at playing herself.

"Oh, yes. The riding crop...Dr. Freud. Absolutely."

"Great! Hey—let's get out of here!" She grabs me by the
hand. "I need fresh air! I need to walk! I need food! Most of
all, I need to learn about *You!*"

In a private dressing room she sheds her rose-colored
Edwardian dress, the diamond necklace, the shoes, and pulls
on a pair of blue jeans a sweater and brand new pair of green
and white Adidas.

"Where can we get oysters?"

"There's Hemenway's—"

She whips out her iPhone...."Philip, a table for two at
Hemingway's in....?"

"It's Hemenway's. About ten minutes."

Waiting outside is an enormous, gold Cadillac Escalade
commandeered by a burly Teamster with a flowing salt and
pepper beard and long hair pulled back into a single braid.
He holds the door for us and we climb in. He's wearing a
black satin baseball jacket with the name of the film, *Belle*,
embroidered in white across the back.

"Look at you," says Aleda. "You look fantastic! Must be
from all the...*exercise* you do and healthy eating. Dan said
you run ten miles a day."

"Not quite. But I get around."

"Will you teach me how to run?"

"If you teach me how to smile."

"You have a beautiful smile."

"But I can only do it when I'm genuinely happy."

"How sweet of you to say that. I think you should keep it that way."

With every moment the years are falling away. She's a little heavier, but the smoothness of the skin is still there, the luster of the hair. A few wrinkles around the eyes, near the mouth. No evidence of the knife or Botox freeze-face. Physically, she looks just terrific for fifty-three, and she has the same exuberant nature.

She claps her hands together, excited like a little girl. "Here we are, together again. How long has it been Swanson?"

"Not that long. About thirty years."

"That's impossible!"

"OK. Thirty-four?"

"Swanson!"

"Yeah. Sometimes life sure does feel quick, doesn't it? I remember when you told me back then that you thought a movie about Isabella Stewart Gardner would be amazing. Now, here you are, making it. *That's* amazing."

"I've never produced a movie before, Swanson. But I think it's gonna work out. I'm glad I just have a small part. Beep Gamble is a great director. Georgette Fanning's fabulous, don't you think?"

"She's Gardner. And the guy playing Berenson. Very sly."

"Marcus Drowne. Very British. But they can do anything."

Downtown at the College Street Bridge we hit a red light.

"Oh, look at this river, Swanson. It looks like a mini-Seine."

"The Providence River."

"Is this where they do that fire-in-the-water thing? I read

about it. I want to go."

"WaterFire. They stack wood in those metal baskets down the middle of the river, and light them at sunset. We'll come one night. They play haunting chant music. Opera. Soulful, contemplative pieces. The burning wood smells wonderful. They give gondola rides."

"I saw a picture of that in a magazine. Providence is very pretty, Swanson. I can see why you live here."

"So, why are you shooting here—if everything Gardner is in Boston?"

"Tax Credits. Rhode Island is giving us major tax credits. And Providence has all the right period architecture. We'll be doing a few exterior shots in Boston. Everything is *much* less expensive here than in Boston The European filming— Paris and Venice locations—has already been wrapped up."

"This movie must have a hefty budget."

"Hefty. That's a good word for it, Swanson."

At Hemenway's we order a dry Graves and a dozen local Watch Hill oysters on the half shell. Then another dozen.

"When you grow up land-locked, you can eat fresh seafood all day long," says Aleda.

"Growing up near the ocean, I took seafood for granted."

Aleda looks out the window. "I grew up on a river. Being near a river makes me feel at home. The ocean is open and honest, but rivers are mysterious." After a pause. "Dan told me about your girlfriend who died. I'm sorry. How long were you together?"

"Seven years. Lila died of a brain tumor at thirty-seven. We were both thirty-seven."

"It must have been hard on you."

"It does cut both ways. I did my best. I just wish I'd done better."

"You were young."

"We were young."

From our table we look out across the river to the center of old downtown, a view of buildings rich with rococo flourishes and decorative ironwork dating from the 1800's and the early part of the twentieth century, the glory days of America's downtowns.

"A lot of those are being converted into lofts," I tell her.

"The empty-nesters are getting bored with the burbs," says Aleda. "And kids today aren't havin' children. They have dogs. Or children and dogs. They must have dogs."

"Very good."

"Hey—I read newspapers. And I have family too, in Georgia, goin' through stuff. But I learned a long time ago, you can't be good-lookin' *and* smart."

"Couldn't they make an exception in your case?"

Aleda reaches across the table and puts her hand on mine. In her face I see a gratitude that surprises me—and months of grueling work.

"So—what do I need to see that's special?" she asks quietly.

"Well, there's a Degas show, but at this point I'm sure you're Degad to death."

"They're just copies. I love Degas! I've been in the house where he was born, in Paris!"

"How long will you be in Providence?"

"Until December twenty-third. But let's not talk about that...."

Leaving the restaurant Aleda cries out, "Oh, look!"

A transit bus whooshes by with a big advertisement

plastered along its side: *Six Friends at Dieppe—Degas at the RISD Museum.*

"Providence: You think it, and there it is!" I proclaim with a sweeping gesture.

"What's R-I-S-D?"

"Rhode Island School of Design."

"I should know that. We have an art authority from there working on the film."

"And the R-I-S-D is pronounced Riz-dee. Everyone around here just refers to the school as Riz-dee."

"I need to stretch my legs, Swanson."

I walk her one block up the hill to the undulating brick and slate sidewalks of Benefit Street. We scuff through crinkly leaves, past charming clapboard colonials with dainty little windowpanes dating back to the early 1700's and magnificent mansions of later periods, including the imposing brick John Brown House surrounded by towering elms.

"Tell me what you're working on now, Swanson."

"Basically, struggling along on a novel about two gay football players—"

"Dan told me about that." A few steps later: "And a girlfriend?"

"No. What about you? Any boyfriend?" Dan's told me she has a fairly serious boyfriend, a real 'man-among-men' type with a ranch and all.

Aleda ignores my question and focuses her attention across the street.

"What's that?" she asks pointedly.

The grey granite building looks like a large mausoleum. Set atop an ivy-covered slope it looms above the sidewalk.

"The Providence Athenaeum."

"Is there anything special I should know about it?"

"It's a library. Edgar Allen Poe used to meet his beloved, Sarah Whitman there—before she dumped him."

"She dumped him?"

"She was society. He was a writer. He drank too much for her. Doubtless made the occasional 'crude' remark. Her friends didn't like him. He never had much money."

"Let's cross," says Aleda.

In front of the Athenaeum is a granite wall-fountain, a stream of water splashing down into a stone basin. Carved above it is the inscription: *Come hither every one that thirsteth.*

Aleda sticks out her hand, catches some of the flowing water and brings it to her mouth. Then I do the same.

"What do you thirsteth for, Swanson?"

"Wisdom, I suppose. Some kind of wisdom."

"That's too big."

"What do you thirsteth for?"

"Getting this film done."

In the next block I swing my arms around. "This is all RISD."

"Beautiful buildings," sighs Aleda. "Nothing like New England for that classic look, in brick."

"And that grassy knoll over there with the kids lolling is called RISD Beach. How do your legs feel?"

"It's wonderful to be walking after sitting in airplanes and cars."

"There's a terrific view of Providence from Prospect Park, a couple blocks up."

"Let's go!"

We cross over the intersection and head up the hill. As soon

as we turn the corner onto Prospect Street, we see police cars
and a news truck.

"Uh-oh...."

The vehicles are in front of Woods-Gerry Gallery, an
adjunct of the RISD Museum. It's a particularly lovely place,
an Italianate stone villa surrounded by old beech trees,
bequeathed to the school years ago and currently housing the
Degas exhibit.

A police car blocks the entrance. Squeezing by, we hurry up
the cobblestone driveway and I spot Susan amidst a throng
on the portico. She notices us and breaks away.

"What's going on?" I ask.

"We've been robbed," she gasps. "We've been fucking
robbed!" She turns to Aleda. "I'm so sorry...I'm just...I was
so looking forward to Swanson bringing you to—" and she
stops, distraught, bringing the back of her hand to her
mouth.

"Hey," says Aleda, and she gives Susan a hug. "Just
breathe....*breathe*...."

Two big breaths later, Abby rolls up on her pink bicycle
with the banana seat.

"Yo, Aunt Susan. Yo, Swanson. S'up?"

Susan pulls away from Aleda and straightens herself. She is
a compact person with square shoulders and straight hips.
With her close-cropped black hair, flecked with grey and
almost non-existent bust, it would be easy to mistake her for
a trim male.

"The gallery's been robbed, honey. Please wait here with
Uncle Swanson and...his friend. God—we have the biggest
show since—and this happens. I can't effing believe it! Could
you please keep an eye on her for a sec? Thanks, Swanson,"

and Susan heads back to the crush.

Abby is shaking a tube of powdered candy into her mouth and examining Aleda.

"Whoa! Lookit that watch." She's staring at Aleda's Rolex. "Are those real diamonds?"

"Yes, they are," says Aleda, holding her wrist out so Abby can admire the diamonds encircling the face.

"Can I try it on?"

"Sure you can," and she slides it around Abby's skinny wrist.

"Where did you get it?"

"Coco Chanel gave it to me," says Aleda.

"What's that?"

Susan is striding back toward us.

"Swanson, I'm gonna be tied up here for awhile. Would you mind watching after Abby? I'm sorry to do this, but—"

"She can come with us," says Aleda. "We were just heading back to my hotel...."

CHAPTER 2

♦

At Hotel Providence. Susan explains theft. Honey butter.
Abby leaves with Aleda's watch

"UNCLE SWANSON?" ASKS ALEDA, raising one eyebrow.

"I can do that, too," and I raise one of my own. "It's an honorary title."

I walk Abby's bicycle down the steep slope of Angell Street toward the river and downtown, while Aleda and Abby walk ahead of me, holding hands.

"Do you have any children of your own?" Abby asks Aleda.

"Nope."

"Why not?"

"I—that's a good question, Abby."

"Maybe you just never met the right person," says Abby. "Where did you say you live again? Sometimes I don't pay attention."

"I don't remember saying where I live. But I live in Los Angeles."

"Oh," says Abby.

"It's in California, sweetheart," I say.

"Oh. Cool. California. Do you have a swimming pool?"

"I do have a pool," says Aleda. "And if y'ever come out to L.A., you can visit me and swim in it."

"OK," Abby accepts brightly, and turns around to smile at

me.

The paneled lobby of the boutique Hotel Providence shimmers with gilt-framed mirrors; enormous cloisonné vases gush flowers. The house dog, Remus, lifts his massive mastiff head and rests it back down with a sonorous snorfle.

While the concierge takes care of Abby's bicycle, Aleda checks at the desk for messages.

"Better Schaefer," she says to the desk clerk, who smiles just enough to show he's in on the conspiracy. Betty Schaefer, the name of a character from Aleda's favorite movie, *Sunset Boulevard*, is the alias she uses when traveling.

She leads us into L'Epicureo, the fancy restaurant on the ground floor. With a wave of his hand, the maître d' gestures to the main dining room.

"Too *dark*," says Aleda. "Let's sit over there," and we follow her into an empty bar that looks out to a charming courtyard fronting busy old Westminster Street and Grace Church with its tall and pointed single spire of dark brown stone.

"Abby!" says Aleda, "What would you like to drink? Are you hungry? Should we get something to eat? I'd like a Ketel One martini," she instructs the waiter.

"Would you like a martini?" I ask Abby.

"Woyt?" Abby has lately taken to pronouncing certain words in funny ways.

"Bring the young lady a Shirley Temple," says Aleda, "and put it in a martini glass would ya?" Scanning the menu, she adds, "And bring us one of the cheese plates and some bread, and—" her face lights up as she looks back and forth from Abby to me—"wait until you taste their honey butter!"

"Honey butter?" says Abby.

"You're gonna love it! It's divine. OK that's all! But leave the menus."

I raise a finger and look up at the waiter.

"Oops," says Aleda, smiling impishly at me and then Abby.

As the drinks arrive, Aleda's phone rings. It's Susan. Aleda insists that she joins us, and arranges to have her picked up.

Susan looks pretty whacked-out and Aleda signals the waiter.

"May we have another chair, please—and this lady is gonna need a drink right away." Susan is breathing hard, pushing off her coat and rearranging her scarf. She's wearing a very pretty maroon beret with a wide green border around it.

"God—I must look like a witch."

"You look gorgeous," says Aleda. "Do you like vodka martinis?"

"I love vodka martinis."

"Waiter—one of these (pointing to her own glass) for her (pointing to Susan). Pronto, por favor. Now don't say a word, Susan. Just *breathe*. Wait until your drink comes."

At the arrival of her bowl of silvery salvation, Susan takes a long sip. "Oh that's delicious."

"Waiter" says Aleda. "I think we'll be having another round."

"Me too," pipes up Abby.

"That's what another round means, sweetheart," says Aleda. "Everybody gets another one, including you."

"Oh," says Abby quietly. "I didn't know that."

Aleda leans over and gives Abby a kiss on the cheek. "If you don't know something, don't ever be afraid to ask. Remember, there are no stupid questions—only stupid answers."

"Oh my god," gasps Susan. "What a day!"

"When you're ready," I say .

"Christ All Mighty—I'll never be ready," and she takes a huge gulp of the martini, draining half the glass, closing her eyes as she swallows and keeping them closed. Abby looks worriedly at me, and I put a finger to my lips. Aleda stares at Susan, observing her carefully. After a deep-deep breath Susan begins to speak, but keeps her eyes shut.

"Today is Monday," she begins slowly. "I like Mondays. I can get things done on Mondays, or just play a little. I left this beret at the gallery." She takes it off and places it on the table. "I was going out and wanted to wear it, so I stopped by to pick it up. I went to the side door and when I pushed my key in, the door just swung open. I thought: did Arrow have a little Halloween party last night? RISD kids are very big on getting dressed up for Halloween and spooking around."

"Arrow?" asks Aleda.

"She's a student and works part-time as a guard. So, I walk in, close the door behind me, make sure it's locked, walk by the guard station, cross the hall into the main gallery and— Gone! All of them. Gone!"

"The Degases?" I say, uncomfortable with how I've just said the plural of the last name of Edgar Degas. Was it plain old Degas for both singular and plural?

Susan nods her head and tosses down the rest her martini.

"Auntie Susan," says Abby, "are you going to open your eyes?"

"In a moment, sweetheart. I just want to stay in here a little longer."

The fresh round of drinks arrives and Aleda places the new

martini in Susan's hand. After taking a long sip, she opens her eyes.

"Gone," says Susan. "All twelve of them. And *Six Friends at Dieppe*...My God, it's a pastel from 1895! Pastel is so fragile—sticky chalk—and this one so old; we never even loan it out. Unless whoever took it knew what they were doing, it's been destroyed. Oil doesn't move. But you shake a pastel, even behind glass, and it shifts like...when it's this old...talcum powder."

"Well, maybe they knew what they were doing and it's OK," says Aleda.

"What happened to the guard?" I ask.

"Oh!" exclaims Susan. "So, I whip out my cell, call 911— can you believe it? They're asking me, *Is this a medical emergency? Fire? Assault?* and I'm screaming: 'I just told you: it's an art theft! The Woods-Gerry Gallery at RISD has just been robbed of twelve Degas! And the dispatcher says to me, and I kid you not: 'What do you mean?'"

"Guess you didn't get the art history dispatcher," I say, noting that Susan has said Degas, not Degases. Still, it seems tricky.

"Anyway, as I try to not have a stroke and explain what 'art theft' means, I hear a noise near the guard's desk, and there's Arrow Amarusso underneath the desk with a goddamn green tennis ball taped into her mouth and her hands and feet duct-taped together. She can hardly breathe, and she'd been like that for hours."

"Did she see them?" I ask.

"They had on masks. It was Halloween! I cut her free, get her standing, get her some water...She's hysterical, beating herself up, shrieking about how stupid she was, and me telling her it wasn't her fault and wanting to scream and jump out a window and I don't know what all, and she's crying and pulling at her own hair....rending her flesh, for chrissake, like something out of the frickin' Bible!"

"This is just terrible," says Aleda. "Was she able to tell you anything?"

"She finally got out that around two in the morning, the front door bell rang. Two Providence Police officers are on the front steps. They tell her that they've received a report about a distur-disturbance on the grounds" Susan stammers, as if remembering something. "Anyway...Arrow...she's a kid...this is pokey little Providence...she lets them in and immediately they bind and gag her."

I notice that Susan's demeanor has gone through an odd shift; she's been completely with us, but is now only half with us, her mind suddenly chewing on something.

"Did she notice anything about them?" I ask.

"She said one was taller than the other...."

"Is the museum insured for a loss like this?"

"No way," cut in Aleda. "Nobody can afford the premiums to fully insure millions in art. Well, maybe Bill Gates can."

Susan nods. "We'd only get a fraction of what they're actually worth." Then she moans and downs the rest of her martini. "God—two kick-ass martinis and I don't feel a thing!"

"It's what happens when you're wired," says Aleda. "The body resists the alcohol—it's too busy dealing with the anxiety. Trust me, when you get home you'll feel it. You'll sleep like a baby. Here—eat some of this wonderful cheese and bread. And you've got to try their butter!" Aleda spreads some on a chunk of bread and hands it to Susan who takes a bite.

"Oh my god! What do they put in this?" asks Susan.

"It's honey butter!" pipes up Abby. "Isn't it *divine?*"

"Yo! Check it out!"

We stand on the red carpet beneath the hotel awning as the same Hell's Angel-looking Teamster who'd driven us earlier in the day lifts the tailgate and lays Abby's bike into the back of the hulking Escalade.

"Whoo," exhales Susan, resting one foot on the running board. Steadying herself she drills her eyes helplessly into mine: "I..." and she sighs deep down. She shakes her head and placing a hand against my chest, leans against me and whispers into my ear.

I groan and offer to return home with her.

"No," she replies. "I just want to be alone."

"It's gonna be all right," says Aleda. "Go home, take a couple Advil, get in the tub...."

"Right," and she seems to rally, blushing. "You know, I loved you in *The Dish and the Spoon.* It was the best TV show ever. You and whatsisname were a great detective team. *Hey! diddle, diddle, the cat and the fiddle, the cow jumped over the moon...*" Susan begins singing the show's theme song. Suddenly she stops. "Where's Abby?"

Abby is already in the back of the Escalade playing a movie.

CHAPTER 3

◆

Wild Boar Loin. The children's real parents. Swanson lets
the closeness sink in.

"WHISH!" ALEDA THROWS BOTH HANDS UP IN
THE AIR. "And off they go! Now, let's go upstairs and get
some dinner. *I'm starvin'!"*

Up in her suite, Aleda immediately disappears into the
bathroom, emerging in white silk pajamas with blue piping.

"That little Abby is so sweet, and—my watch! I didn't get
my watch back from her! I never take off my watch!"

"You never take your watch off?"

"No," snaps Aleda. "Well, hardly ever...."

Just then her cell phone rings. It's Abby, telling Aleda she
has her watch.

"Oh, don't worry about it sweetheart," croons Aleda, as
though it was just a cheap Timex. "I'll send Philip around
tomorrow to pick it up....No, no, he's not my
boyfriend...he's my assistant...sweet dreams to you, too,
love....No, I won't let the bed bug bite." Aleda clicks off.
"Oh, Swanson— she's the most precious thing! I want her to
come out to visit me in L.A. Maybe you could bring her,
darlin'."

"Maybe," I mumble, knowing I don't have the money to
get myself out there, never mind Abby, too.

"Now, c'mon—we have to order something to eat!" Examining the menu, Aleda announces: "I'll have the 'Wild Boar Loin with wilted spinach, crispy risotto cake and Merlot reduction.' Doesn't that sound *fabulous?*"

I shift uneasily in my seat.

"What?" asks Aleda.

"Something about that Wild Boar Loin....I'll have the Vegetarian Platter with—"

"Jesus, Swanson—eat some food, wontcha? I'm payin'...."

"OK-OK...I'll have the...Slow Roasted Atlantic Salmon, etcetera."

"That's better. And we'll have a bottle of champagne." She consults the wine list. "Moët White Star—that's what I keep around at home. Is that all right with you?"

"Here's to us!" she toasts, and keeping her eyes locked on mine, drinks her entire glass of champagne straight down, while I take only a sip of mine.

"No. You have to *swaff* it!" she demands.

"Swaff?"

"Yes. You have to drink it all down at once. Fill my glass again dear, and top off yours. Now, you have to keep looking at me. OK. Here's to Belle and Jack."

"Belle and Jack?"

"Isabella Stewart Gardner and her husband, Jack Gardner." Keeping our eyes locked, we swaff.

"Let's go into the bedroom," says Aleda. "Grab the champagne."

The bell of Grace Church strikes once and Aleda instinctively looks at her wrist. "Quarter past a hair. Right on time." She draws back the drapes and stands in front of the floor-to-ceiling plate glass window and looks up at the clock and the brownstone spire that looms over the room.

"Swanson, what was going on with Susan?"

"What do you mean?"

"She whispered something to you! Now, I don't need to know everything, but part of my training is to be observant, and unless you can't tell me—"

"No, Aleda. There's no big secret. I mean, I can't imagine she would care. She said this theft reminds her of the Gardner theft."

"That's what she said?"

"What she said, was: 'Similar to Gardner. Scares me.'"

"OK. I know about the Gardner theft. I mean, I don't know the details. Our movie ends with Gardner's death in 1924, and the theft was in...."

"1990."

"So, why would she be scared?"

"I don't know. Maybe cause they're never found the stolen Gardner art."

"And she thinks the same people did this and now they won't find this art? What did they take at the Gardner?"

"Your two big Rembrandts that were in the scene today with Gardner and Berenson: *The Storm on the Sea of Galilee* and *Lady and Gentleman in Black*. Vermeer's *The Concert*, that was on the other side of the same room. The Manet, actually, that you referred to, the man in the top hat. And—this is very spooky— a few Degas. Degases. Whatever.

"Well, Jesus. Did they take Titian's *Europa*, too?"

"They didn't. Which is odd. Probably the most valuable piece in the whole museum."

"Maybe they didn't have time."

"Oh, they had plenty of time. Eighty-one minutes, to be exact."

"So, Susan thinks it's similar because Degas/Degases were taken in both?"

"Not just that. Both robberies were pulled off by two thieves posing as police officers. Both places had student guards, and in both, the guards were duct taped up."

"And they never found the art?"

"Nope. Biggest art theft in history. Unsolved. Valued at three hundred million when it was stolen back in 1990. Today, it's probably worth twice that."

"How do you know so much about the Gardner theft, Swanson?"

"My best friend from college ended up in Boston doing graduate work at the Museum School, the school associated with the Museum of Fine Arts, which is across the street from the Gardner. He married Susan's sister, who also went to the Museum School and was working as conservator at the Gardner when it was robbed. Not *at work* when the museum was robbed, but employed there. That's another similarity— both robberies took place around 1:30 in the morning."

"Weird. And here I am, doing a film about Isabella Stewart Gardner."

"I didn't wanna say it."

"Am I gonna become a suspect?"

"I don't know. It is pretty coincidental."

"Swanson!"

"Don't worry," I laugh. "I'll vouch for you. But come to think of it, we weren't together last night, were we?"

"I called you."

"Yeah, but I was asleep."

"I went to sleep right after."

"Tell it to the police. I'm sure they'll believe you. You don't have any criminal record, do you? None of that Hollywood starlet kleptomania?"

"This isn't funny, Swanson. I don't have time for a police investigation."

"I really wouldn't worry about it, Aleda."

Just then, there's a knock at the door. We look at each other wide-eyed.

It's the food, and the coffee table and the writing desk become a mass of silver and covered dishes.

"Here —let's bring it into the bedroom. I like that room better."

On a table next to my side of the bed is an exotic fish swimming in a bowl of freshwater grass.

"This is kinda cool," I say.

"A friend sent it to me. I told him I didn't want it. Now I have to worry about feedin' it. So, finish your story. I had no idea you were such an authority on art theft."

"I'm not. I only know about the Gardner and now this one. Oh, the Gardner was robbed in the wee hours after St. Patrick's Day, and this theft happened in the wee hours after Halloween. That's kind of a similarity, happening around events that could be a distraction."

"And you said your friend's wife was working at the Gardner? And she's Susan's sister?"

"Yeah. My friend, Ray, married Susan's sister, Julie, who studied art conservation and was working at the Gardner, helping maintain the collection."

"How interesting. Is she still working there? God—this wild boar's loin is fantastic! Have a bite."

"No thanks. I'll stick with my salmon. You wanna bite?"

"No, thank you. I'm pretty excited by this boar's loin. I wonder if he had big tusks. So, your friend's wife who works at the Gardner...."

"Not anymore. She died. So did my friend, Ray."

"Swanson! What happened?"

"Electrical fire in their car. They were trapped. Horrible-horrible-horrible."

"Oh my god. I would say so. Swanson, your friend Susan has been through a lot. Well, at least she has that darling—wait a minute—Abby calls her Aunt Susan. Was Abby's mother...."

"Yes. Abby's mother was Susan's sister, Julie. Susan became the legal guardian of Abby and her brother, Eric.

"Oh, Swanson. When did this horrible thing happen?"

"2004. Abby was three and Eric was six."

Tears begin spilling out of Aleda's eyes. She reaches over and takes my hand.

"The most important thing was making sure Abby and Eric were cared for. Susan's done that, and *Uncle* Swanson tries to help out, in his crippled way."

Aleda leans across the bed and hugs me. The side of her face fits nicely against mine. She smells good, some perfect perfume, and I do something I should've done when I had the chance, more than thirty years ago—I keep my mouth shut and let the closeness sink in.

CHAPTER 4

◆

Eric and Abby clean Swanson's spooky house. Five
million dollar Gardner reward.

NEXT DAY, THE THEFT IS BIG NEWS but still no
leads. Susan phones the following morning.

"Swanson," she despairs, "I don't know what I'm gonna do.
I feel like swallowing a bottle of Xanax."

"How about a break?" I suggest. "Why don't I take the
kids for a day or two? I'll pick them up from school this
afternoon."

Doesn't take too much arm-twisting for her to agree to
that.

I sit on a bench across the street from the Wheeler School
on Hope Street where Abby is in the fifth grade and Eric, the
eighth. Eric is entering the moody stage and beginning to
bully his sister. He is neither fish nor fowl. And he's addicted
to *RuneScape*, an online computer game.

Abby is starting to develop little breast buds and trying to
get away with wearing makeup, and some kid named Brad
has a crush on her and wants her to come to his birthday
party this weekend. "We'll have to see about that," I muse.
I'd never cared for the name Brad.

Eric comes up behind me, his thick brown hair hang

almost into his eyes. I push it off his forehead and he pushes it back down.

"Where's Abby?" I ask.

"I dunno. Probably she's still inside, talking to her girlfriends. That's all they do, is talk to each other all day."

"They're prepping themselves for the rest of their lives. They're plotting and planning relationships while you guys are dorking around with *RuneScape*."

"It's a good game."

"It's gonna rot your brain. I don't even understand what it's about."

"It's because you're *old*," teases Eric.

"It's because I have a brain. It's because I like to get outside. Hey—go find Abby, will ya."

"Why don't we just leave her?"

"Eric. Please do this for me, will you? These are tough times. Your Aunt Susan is about to commit hara-kiri."

"What's that?"

"Japanese ritualistic suicide. They stick a knife in their own stomach and draw it up to their chin." I feign slamming a knife into my gut—"Eeeeeee-Yaaaaaa-Oooooh"—rotating it up my torso to my clavicle. "But don't think about that stuff."

"Holy shmoly!"

"Holy shmoly, indeed. Please find Abby—there she is. Who's that she's talking to?"

"Chris Meglio. His family's really rich. They own like twenty supermarkets or something."

"Hi Swanson!" chirps Abby, doing a little hop jump toward me. I place my hand on top of her warm head, pat the pink backpack on her back. She's wearing a necklace of little blue beaded stars I gave her for Hanukkah last year.

"This is my Uncle Swanson," says Abby. "He's not my real uncle, but he's my uncle."

"Hi" says the boy.

"Wuddup, *duuude?*" I squawk.

"Urrrrhhhhhhhh...." growls Abby, glaring at me.

"OK, C'mon kids, hop in the car. We're going to my house!

"Why are we going to your house?" asks Eric.

"Your Aunt Susan needs a little break. We can swing by your house, pick up whatever you need and then maybe do a little grocery shopping. It'll be fun."

Is your cable connection solid?"

"Yeah it's fine. Why?"

"*RuuuuneScape,*" he grins.

After a pit stop at Susan's, we drive across town to my place.

"Welcome to Count Dracula's Castle," says Eric. "Look— there goes a bat!"

"Stop it Eric," says Abby. "There aren't bats over here, are there?"

"There are bats everywhere," says Eric. "We have bats over on Cushing Street, pea brain."

"Eric," I say, "don't be yourself. Be someone a little nicer."

We pile out of the car and drag stuff across the porch and into the house. Eric grabs the newspaper sticking out of the pyracantha bush by the front steps. Little Guy, who's been asleep on a blanket on the porch swing, stands up, arches his back and stretches. "Little Guy's hungry," Abby says, hugging him. "Can I feed him?"

"Here's your newspaper," says Eric. "I heard they were gonna stop making newspapers."

"Thanks. Yeah. We're all just gonna sit in front of computers and turn to slush."

"You can get it on an iPad."

"Glorified portable TV. Maybe we'll just get rid of words altogether—they are kind of a pain in the ass to read."

"Am I in the back room?" he asks, remembering where he'd stayed last summer when Susan had gone to Italy for a couple of weeks.

"No. You're in the front room on the side facing the Lunas."

"Oh—so I get to listen to Spanish people yelling at each other."

"Hey—you're taking Spanish. Maybe you'll pick up a few things."

"Chinga tu madre."

"And don't forget the black people too, pampered white boy. You can bone up on your hip-hop street shit, you know what I be thayin' mang?"

"Yay. I can git jiggy wit dat, muthafucka. Hey there's this black kid in my school and—"

Abby comes zipping out of the kitchen and I make a quick hatcheting motion to Eric.

"Oh. O-K," she says. "Something I'm not supposed to hear. That's cool. I don't wanna hear it anyway. Can I take a bath?"

"Good idea, Stinky," says Eric.

"Can I use the tub in the red room?"

"Of course you can, sweetheart." My monstrous house has three full baths, all with ancient claw foot tubs.

"Goooooooody!!!" and she flies up the stairs past Eric

"Excuuuuuse me, Dummy!"

"Wait! Put on the brakes, please. Before we do any bathtubbing or computing, I need you guys to help me out." I tell them Aleda might be coming over soon. "So, I need to clean up a little around here, OK? Many hands make light the work."

"Wait a minute," says Eric, trying to be tough but unable to contain a smile: "Are you saying you brought us over here to clean your house?"

Eric is thirteen now and resembles his father as much in the stoutness of his body and broad features, as Abby does her mother's slenderness. And he has his father's thick, dark brown hair.

"Don't be selfish, Eric," says Abby.

"No, I did not bring you over here to clean my house. But now that I've got you here—may I suggest you take a look in the kitchen?"

Eric peers in. "Holy Shmoly!"

"That's riiiiight. So, if we want to eat tonight, we've got to start cleaning."

"Well you can clean in the kitchen," says Eric. "I'll do the living room. I don't mind vacuuming."

"Vacuum's in the foyer closet."

"Is it an upright? I don't do uprights."

"Listen to you. How do you know so much about vacuum cleaners?"

"Because Wheeler gives us chores to do, and one of them is to vacuum the Common Room. They have an upright and a canister. I prefer the canister."

"Well, dude, you're in luck, then."

Abby and I start in the kitchen. Her skinny ten year o'

legs stick up like broomsticks out of her pale pink Uggs, and her big blue eyes are happy and ready for adventure. Her skin glows the color of ginger ale on her prominent, rounded forehead. She has her father's large mouth and full lips, but she has her mother's bright blonde hair and willowy frame.

"So, if you ever had a daughter, you'd want her to be just like me, right?" asks Abby, a big pink sponge dripping in one hand and apprehensive eyes rolled up beneath her eyebrows.

"Absolutely correct."

"And you'd never want a son like Eric, right?"

"Not true. If I had a son, I'd want him to be just like Eric."

"So then, why don't you have children and you could raise them to be just like us!"

"Because I have you two. And I guess because I never met the right person."

"And you can't marry Aunt Susan because she's a lesbian."

"It's not that I can't marry her because she's a lesbian, it's more like she wouldn't want to marry me and I wouldn't want to marry her."

"But you still love each other."

"Yes, we do. Like brother and sister."

Abby trudges over to the sink to rinse out her sponge. In those Uggs, she might as well be tramping through snowdrifts in the Klondike, and I remember a pair of Spanish riding boots I had when I was fourteen.

"My Uggs," I mutter.

"You talk to yourself," says Abby.

"So what?"

I check on Eric who's busy vacuuming the foyer and living room. I come up behind him and squeeze his shoulders.

"Thank you, Eric," I shout over the roar of the vacuum. He nods, seriously at work. He is such a good kid.

"So, did this movie star who's coming, did she used to be your girlfriend?" asks Abby.

"No....She was already way up there when I met her. I was just in college."

"But, did you *wish* she was your girlfriend?"

"Yeah, I guess I did."

Understatement of a lifetime.

Warm western light drenches the living room in red gold, and I slide the newspaper out of its plastic bag. Page one: Sex-Death-Sex-Death. Page two: Blah-Blah-Blah. Page three: Photograph. *"What?"* Here, in living color as they used to say, is a splashy picture of Aleda and...Me! The caption reads: *Movie Star Aleda Collie leaving Hemenway's Restaurant with friend, Swanson Di Chiera. Collie is in Providence producing and acting in the film Belle, about the life of Victorian art collector Isabella Stewart Gardner.*

"Oh, *borther*...." Just then, Eric comes into the room all smiles.

"Well, *oh, borther*—you got a computer in my room!"

"Yeah. Zack Ball's Used Pooters strikes again. He just about gave it to me."

"Still, it's a P4. That's pretty cool! What's *borther?*"

"It's like, Oh *brother!* It's from a book I wrote about operators who relay phone calls for deaf people. Deaf person types in, operator sees it on their screen and reads it to the hearing person. The deaf person typed, *oh borther* but meant, *oh brother*—transposed the o and the r. Oh, *borther!*" I moan again.

"What are you oh borthering about?"

I hand Eric the paper. He looks at the picture and reads the caption out loud.

"Whoa. Dude. Your new girlfriend is a movie star? Cool! Abby told me about her, but I didn't believe her. Is it true she has a DVD player in the back of her car, and a refrigerator?"

In my bedroom getting dressed after a bath, Abby calls through the door: "It's like, *freezing* in here. Can you turn on the heat?"

"Really? You're cold?" I knew it was pretty chilly—I was somehow hoping they wouldn't notice.

"*Yeah-uh!* I've been holding Little Guy just to stay warm!"

"OK. I'll turn on the heat as soon as I come downstairs."

Could I pay the bill with a credit card? I'd never done that before. Crap. But what choice did I have? I couldn't let them be cold.

After dinner, homework, a little TV and then tucking the kids in upstairs, I pour myself a glass of red wine and ghost around the first floor. It feels good with them here—like a home. In the distance, but still in the house, I hear an indistinct noise. It's probably Ina, flushing her toilet or closing a door. Ina is a nursing student I rent a small apartment to at the back of the house, up on the third floor.

"Thank God," I sigh. Having that apartment paid the mortgage. "This is the perfect moment." Then the phone rings. I pick it up fast, so it doesn't wake the kids. It's Aleda.

"Boyfriend!" she gushes.

"Girlfriend," I reply with a bit more reserve.

"Did you see the picture in the newspaper?"

"The paparazzi find Providence."

"We make quite the handsome couple. So what are you doin', darlin'?"

I tell her about the kids being over.

"You're a good man. I don't know why I didn't marry you instead of those other idiots."

"Let's see—Because you were rich and famous and I was a nobody. Because you lived in L.A. and I lived here. Because I didn't have enough money. Because I might have been married at the time."

"You've never been a nobody, sweetheart. Well—maybe when I first met you. You were cute, though. Hey, we gotta get some money into you. Is RISD offering a reward? How about the Gardner?"

"I dunno...I'll have to look into that."

"Do it. So listen—why don't ya meet me on the set tomorrow? We're on that Benefit Street, near the museum. We found a house to stand in for Gardner's Beacon Hill house, before she built Fenway Court. You'll see the signs and trailers. Then we can have lunch together. I wanna go back to Hemingway's and eat oysters!"

"Hemenway's."

"Right. Hemenway's. I don't know why they named it that. It's so confusing."

"I dunno. It's like, why did they steal Degas, or Degases? Couldn't they have stolen some Picassos? We know his name is Pablo Picasso. A bunch of his paintings are called Picassos. But what's the deal with Edgar Degas? His name is Edgar Degas, but are a bunch of his paintings Degas or Degases?"

"You are funny, Swanson. You really are."

"Well, you know what they say—got a little dick, you better have a good sense of humor."

"You don't have a little dick!....Do you?"

"You'll never know! Ha-ha-ha! Hey—go to bed. I'll see you tomorrow."

"But, now I'm thinkin' about your dick."

"That's good. Keep thinkin' about it—I gotta work on getting rich!"

After hanging up I tell myself: "Bloody relief she knows you don't have any money." There's nothing worse than pretending to a woman you have money when you don't.

I wake up my computer and go to the RISD site and the *Providence Journal* site...nothing about a reward—not much about the theft, period. Go to the Gardner Museum site. Nothing up front...click here...click there...finally have to search "theft" and it comes up under something called "Resources." Open PDF document. "Jesus...." OK, here we go...."Oh, yes-yes-yes *darlin'*"—a five million dollar reward!

"Tucked this sucker away, didn't they?" Face it—major league humiliation. Bend over and take it with a torpedo. Biggest art theft in history and it happens at your place? OK. Five million dollar reward...blah-blah-blah...photographs of stolen art, click here...."Voila!"

Two big Rembrandts and a teeny, postage stamp-size Rembrandt self-portrait etching; Vermeer's *The Concert,* and ere were only, what, thirty or so Vermeer's in existence? e Manet painting, *Chez Tortoni,* of a man in a top hat; five is drawings (horses, neck of violin); a Govaert Flinck, *ape with an Obelisk,* 1638...and the two very oddball the bronze Chinese drinker beaker, called a Ku, from g Dynasty of 1200-1100 B.C., and the eagle finial off the top of a Napoleonic flag.

Looking at the Ku and the eagle finial, I have the same reaction I had years ago when I first learned of the theft: This stuff was taken because it could be. This theft was a lark. No serious thieves would ever stop to take the Ku or the finial.

The Degas (I am preferring Degas to Degases) taken from the Gardner were minor works on paper: small, no more than a foot square, some watercolor; embellished sketches, really. The Degas taken from the RISD museum were large and involved. Was someone trying to balance out their Degas collection?

I find myself reaching for the phone. I want to talk to Susan, but stop. Leave the woman alone, for God's sake. Can talk to her after I bring the kids back. Let her relax.

"Cigarette would be good now. How about a Number Two Special?" and I bust a pencil in half, stick it in my mouth and inhale.

I remember conversations I had with Ray and Julie about my "Lark Theory." They'd said no, place was left a mess. The robbers were just brutes. Most big time art heists were just glorified smash and grabs. OK, fine. But the Ku and the finial? What about that huh? They shrugged. Who knows?

But maybe, I'm thinking now, the thieves made it look brutish to put investigators off the scent. Make it look like your typical art theft, when, in reality, it wasn't.

When you have very little money, but very large ambitions, the thought of acquiring five million bucks does have a way of stimulating the imagination.

CHAPTER 5

◆

Royal Madeira on the set of *Belle*.

"SWANSON."

"What?"

"It's time for us to get up."

"What time is it?"

"Six-thirty."

"God help us."

"Woyt? Eric and I have to be to school by eight. And we need breakfast. Could you please open your eyes, please?"

I whisk together some pancake mix with a few eggs, some frozen blueberries and milk, and pour it all into an enormous Lodge cast iron skillet I'd found at a yard sale for a buck. What flops out ten minutes later is a pancake the size of a hubcap.

"Holy shmoly!" says Eric.

"This," I proclaim, cutting it into thirds, "is a *pan* cake!"

"See—you could have kids," says Abby.

After dropping them off at school, I stop at the public library and sign out their only two books on Isabella Stewart Gardner, recognizing one of them as the very book about Gardner that Aleda was reading the summer we first met. I'm not sure why I think absorbing information about

Gardner might help me solve the theft, other than having learned over the years, both as a writer and photographer, that background information helps to set off and make more visible the subject matter at hand.

I also pull a few books about art theft in general which I dive into immediately, learning that hundreds of art thefts occur every year, all over the world, including New England. Smaller museums and private collections are often targeted. Missing are Picassos, Cezannes, Van Goghs....just about every famous artist past and present has been stolen, and many of the works have yet to be recovered.

What artwork does find its way back to the owner is in return for insurance money or just outright ransom cash. Conjecture for many unrecovered pieces is that they are being used as collateral in the international drug trade: I give you the art, you give me the dope; I sell the dope, pay you back, you return the artwork to me.

Most art thefts, even those unsolved have *something* to go on. What sticks out about the Gardner theft is—no leads. Zippo. Nothing. And not one piece has surfaced. Thirteen pieces of art, including the finial and the Ku was a lot of art. After all this time, wouldn't money-driven thieves have tried to cash in? Twenty years is a long time without *somebody* opening their yap.

"It's not about the money," I muse. "It can't be about money."

Full-bore Hollywood movietime. Enormous white trailer trucks filled with generators and instruments, switches and dials; hundreds of feet of heavy black electrical cable running down the street and a long row of white trailers for cast and wardrobe. Klieg lights bleaching the fronts of buildings and trees and big silver reflectors and cameras and monitors and tracks for follow shots and people-people everywhere. Scrungy kids in jeans and plaid flannel shirts with walkie-talkies mingle with mutton chopped actors in Derbies and corsets and puffy-sleeved garb of the 1880's and '90's...and somewhere in all of this....

Yes, there she is coming down the front steps of a townhouse in conversation with a striking-looking man—heart-shaped face, big, dark, mirrory eyes and a widows peak of blue-black hair. You can see he's a ruined man, although not old, who seduces you even as you want to draw away.

I'd once had an exasperating encounter with this person.

Aleda sees me and waves. She breaks off and crosses to me.

"Let's go," she says, taking hold of my arm. "I'm starvin'."

"How do you know that guy?"

"Royal Madeira?"

"*That's* Royal Madeira?" I ask. I know the name. Royal Madeira is head of the Painting Department at RISD, and his name pops up every now and then in the newspaper. But I'd never connected the name with the person who'd so irritated me a few years back.

"We hired him to be the art consultant on the film. He's a big authority on Gardner and her collection, and Bernard Berenson, and Sargent and that whole period. We're usin' him to make sure the scenes, the artwork all look authentic. He's very bright. He's a gorgeous man."

"You think he's *gorgeous?*"

"He's almost too good-looking for a man. Whataya have against him anyway?"

"Why do you think I have anything against him?"

"Rivalry is thick in the air."

"We had a little run-in a few years back. Just a local issue sorta thing. How'd you get to be so smart?"

"Why, thank you for saying that, Swanson. I got to be so smart because I had to. I saw early on that it's very important for a woman to have her own money. I wasn't gonna get any by being stupid."

Late in the afternoon, I sit at my writing desk in the bay window watching Abby ride her bicycle up and down the driveway and Eric shooting baskets. I kicked them out of the house before it got dark so they'd get some exercise.

I'd once had such high hopes for myself. I really believed that one day I'd make it big and have a family. Now I live in fear of Providence Water showing up to turn off my water, or the gas company to shut that off, or Linda from the dentist's office calling about my bill, or the retina specialist squeezing me for his final hundred bucks.

And then there's the side fence falling down, slate shingles sliding off the roof, peeling paint on the ceilings, the old wallpaper...the split carpeting going up the staircase.

How had I managed to blow it?

I walk across the room to the bookcase.

"You have this," I say, touching the spine of *What Mean?* my first novel, a story about people who relayed phone calls for the deaf. Published twenty years ago, it hadn't been a big bestseller, but it had sold well enough to provide the down payment on this house.

"And..." my finger ripples down the row of books, stopping at *Debris Creatures*. This one sold moderately well, for a book of photographs. It portrays objects on the highway—a wet cardboard box that for one, heart-stopping moment you think is a dog...a crumpled sweater or a crushed grocery bag that might be your cat. It had paid for the renovation of the small apartment I rent at the back of the house.

"I'm a double-threat!" I exult. Well, I *had* been a double threat. Novel number two never made back its advance, and novel number three had been rejected by my publisher...and every other publisher.

"But I am working on novel number four!"

And I regularly sell essays and photographs to the Op-Ed pages of the *Providence Journal*. I also freelance articles and photos to various magazines...all of which allows me to *almost* pay my bills on time—except for health insurance, which I don't have.

"I'm on the Colt Plan. Get real sick, and—" sticking a finger against the side of my head, I am about to pull the trigger when I look out at the children and put it down.

After dinner, the phone rings. Because it's so often someone tracking me down for money, I always let the machine pick up.

"I'll get it!" Abby yelps, and answers it as I let the words, "Let the machine get it," die on my lips. She comes into the kitchen, the phone huge against the side of her head. "OK...I   will...Yup...OK...Here's   Uncle   Swanson. Byyyye..." and with a big smile she hands me the phone.

"Swanson, you musta done something right in your life to have that little girl to take care of. I told her if she'd let me take you away to Newport tomorrow, I'd take her shopping sometime."

"Newport. My hometown. Yeah. What's the occasion?"

"I have to go down there for the weekend."

"OK...." Aleda doesn't volunteer any more information, and I don't ask. Take the good as it comes.

I phone Susan and tell her about Aleda's invite.

"You go and enjoy yourself, Swanson. I'll pick them up after school. Does Aleda have children?"

"Nope. That's one thing we do have in common."

"Thank you for taking them, Swanson. I so appreciate any time you spend with them."

"Hey—they helped me clean up my house, Sue! They're little particles of light bouncing around. I get to gather them up in their excitement. I get to have them when they sparkle. It's you who has them when they're dull and demanding. I'd never be able to do it day in and day out."

"Swanson—never underestimate what you can do."

"You're sounding better, Sue."

"I'm OK. I've been thinking about some things I haven't looked at in awhile. I'm feeling focused, Swanson. I'll tell you about it when you get back from Newport."

In the morning, I drop the kids off at school and give Eric a hug and a kiss on the side of his head. "If I had a son, I'd want him to be just like you. You know that, right?"

"Uh-huh."

"OK. Be good. Work hard. Have fun today. And look after your sister. OK?"

"OK."

"I'm serious. We have talking to do about girls. They're not like us. They are very, very, complicated—like old-fashioned watches with lots of intricate little moving parts."

"I don't see why they just can't go digital," Eric grumps.
"Hey—that's the beauty of life, Eric. It's not digital.
Digital is just something people made up. Life itself is very,
very old-fashioned. Trust me."

CHAPTER 6

◆

To Newport with Aleda. Chanler Hotel and Cliff Walk.
Susan Disappears.

THE MORNING TURNS SUNNY AND MILD, a genuine Indian Summer day, and I give Veronika a quick rinse in the driveway before heading downtown to pick up Aleda. V is the last of the big box Volvo wagons. A stately dark blue, I bought her used from a wealthy cardiologist who'd won her in a raffle. Ain't it the way? At her helm, I look positively prosperous.

I pull up in front of the awning of the Hotel Providence and the doormen spring forward, followed by Aleda sweeping out of the lobby with Philip and—*Royal Madeira?* Now, what the hell is he doing here?

"Royal," says Aleda brightly, "this is my dear old friend, Swanson Di Chiera."

"The writer," says Madeira extending his hand. Taking it I look at his dark eyes, glossy mirrors.

Philip appears, carrying a black nylon tote and a big duffel. "I've got a few of *Betty's* things to put in the car...."

I open the tailgate and Philip loads the bags in. He's been Aleda's personal assistant for five years now and is in his early thirties with short dark hair and an open, fair face. A light sprinkling of freckles decorates his nose and cheeks. His dark brown eyes are friendly, yet observant and protective.

As I'm wondering who all is going down to Newport, Aleda clarifies the situation.

"Royal. Thanks for everything. Call if you need to."

Madeira takes her hand in both of his and kisses it. *"C'est mon plaisir,"* he purrs.

"Oh *borther!"* I mutter under my breath. He's probably a terrific dancer, too. Aleda gives a few final instructions to Philip and we're off.

"There's a sandwich for you in the door pocket," I say, accelerating out of downtown. "Would you like to take the scenic route through small towns like Bristol and Warren, or the faster way down Route 95 and over the Newport Bridge?"

"Let's just get down there. Thank you for bringing me a sandwich. What kind is it?"

"Turkey. The Hudson Street Market, my neighborhood market, makes great sandwiches."

"And look at this." Aleda unfurls the cloth napkin I'd tucked inside the bag. "You are sweet." Unwrapping the sandwich, she says, "You really don't like him, do you?"

"No. I don't."

"Why?"

"Because he's a self-serving prick."

"Aren't we all?"

I've really been looking forward to this day, going back to my hometown with Aleda, and I don't want it to start off on the wrong foot. But I just can't let what she said slide.

"Not always," I say. "Not when lives so much less fortunate than one's own are at stake."

"OK," she sighs. "Tell me."

"You don't really want to hear."

"Please don't tell me what I want to hear."

I smile. I'd long noticed that women, more so than men, have a way of unwittingly saying things that carry a double entendre.

"OK. A few years ago, the famous urban planner Flavio Suvari came to Providence and held some charettes to try and understand how the city might improve itself. I went to one of them, and Madeira—I didn't know who he was at the time—stood up and whined about how the East Side, the money side of town—where Brown and RISD are—needed more trees and street improvements, blah-blah-blah, while my side of town has nothing. In particular, he gassed about how a pretty little area called Wayland Square needed to be made even prettier, while the geographic equivalent on the West Side, my side of town, hardly has a single tree. Instead of having a Starbucks, it's anchored by a blood plasma center—where poor people go to sell their blood!

"I listened to him go on and on, watching Suvari suck it all up. As soon as he finished, I stood up and straightened Suvari out upon the real needs of Providence."

Aleda has no comment, seeming more interested in her sandwich than to what I am saying.

"Is it good?" I ask, trying to hide my irritation.

"It's delicious."

"C'est mon plaisir...."

"Oh for chrissake, Swanson—let it go! He didn't commit a crime. He could help you. You live in the same town. He has a lot of influence. Frankly, he's a fascinating person."

"What are you saying?"

"I'm saying that—nobody's perfect. So he pissed you off at

that meeting, whatever it's called."

"Charette."

"The charette. He was sticking up for his side of town, his neighborhood. He's probably never seen a blood plasma center."

"Don't count on it."

"What are you talking about?"

"The guy's a fucking vampire."

"Swanson—knock this shit off! Maybe this is why...."

"This is why what?"

"Forget it."

"No. This is why what? Why I've never gotten anywhere? Because I don't kiss the asses of people who can 'help' me? Because I don't write stories about vampires?"

"Maybe. I don't know. Maybe your standards are too high."

"You mean I expect too much from other people?"

"No. From yourself."

I twist my grip on the steering wheel and stare hard down the road. Aleda reaches over and squeezes my thigh.

"C'est mon plaisir," she smiles.

Crossing over the Newport Bridge, I point out the Newport Naval Base. "That stone building is the Naval War College. And over there," I point to the other side of the bridge, "is Rose Island. See where the lighthouse is? Ray and Julie and the kids lived there for two years, until the accident."

"How did they get to live on an island?"

"The foundation that owns it was looking for a caretaker. Ray was able to do his sculpture and Julie found work restoring art in the mansions in Newport owned by the

Preservation Society. Susan was here, too. She was hired for her first museum director job at the Newport Art Museum."

Entering Newport, we roll past the old graveyard on Farewell Street then turn right onto America's Cup Avenue, a sweeping stretch of asphalt designed to funnel the tourists into downtown. The ruination of little streets and destruction of a modest old neighborhood to accommodate this monstrosity always makes me wince—every change to my beloved hometown has been for the worse.

Aleda unfolds a sheet of paper with information off the Internet. "We're lookin' for The Chanler Hotel."

"Never heard of it," I sniff.

"Maybe it's *neeeew,*" she teases in a spooky voice.

"Oh, no—not *neeeew,*" I quaver back. "Oh, *deeeeeear....*"

"It's OK, sweetheart. We'll bring you into the present yet. It's at one-seventeen Memorial Boulevard."

"Don't wanna be in the present, Miz Aleda. Me skeered. You know that Nike ad, *Just Do It?* I says, *Just Don't Do It.*"

"No, darlin'," Aleda pats my leg. "We gonna get some Nike into you."

"You mean we gonna Do It?"

"Maybe. But first, you're gonna do it."

"I'm skeered."

"That's OK. It's good to be skeered sometimes."

Coming to the end of America's Cup Avenue, we make a left and head up the hill.

"That's St. Mary's Church—where JFK and Jackie were married."

"Looks like the church across from my hotel."

"It does. OK, Miss Aleda....This is Memorial Boulevard, so I guess we better start looking for numbers."

"I'm not good at looking for numbers. It says here...The Chanler at Cliff Walk."

"Oooooh...." I croon. "I bet I know where it is."

Sure enough, as we proceed onto the downside of Memorial Boulevard overlooking the ocean, we come to what had been the seedy old Cliff Walk Manor Hotel when I was growing up, now restored to its original glory and then some, recast according to an elegant sign on a driveway pillar as *The Chanler*.

I pull Veronika up beneath the porte-cochère where the hotel manager and valet laying in wait, pounce on us. The manager in his dark blue suit and pencil mustache butters Aleda, oils her with his aura. He ushers us into the grand foyer where the entire staff dressed in black and white like toy soldiers snaps to attention. The one, the only Aleda Collie has arrived!

He leads us up the gleaming mahogany staircase to the second floor. At the head of the stairs he opens the first door on the hallway and we step into the Renaissance Room—a little brass plaque on the door says so. It is a sumptuously appointed, chandeliered room of Wedgwood blue walls, ornate white woodwork and a canopy bed right out of La Belle Époque; creamy, floral-painted Louis XIV chairs and bureaus and old oil portraits—or at least respectable copies—a balcony with sweeping views of Easton's Beach and the Atlantic Ocean. Isabella Stewart Gardner would've felt right at home...until she noticed the discreetly curtained LCD screen and DVD player.

"This is the most beautiful room I've ever seen," declares Aleda.

The gas fireplace is already lit. There is champagne on ice

and exotic fruit pieces and lines of nuts arranged on a square plate of frosted glass. Before leaving, the manager invites us to "be our guests for dinner tonight."

As soon as he's gone, Aleda spins around. "Isn't this fabulous! Open the champagne, darlin'!"

"And dinner on the house!" I exclaim. "Their restaurant, The Spiced Pear, is supposed to be world class!"

After swaffing a couple glasses of champagne, Aleda urges: "C'mon—let's get out and walk while it's still light! What should I wear? Do you think it's cold out?"

We cut across the sweeping back lawn and down to the gravel path of the Cliff Walk that meanders along the rocky coast, the Atlantic on one side and the famous mansions on the other: replicas of European chateaux and castles, places with names like The Breakers...Rosecliff... Marble House...Chateau-sur-Mer...Miramar....

I am once again awash in the sensory impressions I've carried since childhood; the glittering, breathing ocean...the little island of Cuttyhunk, way, way out there...the smell of the ocean mingling with hedge and lawn smells....

"Aleda—sometimes I think I am too sentimental...and that it's held me back. Do you think of yourself as sentimental?"

"That's a big question," she replies. "I'm not sure what you mean."

"I mean, I think I spend too much time living in the past."

"But isn't that what writers do?"

"I mean a nostalgia for the past."

"No. I had a shitty childhood. I am not nostalgic for the past."

"I had a wonderful childhood. Sometimes I feel like I'm the

victim of a happy childhood."

"Your present never lives up to your past. I see how that could be a problem. You need a great challenge. I had to become successful to take care of my parents and my brother and sister."

"I didn't have to do anything except pursue my dreams."

"That's not enough."

At a juncture along the path known as The Forty Steps, named for forty cement steps that lead down to the rollicking ocean and from which more than one person in despair has plunged to their death, we come upon two police officers blocking the path. They're looking down at the screen of some handheld device like two boys who are seeing porno for the first time.

"Sorry," says one, pulling a cigar from his mouth. "You're gonna have to go around," and he motions up toward a town road leading away from the ocean path. They are staring at Aleda, knowing she looks familiar. Suddenly one of them says, "Aren't you—"

Aleda pushes a shock of hair away from her face and assumes one of her trademark, sultry expressions.

"I thought so!" says the other one, and they both beam at her, starstruck.

"What's goin' on?" I ask, looking off to the big white tent set up on the lawn behind one of the mansions. A voice can be heard coming through a microphone inside the tent.

"The Dalai Lama is giving a talk at Salve," says one of the officers. Salve Regina is a small Catholic college in Newport that has bought up a number of the mansions as their enrollment has expanded.

"Well," I say humbly, "don't you think, you know" and I

dart a glance at Aleda, "you could let us by?"

"No!" says Aleda, grabbing me by the arm. "This is how it was meant to be—the Dalai Lama is forcing us to take the high road!" Holding onto the sleeve of my jacket, she waves good-bye to the officers and pulls me off the path.

We walk down a quiet street of mansions closed up for the winter, beneath gargantuan copper beech trees with their grey, elephant hide bark; past high stucco walls and black, wrought iron gates tall as giraffes, gravel drives disappearing between jungle-size rhododendrons.

"We are walking in the world of Belle Gardner," observes Aleda reverently.

"Imagine what it was like to grow up surrounded by all of this—to have it on the periphery of my middle-class life. To have appreciated it. Not all of my friends did. Why did I? And then in high school, I won the school art prize."

"You have a strong feminine side. All artists must. You are well-suited to solve the Gardner theft."

"Because I understand her world?"

"Because you understand her world—but you are not part of it. When you are part of something you cannot really see it. You think like everybody else in that world. *You* have the advantage of appreciating great art without ever having been able to own it. Therefore, you feel its theft keenly—it belongs to you in a way that really is irreplaceable."

"And that gives me special insight into what might have happened?"

"It could, because the loss bites into you. It is not comfort that fuels the imagination. It is desire."

I sling an arm around Aleda's shoulders.

"What do you want to say, Swanson?"

"I don't know. I am just feeling very full. And very close to you."

Aleda puts an arm around me. Her hand drifts down my back.

"Is there anything you would like to say?" I venture.

"You've got a very cute ass, Swanson."

Back at the Chanler, Aleda sits with her feet up on the white and gold brocade couch in front of the fireplace. I lounge in a blue-checkered wingback. Behind me, the setting sun bathes the waves, turning them an iridescent purple. Suddenly, tears start spilling down Aleda's face.

"Gash is comin' in tomorrow night," she says.

"He's gonna love this," I manage. Gash must be the boyfriend—the trainer of Navy SEALs...the one with a ranch. My face is burning. What a fool I was to think this was for me!

She stands up. "I'm gonna take a shower before dinner," and she goes into the bathroom, closing the door behind her.

I pour myself more champagne and open the French doors and step out onto the deck.

In the gathering darkness, line after line of gently rippling violet waves follow one another onto Easton's Beach, where at eight years old, I'd dug in the sand for numbered wooden blocks that were redeemed for prizes—an annual hunt sponsored by the city to help keep kids occupied as winter staggered into spring. Where at thirteen I'd lost an entire week's pay—a hundred and twenty dollars stuffed into my cut-offs—running into the surf after loading bales of hay for a farmer all week.

Aleda emerges, wrapped in a big, white bathrobe, moist and soft.

"Step out onto the deck with me….See the spires of that gothic chapel over there?"

"Yes."

"That's where I went to prep school. It's the chapel of St. George's School. It was my mother's dream that I go to school there. My parents gave up a lot to pay for it, and that was even with a partial scholarship.

"My Aunt Marie worked there, in the kitchen. She served food at lunch and cooked cakes for the teas we had after sporting events. Nobody knew she was my aunt. We behaved as though we were strangers when we saw each other at school.

"My fellow students referred to her and the other workers and maintenance people as wombats. Small, strange-looking, insignificant animals. I never took up their cause, never defended them. I fell in with my friends."

Aleda strokes my arm. "And now you feel ashamed."

"I am disgusted with myself."

"You were just a boy, trying to fit in."

"Still, I should have been better. It makes me sad."

"It can also make you wise." She places a finger on my chin and turns my face toward hers. "While it does, let's enjoy dinner together, love."

In the dining room of The Spiced Pear we're brought samplings of everything on the menu, accompanied by an appropriate wine. Each dish is introduced and explained. We giggle like children when the waiter announces—"Peekytoe crab."

"Oh my goodness!" cries Aleda. "You mean I have to eat crab toes?"

At that moment the hotel manager approaches the table. He looks positively stricken. Even his mustache appears crooked.

"Miss Collie: I am *so* sorry to disturb you, but you have a call," and he holds a phone out to her.

"What's *that?*" snaps Aleda. "That's not my phone!" Looking at me, she says, "I purposely did not bring my phone to dinner."

"It is my phone, Miss Collie," says the manager. "I never would have disturbed you, but they said it was an emergency."

Aleda clenches her jaw and holds out her hand. The manager places the phone in her palm and backs away to the horizon. "This better be good," she says, before whoever it is can even speak. I am shocked to see her break into a big smile and gush, "ERIC! Hi, it's Aleda. I've been *dying* to meet you! I've met your sister, but I haven't met you yet, and Swanson has told me so much about you! Yes, he's right here. Hold on, love."

Handing the phone to me, she whispers, "There's a problem. I hear crying."

I listen to Eric and barely say anything, except: "I'll be there in an hour. Good-bye."

"What happened?" asks Aleda.

"Susan didn't come home after work. They found her car running in the museum driveway...but she was gone."

"She's just gone?"

"That's what Eric said."

"Are they alone? Where are they?"

"There's a police officer with them. They're at home. At Susan's."

"This doesn't sound good, Swanson. Was there any evidence of...any evidence?"

"Nothing, according to Eric. But who knows what they've found out. I gotta go." I stand up and so does Aleda. Behind her the moon shimmers upon the ocean.

"Do you want me to come with you?"

"No. No, Aleda. Enjoy your visit to Newport. And your friend will be coming tomorrow."

"I wish he wasn't. He isn't supposed to be here."

There is only one response to that and I give it to her: an unforgetable kiss.

CHAPTER 7

♦

Old college photo of Madeira, Susan, and children's parents.
Detective Umberto "The Hydrant" Porcaro.

WALKING INTO SUSAN'S HOUSE it's almost as though
nothing is wrong. A female police officer is sitting in the
living room watching an episode of "House," and Abby is
online with Susan's laptop. Eric is in his bedroom playing
RuneScape, but comes whipping down the hall as soon as he
hears the door open.

"Hola," he says, stretching up on his stocking feet to touch
the top of the doorway. Eric is taking Spanish I.

"Hola, dude. Qué pasa?"

"No sé," answers Eric.

"Hi, Abby." She is staring into the computer screen and all
of a sudden come the big tears.

"It's all right, Sweetheart," and I pick her up from her
cross-legged position in front of the coffee table. "It's gonna
be all right." She sobs and clings to me like a monkey. Eric
stands by my side and I notice he's gingerly holding Abby's
bare foot.

I introduce myself to the officer, who calls herself Officer
Drummond. I can tell she is OK by the way Abby stops
crying and twists in my arms to look at her. She is probably
in her early thirties. Beautiful dark skin, the color of smooth

chocolate ice cream. Nice figure, even with all that police stuff hanging off her. She already seems to know enough about me to be on her way. First she radios a superior with the information that I am here with the kids.

"Yeah. Their uncle is here with them now," she reports. I look at Eric who gives me a big wink. Officer Drummond tells me nothing more is known about Susan. Do I have any idea where she might be or if anyone wanted to harm her?

"No and No," I answer.

"A detective might be here to talk to you tonight, or in the morning. Will you be here?"

"Here or at my place," and I give Officer Drummond my address and phone number. "Either way, the kids will be with me."

"Very good," she says. "Then I'll be going. Frankly, unless there's some news, I don't think anybody'll be here tonight. It's kinda late." She smiles at the kids. "Good-bye, Abby. Good night, Eric," and she shakes Eric's hand. To me: "If we know anything we'll call you."

"Ditto."

As soon as the door closes, I deposit Abby on the couch. "Eric, your Aunt Susan has a bottle of vodka in the freezer. Could you please bring that to me? And a glass, not that I need one, with some ice in it? Thank you!"

"Sure thing!" says Eric, zooming off and sliding around the corner in his stocking feet. "Are you gonna get shit-faced?" he calls from the kitchen.

"Possible...possible...."

"Can I too?"

"No."

"Can I get shit-faced?" asks Abby, wiping her eyes with her

palms.

"Negative. Hey Eric, see if there's some ice cream in there for your sister, will ya." I rub my face and sigh. "Oh, borther...."

"What's *borther?*" asks Abby.

"Wait! Let me tell her!" shouts Eric, and a few moments later he comes into the room with the bottle of vodka, a glass with ice, and a big bowl of ice cream for Abby balanced on top of the glass. "It's like, 'Oh, *brother*,'" says Eric. "Only Swanson wrote it in a story about deaf people who spelled it borther instead of brother. They just reversed the r and the o."

"Oh," says Abby, reaching for the bowl of ice cream.

"Are you having anything, Eric? Cripes—have you kids had dinner?"

"Yeah. Jeanette, I mean Officer Drummond, ordered us a pizza."

I take a long pull on the glass of vodka. Goddamn—a nice, unfiltered Camel would hit the spot right about now. I take another healthy slug. "Uhhhhhhhhhhh...."

"Oh *borther,* huh?" says Abby.

"Oh *borther,* indeed. Well, do you wanna spend the night here or my place?"

"Here," says Abby. "Here," says Eric. "Maybe Aunt Susan will show up. Whataya think happened, Swanson?"

"Guh—I just have no idea. You say her car was just sittin' there, running?"

"Yeah," says Eric. "When she wasn't home by six, I called the museum and they said she left forty-five minutes ago, so I called her cell and she didn't answer, so we rode our bikes down and her car was sitting right, you know, inside the gate. It was running and nobody was in it, and the driver's door wasn't closed all the way. I mean, it wasn't open but it wasn't pushed all the way in."

"Was her purse in the car? Anything just, you know, sitting on the seat?"

"Nope."

"Hmmm. Abby—did you notice anything?"

"Woyt?" Abby was busy working on her pile of ice cream.

"Never mind. Uuuuuh…" I pour more vodka into the glass and Eric comes over so all three of us are sitting on the couch. Both Abby and Eric lean on either side of me and fall asleep. No wonder—it's almost eleven.

I'm asleep when the phone rings. I can hear Aleda's voice coming out loud and clear from the answering machine in the kitchen. Like little robots, Abby and Eric get up and sleepwalk into their bedrooms. I go into the kitchen. I pick up the phone and start filling in Aleda while I check on the kids. They have both fallen asleep with their clothes on.

"If she hasn't turned up by morning," says Aleda, "the cops'll be back to go through the house for clues. Is there anything you don't want them to find? That she wouldn't want them to find?"

"Right. Good thinking. I'll poke around."

"It's beautiful here, Swanson."

Feels like a hatchet has just been planted in my chest.

"I know."

After we hang up, I go to the hall closet where Susan stuffs the recycling and the vacuum cleaner. I grope along the shelf above my head until my hand finds the wooden box with the pot in it.

"And the *paraphernalia*," I moan in a quavering,

Vincent Price voice. God—when would they finally legalize this stuff?

I roll myself a nice, fat joint. Aleda is right. Unless Susan turns up, they'll have cops over here tomorrow combing through the house. Pot's no big deal—or is it? Susan is the legal guardian of the kids...don't even give the dildos something to chew on. I'll take it back to my place, and stick the baggy and rolling papers in my pants pocket. Going down to the basement I quietly open the glass slider and step outside.

Susan's back yard is fairly small and heavily landscaped with slate, ornamentals, and overarching trees, keeping it private from the neighbors. I light up. Good pot. Interesting how I can smoke marijuana but not be triggered into taking up cigarettes again, but if I had a cig, I'd be a goner.

I look up the side of the house. Needs a paint job. And those wooden gutters need to be replaced. Man, they have grass growing in them. Suddenly, I have the feeling I'm not alone out here and step back inside, glad to lock the door behind myself.

OK—time to have a look around—see if there isn't something else the police shouldn't find, and maybe turn up some clues myself.

First the obvious—Susan's bedroom. On the wall are photographs of Abby and Eric when they were babies. They used to be on Julie and Ray's walls. There's a framed piece of stitchery Julie had made: a heart of flowers encircling the inscription, *A Sister is a Forever Friend*. Next to it is a framed color photo of Ray and Julie. Ray is wearing one of the incredibly ugly flower shirts from the sixties he collected, and Julie with her long straight blonde hair looks like Mary

Travers, from Peter, Paul, and Mary. They both have on bell bottoms. They were flower children, something out of a Peter Max painting. How funny. That's not how I thought of them, but that's what a stranger would think from this photo.

"We're a lot of people" I whisper, and touch the glass over the photo.

Sue's ironing board is set up in front of the windows overlooking the backyard. A TV, VCR, and DVD player are all stacked together near the foot of the bed.

"Sorry Susan." I slide open the drawer of her bedside table. Keys...couple books of matches...emery board...a vibrator. Oh, borther. Leave it. Probably normal enough.

From there I go to the bureau: underwear...sweaters...socks...tops...good....Next, bookcase: books, DVD's—nothing weird or kinky. College yearbook...SMFA—School of the Museum of Fine Arts 1989....I open it and sit down on the bed and read a few of the inscriptions inside the cover. Stuck between the pages is a photograph from that time. Susan and Julie, and Ray, and just behind Ray and Julie some woman who's a real looker. "Jesus, Ray—where were you hiding *her?*" Resembled Audrey Hepburn with her short dark hair and big eyes. "Big hands, too." One of them gripped Rays shoulder. I move over closer to the table lamp to get a better look. Pretty mouth and dark eyes. Quite exotic-looking, actually. Then suddenly—

"Holy chit, mahn!" I realize the woman I am admiring is— Royal Madeira!

I turn the photograph all the way around twice. It's still him.

"Carumba." I place the photograph back between the pages of the yearbook and shut it. "This goes home with the pot, señor."

The only other item I find that gives me pause is a large, black portfolio tied shut at the top. Untying it, I bend over and leaf through the contents: several large charcoal drawings of a house with stone terraces overlooking the water; some nudes of both men and women...nudes of women together....various landscape drawings...."Take it," I mutter. I close it up and bring it outside, where I slide it flat into the back of Veronika's cavernous storage space. Placing the yearbook with the photograph stuck inside of it on top of the portfolio, I drag an old army blanket I keep in the back over top of them.

A search of the rest of the house turns up nothing unusual; nothing the cops might use against her, or give them cheap thrills.

There is an address book on the kitchen table. I tuck that into a pocket of my sport coat and at 3 A.M. collapse across Susan's bed.

The aroma of coffee. Is she back? I stagger out to the kitchen just as Eric is pushing the plunger down into the big glass coffee pot.

"First time I ever did that!" he announces proudly.

"Perfect Eric. You did it perfectly."

"Yeah. I've watched Aunt Susan do it about three hundred times. Actually, probably more than that if you think about it."

"¿Donde está Abby?"

"Ella...está...dormida. Still."

"Muy bien, señor. You're gonna fit right in over in my barrio."

"You mean we're gonna go over to your house?"

I shrugged. "That's the general idea. What else can we do until your aunt comes back?"

"Stay here."

"No can do. I've gotta get back to my life."

"What about my life?"

"You've got a portable life."

"Well, what if Aunt Susan doesn't come back?"

"Inneresting question...but let's not worry about that right now. Let's just 'stay in the moment.' And that moment says it's time for Swanson to drink some of that expertly-made coffee. Black. No azúcar. Like Bond. James Bond."

Just after nine, a detective shows up. He looks like a fire hydrant. He is barely five feet tall, with a head shaped like the Capitol dome set directly upon chunky shoulders that simply drop straight down to the floor. He has short, thick arms, and the sleeves of his suit jacket are too short for them, so his cuffs stick about four inches out. It must be a nightmare for the guy to buy clothes, and clearly he's given up.

I ask about Susan, and Detective Umberto Porcaro rotates his head back and forth.

"Nuttin' so far."

"But it's just too weird. Did Martians come down and abscond with her? I mean, what the hell?"

"We just dunno, at this point," says Porcaro, his big droopy eyes lazily scanning the room. "Do you have any idea there might be somebody who's having a problem with her?"

Fair or not, I make a quick judgment and decide that showing the photograph I found to this guy would only complicate matters. Keeping it to myself, I might at least be able to figure something out.

"No. I mean, the woman's a museum director. She's the legal guardian of her sister's two children. She should be getting a *medal,* for God's sake."

"I understand," says Porcaro. "Sounds like somebody who everybody would like."

"But there's always somebody who doesn't like you, right?"

"I think that is true. Unfortunately. Look, um, I'm gonna hafta have a look around—well, more than just a look. I'm gonna—"

"I know. You're gonna have to go through things. I understand. And if it helps you figure this out, be my guest. In the meantime, I've gotta take care of business. I've gotta take care of the kids and get us set up over at my house. I can't stay here. I work from home."

"So you work at home? That must be nice. I saw your picture in the paper with Aleda Collie, who's making the moving here about that woman, what's her name...."

"Isabella Stewart Gardner."

"That's the one. Funny how you don't hear anything about art, then all of a sudden they're making a movie in Providence about a big art collector, and then that art is stolen from the RISD museum, then your sister disappears."

I am about to correct Detective Porcaro and tell him Susan and I are not actually related, but at this point, why? Again, it would probably only serve to complicate matters. There are no other relations of the children within a thousand miles. The closest blood relative is a cousin of Susan's out in

Iowa. Or was it Idaho? Oh, *borther.*

By late-morning, I have Abby and Eric ensconced back at my house with their necessary items of practicality and pleasure.

"Do you think they'll find her?" asks Abby.

That question sure cut to the chase.

"Oh, yeah," I answer. "People just don't disappear very often."

"But what if they don't find her?" asks Eric.

"Highly unlikely, and it's not worth worrying about right now."

"I know—but I'm just saying, *what if?*"

"Yeah," chimes in Abby. "Like if they don't ever find her, will you take care of us?"

I've fallen short at everything I'd hoped to accomplish in life, all of which had to be easier than raising children. Still, my heart speaks right away: "Of course I'll take care of you."

But the very thought scares me to death. I can barely take care of myself; what would I do with two children?

CHAPTER 8

♦

Swanson researches life of Isabella Stewart Gardner.
Bugatti Veyron in Madeira's driveway.

STANDING IN THE BAY WINDOW behind my desk, I examine the photo of Susan and Julie and Ray, and Madeira. The background is pretty generic; brick, part of a bush...the edge of a window. Probably somewhere around the Museum School.

I prop it up against the desk lamp and jump onto the RISD website...Faculty...here it is: Royal A. Madeira. Head of Painting. Lecturer Art History. Boston University, BA. The School of the Museum of Fine Arts, MFA. Bingo—it is her. Or him. Or whatever. Ray and Julie and Susan *and* Madeira all knew each as far back as the nineteen eighties.

"I gotta talk to this *bastid,*" I say aloud, applying just the right New England twang to how I feel.

I open the phone book and look for a listing. "Nuttin," I grumble, inhabiting for a moment the persona of Detective Porcaro. I go online to Switchboard.com. "Nuttin."

I remember the contact book I'd taken from Susan's and find Madeira's address in there.

Eric is upstairs in front of the computer playing *RuneScape.* "Eric—I need to go out for about an hour. Will you be OK alone?"

"What do you think?"

"Where's your sister?"

"I dunno."

I check Abby's room, but she isn't there. I run up to the unheated rooms on the third floor—not there. I go back to the first floor and check the kitchen. Finally, I go down into the basement. She isn't down here either, unless—I open the door to the cedar closet and she's sitting on the floor cradling Little Guy.

"Eric closed the door on me."

The inside knob has been missing for years, but there has never been any need for me to worry about that—prior to now. I return to Eric's room.

"You're coming with me."

"Whataya mean? I thought—"

"Don't think, cretin. I can see now that I can't trust you to stay here alone with your sister."

"Whataya mean? I was just—" But I already have him by the back of his collar and leading him downstairs.

"C'mon Abby, We're goin' for a ride."

"OK," she chirps. Honestly, age ten must be the best; she's just so perfectly sweet and agreeable.

We roll slowly down Viceroy Avenue...number 21...comfortable Craftsman-style bungalow. There is a very exotic-looking sports car in the driveway.

I pull a U-turn and park in front of the house.

"Will you two not kill each other if I leave you in the car for a few minutes?"

Abby looks at Eric with big worried eyes and a furrowed brow, and he grins devilishly back at her.

"You're both coming with me. Hop out." Nobody moves.

"Fine. Then sit in the car and behave. I'll be back in a few minutes."

I walk up the flagstones to the front door. The door is curved at the top and is made of strips of golden oak and has a speakeasy window at eye-level with bars over it. I ring the doorbell, but no one answers. I ring it again, then walk along the driveway side of the house and peer over the fence into the backyard. There doesn't seem to be anyone at home. On the way out, I glance at the super-spiff sports car in the driveway. It is a brand new, two-tone blue and grey Bugatti Veyron with Massachusetts plates. I've only seen a Veyron before in photographs. It costs a million six and tops out at two hundred fifty-three miles per hour. At that speed, it runs out of a full tank of gas in twelve minutes. Even parked, it looks like a car shooting out of its own skin.

Returning home, I take Abby and Eric into the backyard and we stand at the border of the flower garden.

"See that cement frog? Underneath it, there's a key to the front door. Eric, you can get it."

I have Eric unlock the door and open it.

"Good. Now lock the door."

Eric puts the key back in, turns it in the opposite direction and removes the key.

"Locked!" he says.

I turn the handle and open the door. "Not locked. With this lock, you have to turn the key twice around to lock it."

I have both Eric and Abby lock and unlock the door a few times until they get it.

"Good. I'll put the key back under the frog, so if I'm not here, or you ever get locked out, you'll be able to get in."

"Does this mean we officially live here now?" asks Abby.

There's a message on the answering machine from Detective Porcaro: nothing turned up in Susan's house that shed any light on her disappearance. Has anything occurred to me? Well, give a ring if it did.

I decide to give him a call, just to be in his face. I don't like the indifferent attitude in his voice. When he picks up, it sounds like he's eating something.

"We don't know anything at this point," he says.

"Well, what the hell do you think happened? Is there a statistical probability in cases like this?"

"In cases like this, the missing person usually has some hand in their own disappearance."

"Meaning?"

"They're running away from debts...a bad relationship. Usually some life-pressure drives them to extremes. She been under any unusual pressure lately that you know of?"

"Only the theft of a few million bucks worth of art," I reply dryly. "Do you think there's any *link* between her disappearance and the museum theft?"

"Are you saying she mighta stole the art herself?" asks Porcaro.

"Good Lord, no! I just thought here you have two unusual events happening on top of each other at the same location, that's all."

"You think there's a connection?" asks Porcaro. "Why might you think such a thing?"

I hold the phone at arm's length and count slowly to five. I want to drop a cinderblock on this guy's head, but it might ruin a perfectly good cinderblock.

"No reason," I say.

I want to call Aleda. She would understand my frustration. She would have some ideas. "Goddamnit!" I look at my watch. The boyfriend will be coming in from California about now. Will she be meeting him at the airport? Of course not. Will she send the Escalade? Maybe. She said he wasn't rich, but what did that mean—he's only worth a couple million, not ten? Probably rent a Corvette. Dan said he owned a ranch in Solvang, near Vandenberg Air Force Base. I get out my old Rand McNally Road Atlas and find California. I find Bel Air, where Aleda lives then locate Solvang. I dig out a wooden ruler...the conversion table says one inch equals twenty-five miles....so it's about four inches, or a hundred miles away as the crow flies...a two hour drive, minimum. She couldn't see him *that* often. God this is stupid! and I slap the ruler down. It's like getting a hard-on and finding a ruler to measure your dick. It is what it is— measuring isn't going to change a goddamn thing. Either it works or it doesn't.

Abby comes bounding into the room. "Aoibhinn wants me to come to her house for a sleepover."

"Let me think about it," I say distractedly.

"But she's on the phone now."

"If you need an answer right now, then the answer is no."

"What about if I need an answer in five minutes?"

"Then it's maybe."

Abby starts talking excitedly into the phone and zips out of the room. I like Aoibhinn. She and her family moved to Providence from Ireland two years ago, and live one street over. She is smart and polite. It is a friendship I am happy to encourage.

Eric comes swinging in, grasping the top of the doorway with his fingertips. "Hey Swanson, do you have anything to eat? There's only some old, I-don't-know-what-it-is, in the refrigerator."

"Tempeh burger. Toss it. Yeah. I need to do some grocery shopping."

"If you get the ingredients, we can make a pizza."

"Eric, that's a brilliant idea."

When Abby returns, she looks at her wristwatch and then at me. "OK," I say. "You can have your sleepover."

"Yes!" she exults with an air punch.

"But it's gonna be here. Aoibhinn can come here. We're gonna make pizza."

"Woyt?"

"I just want us to stay together this weekend, OK?"

"Yeahbut—"

"Humor me this one time, OK? We're gonna go out grocery shopping and we can pick up Aoibhinn. And guess what—you girls can stay up as late as you want!"

"We do that anyway," sulks Abby. "And you don't get the Disney Channel...."

"We can play Scrabble. You like Scrabble. We can stop by your house and pick up whatever you want. We can play the Barbie Game...."

After dinner, Abby and Aoibhinn disappear upstairs to Abby's room. As fanciful and fair is Abby, Aoibhinn is solid with dark hair and a droll Irish wit.

Happy pop music bops out of Abby's boom box, accompanied by absolute gales of laughter, wild giggling and howling. It goes on and on, as well as frequent excursions to the bathroom. Eric has barricaded himself in his room practicing his guitar, except for a trip downstairs to get some ice cream.

I glance at him from my desk where I'm reading up on Isabella Stewart Gardner.

"Retards," he says, lifting his eyes upward.

"They're young women, Eric."

"They're retards."

"Eric. You fantasize about being a musician? Playing in a band?"

"Yeah. So?"

"And I write novels."

"So?"

"So...most of the music in this world and most of the novels in this world are bought by women. Do you want to think that retards will buy your music? Do you think you will ever sell any of your music if you view girls as retards?"

He stares at the blob of ice cream on his spoon.

"Carry on. And be careful going up the stairs. I still have to do something about that carpeting."

OK...Isabella Gardner....Basically, it comes down to this: Born Isabella Stewart in New York City, April 14, 1840. Stewarts are a wealthy family, she travels, goes to school in France, meets sister of Jack Gardner. Introduced to Jack. Four days before she turns twenty, she marries Jack. Though from wealth, it's nothing like what the Gardner's have. The Gardner fortune comes largely out of their shipping business in Boston.

She moves to Boston, and she and Jack Gardner take up residence in an imposing house on Beacon Hill—built and paid for by her father.

"Thank you, Daddy-o."

She settles into being a rich Boston society lady. Some take to calling her, "Mrs. Jack." In 1863, Belle and Jack have their one and only child. A boy. Jackie. Two years later, in the early spring of 1865, the child dies of pneumonia.

Isabella goes into a tailspin for the next two years, never leaving the house. Finally, under the advice of a doctor who declares that this woman desperately needs a change of scene, she is literally carried out of the house and aboard ship for a trip with her husband to Europe.

The trip is a success, reviving her interest in living. It also ignites in her an interest in spending money on beautiful things, first and foremost designer clothes. The famous Parisian couturier Charles Worth designs dresses for her and if she has an unremarkable face, her sexy little body returns to staid Boston draped in styles that become the talk of the town.

More trips abroad follow: Egypt. Venice. Turkey. Greece. France. Italy....Palestine. Cambodia. China.

She begins attending the lectures of Harvard scholar Charles Eliot Norton, who encourages her to collect rare books, specifically those of Dante, about whom he's an authority.

Isabella Stewart Gardner finds that she enjoys the company of writers, artists, and musicians, and collects as many of these as she can, too, bringing them to her Beacon Hill home for recitals and readings. The author, Henry James, and prominent painter, John Singer Sargent both become lifelong friends.

Through her Harvard connections, she meets a student,

Bernard Berenson, whose desire to study in Europe is enabled by Gardner's financial support, and who later uses his art knowledge and business savvy to help Gardner acquire many works, including Rembrandt's first self-portrait.

From what I can glean between the lines, it appears that Jack Gardner is utterly supportive of his wife's collecting interests, both with his checkbook and his heart. I find this touching in an age when many men, certainly of his class, regarded their wives principally as *châtelaines* and bearers of heirs.

By 1896, the Gardner's 152 Beacon Street home has become crammed with so many paintings and other art objects, that all of the wall space is covered, the overflow leaning against chairs and sofas and stacked upon bureaus and desks.

Deciding against enlarging their house, Isabella and Jack Gardner begin conceiving a new home that they will build for themselves and their art collection. Toward this end, they purchase land outside of the heart of downtown Boston, on the Back Bay Fens, eventually to become known as the Fenway. The former tidal marsh that their newly acquired land overlooks has recently been re-designed by the prominent landscape architect Frederick Law Olmsted into a winding, countryside lagoon that retains its communication with the ocean, not unlike the lagoons of Venice.

Two years later, at the age of sixty-one, Jack Gardner suddenly dies. Still, Isabella forges ahead with their construction plans and builds a Venetian "palazzo" on the Fenway.

Fenway Court, as she calls it, is completed in the winter of 1901-02, and Gardner moves into her apartment on the fourth floor, above the galleries.

Isabella Stewart Gardner has twenty-two more years of earthly life remaining, until July 17, 1924, and she does not languish. Concerts by the Boston Philharmonic for two hundred guests are given at Fenway Court.

"I was there!" I exult, recalling the filming at the armory.

John Singer Sargent is a frequent lodger, setting up in the Gothic Room to paint portraits of the posh and the prominent. And more art is acquired, often with the guidance of Berenson, who is living in Europe and is crucial to the authentication of paintings during a time of rampant fraud. So many acquisitive rich Americans, so little real knowledge of art.

There is one item that really disturbs me, though: Isabella's husband buys his way out of fighting in the Civil War. When conscription comes to Boston in 1863, Jack Gardner pays the government a three hundred dollar exemption fee for them to get a Union Army substitute.

"Just gotta love money! Literally save your fuckin' skin! While the boys are getting blown to bits, you and your Isabella are travelling Europe, living it up, buying art....Kiss my ass, muthafucka."

Better check on the kids.

The weekend passes without any news about Susan. The police are stumped. I feel bile rising to spill over Porcaro, but then I think of Jack Gardner buying his way out of battle, and I feel sympathy for Porcaro...and all of us who have to keep jumping out of the way of the teeth of the machine.

CHAPTER 9

♦

Swanson to Boston with Aleda. Shows her a shocking
photograph.

ALEDA RETURNS TO PROVIDENCE on Monday night.

"Did you have a good time?" I ask meekly, hardly wanting
to know.

"We ate a lot of good food. Why don't you come down for
a drink."

"Can't. There's been no luck finding Susan. The police have
squat. The kids are staying with me."

"But Swanson, you've never had kids!"

"So what? I was a kid, once." Remembering the
photograph I'd found stuck in Susan's yearbook, I ask Aleda,
"What is a transvestite, exactly?"

"A man who acts and dresses like a woman, or vice versa.
But usually it's men who indulge."

"Why do you think somebody would want to do that?"

"Probably because they're not happy with how they were
born."

"Ugh. What could be more fundamentally terrible than
that? Do you think that, as with gays, there's become a much
broader acceptance of cross-dressers? That's what
transvestites are, right?"

"Swanson—where have you been? Police departments, fire

departments...major corporations...The whole thing today is *diversity;* tolerance for LGBTQ lifestyles. In fact, I'd say it's about encouragement! White, middle-age guys like you are *out!* You *het,* you little *breeder.* It's not the world we grew up in, Swanson. Look at it this way: maybe it's nature's way of taking care of the overpopulation/pollution problem."

"What does BLT...QRST blah-blah-blah mean?"

"L-G-B-T-Q. Lesbian, Gay, Bi-sexual, Transgendered or Transsexual or Two-spirited, Queer or Questioning. Or maybe it's Questioning or Queer. I dunno. It's a mess."

"How do you know about this stuff?"

"It's my job! And it should be yours, too! People need to like me. And you need them to like you, too!"

"But do you believe in all this LBJ stuff?"

"Believe? Swanson, I believe in myself! I don't care what anybody else wants to do with their genitalia. I am an accepting person. You are a struggling person. You like to fight with people."

"Is that why you're rich and famous and I'm...still struggling?"

"It could be. Swanson—these people—they are *harmless.* And they are not procreating. This is a good thing for the planet. Look at the bright side, OK? You have to start looking at the bright side!"

I am silent. What was the bright side of Ray and Julie being dead? And Susan disappearing? The RISD Museum being robbed, and the Gardner? And did this Madeira person fit into any of it?

"Hey!" says Aleda. "You wanna go up to Boston with me tomorrow? I've gotta meet with some people, but not all day. Just for an hour or so. Then we can have lunch."

"Boston? Yes. I do. I most certainly do."

Aleda swings by early enough so we can drop the kids off at school.

"Whoaaaa...." yowls Eric when the enormous Escalade comes heaving into the driveway. It's captained by the same Hells Angel-looking dude who drove us from the set that first day. We climb into the back with Aleda, who's watching the "Today Show" on the bright plasma TV.

"See, I told you," says Abby, as Eric twists his head around in amazement.

Aleda's attired military-chic in a marine blue pantsuit, red piping on the lapels and down the legs.

"Does anyone want juice? We have orange, grapefruit...." Aleda peers into a refrigerator that's part of a mahogany built-in that also features a bookcase, a full bar and an array of violet-lighted buttons and switches. "And we have bagels and lox and cream cheese, blueberry muffins....egg and English muffin sandwich...."

Just to make sure they're properly envied, Eric and Abby hoot and holler to their friends as they jump out. Even though some pretty fancy rigs dock at the Wheeler School delivering their *bébés à bord*, all eyeballs float to the surface when this frigate sails in, Blackbeard's badass uncle hissef at the helm!

After we pull onto 95 north to Boston, I show Aleda the photo I'd found at Susan's.

"Recognize anybody?" I ask.

"Nope. Waitaminute....is that your friend from the museum—Susan?"

"Yes, it is. That's her in graduate school in Boston. And the girl next to her is her sister, Julie, and the young man next to Julie with the big grin is my old pal, Ray Mendelsohn— Julie's husband."

"The children's mother and father," says Aleda wistfully.

"Yes—the children's mother and father. Now—guess who the person is, standing behind Ray and Julie."

"She looks like Audrey Hepburn."

"That's exactly what I thought at first. But, guess again."

"Have I met her?"

"Oui, madam."

"Gimme that," and Aleda snatches the photograph out of my hands. Scrutinizing it, she suddenly exclaims, "She looks like Royal Madeira's twin sister!"

"LBJ...IRT...Queer-Questioning-Diversity strikes again, baby!"

"What the hell are you blathering about?"

"I'm talking about what you lectured me about last night," and I break into the old Kinks song: *"Girls will be boys and boys will be girls, it's a mixed up muddled up shook up world except for Lola, Lo-Lo-Lo-Lo-Looo-laaa....Lo-Lo-Lo-Lo-Looo-laaa...."*

"No...." says Aleda in disbelief, looking back down at the photograph.

"Oh, yeeeees....The hands, Aleda—look at the hand on Ray's shoulder. That's a big hand. That's not the hand of a woman. That's the hand of a man."

"But Swanson," gasps Aleda. "How...I mean, why are Susan and the kids parents and—why are they all in this picture together? Where was it taken?"

"It was taken in Boston, sometime in the late nineteen eighties. After we graduated from college together in

Baltimore, Ray eventually ended up in Boston and enrolled in graduate school at the Museum School. That's where he met Julie and Susan, who were also both at the Museum School."

"And Madeira, too?"

"Yes. I checked out his bio on the RISD website. That's where he got his MFA."

"Wow. What do you think it means, Swanson?"

Looking at her reflection looking at my reflection in the window, I say, "I think it means that Madeira might have something to do with Susan's disappearance."

"And the theft from the museum?"

"Possibly."

"And the Gardner theft?"

"It has crossed my mind."

"I don't normally drink in the morning, Swanson."

"Nor do I."

At the press of a button, two shot glasses are filled with vodka.

"Here's mud in your eye."

"Santé."

"Jesus, Swanson."

"Sorry. I've never been able to get Paris out of my system."

"I wasn't thinking about Paris."

"I was. It was the foreign city I wanted most to see. I was not disappointed."

"How are the kids doing?" asks Aleda.

"They're fine. They've voiced some concern about: 'What if they don't find Aunt Susan? Will you take care of us?' I told them they'd probably find her. 'But what if they don't?' I told them not to worry, of course I'd take care of them."

"Haah!" Aleda brought a hand to her mouth to prevent vodka spraying out.

"What's so funny?"

Aleda shakes her head. "Actually, you probably would make a pretty good father."

"A course I would. But I think they're gonna find her. Don't you?"

Aleda shrugs and rolls her eyes. "I dunno. But listen—did you show this photograph to the police? Last thing we need is Madeira pulled off the movie. On the other hand, a scandal could be good for publicity."

"I didn't. I was gonna, but then I thought, no, the police are gonna fuck this up."

"I don't think that's what you thought, Swanson."

"Oh, really?"

"Oh, really. I think you wanna figure this out yourself. You want to solve the Gardner theft! You're a writer—of course you're a control freak!"

"How did you get to be so smart, Aleda?"

"You asked me that question before. And now you're startin' to smarten up yourself. You want that Gardner reward money without any complications."

"Yes, I do."

"And you're willing to throw Susan on the sacrificial altar?"

"No."

Aleda hands me her phone. "Call the police right now."

I just stare at it. Might as well have been a moon rock.

"Here, give it to me." She calls information for Providence Police, presses some numbers, hands the phone to me. I ask for Detective Porcaro. When he comes on, I briefly explain the relationship between Susan and Madeira, and suggest they check him out. Porcaro thanks me, and that's it. Sounded like he was eating something again.

I hand the phone back to Aleda.

"There," she says. "Don't you feel better now? Who's Porcaro? Sounds like something we had for dinner."

"He's the detective on the case. You should see him—he looks like Tony Bennett, dwarfed. He does have a nice head of hair—tight curls, generous with the grease....the color of roasted chestnuts."

"Well, be nice to him," says Aleda. "And don't pull the sarcastic shit. Cops don't understand it. I might know you're kidding around, but other people don't know you. They'll peg you as an asshole, and that'll be the end of it. Don't go out of your way to make enemies, Swanson. Go out of your way to make *friends*. I do know Tony Bennett, you know."

"I know."

That vivid, Technicolor summer night over thirty years ago—I was picking her up at Kennedy Airport. Coming down the arrival corridor she was talking to Tony Bennett. I remember everything about that night. But the way she spoke now, the way she mentioned Tony Bennett when we had all been in the same moment together, gives me the insecure feeling that our long ago night, so magical to me, is something she doesn't remember at all.

CHAPTER 10

♦

Museum School. Tiny sets off a "pencil." Hermès store.

ALEDA'S MEETING IS IN A GLASS OFFICE TOWER ON STATE STREET.

"I'll call when I'm finished." She tells the driver to take me wherever I want.

"Where to, Magoo." His voice comes from somewhere near the television set.

"It's Swanson. What's your name?"

The driver shakes his head. "I can't hear you. See the row of blue buttons above the bar? Press the last one on the right."

I did. "Can you hear me now?"

"Why, yes, I can," says the driver. "I certainly can. Ain't technology beautiful?"

"My name is Swanson. What's yours?"

"Tiny."

Tiny....."OK, Tiny," and I pull out my notebook. "We want to go to the School of the Museum of Fine Arts, located at 230 The Fenway."

Tiny speaks the address into the GPS, and we're off.

I push a button and freshen my coffee. I try one of the bagels and lox. Mmmmh....This car is nicer than most people's homes.

"Tiny, you want something to eat? There's a whole

delicatessen back here."

"No thanks. I'm good."

In ten minutes, we pull up in front of the Museum School.

"I'll call you if I hear from Aleda," says Tiny.

"I don't have a cell phone."

"OK, we'll do this: if she calls, I'll set off a pencil."

"What the hell's that?"

"See this button here? I hit it and there's a little cylinder mounted near the rear window. It sends a mini-missile about the size of your thumb a hundred feet straight up and it explodes. Only it doesn't sound like a cannon. Can't do that. It sounds like a giant pencil cracking. And there's no smoke. Nuthin' to see and pinpoint it. If you're listening for the sound, you know exactly what it is. If not, you just figure it's some noise of the modern world. But trust me—you could be in the catacombs under Fenway Park and still hear it."

I find my way to the alumni office and ask if there's any general information about notable alumni.

"Not really," says a young man, pale as a peeled cucumber.

"If I was writing a story about 'Famous People Who Attended the Museum School,' wouldn't there be some sort of list or compendium I could look at?"

"Not really," says the young man, repeating his favorite phrase.

"Then what would you suggest?"

"The Internet?"

Under my breath I mutter heresy: "Fuck the Internet." More audibly I say, "That's a brilliant idea. Why didn't I think of that? Thank you very much for your help."

Drifting back out into the hallway, I wonder what to do

next. Have another bagel and lox?

Pray to Saint Anthony! my mother's voice admonishes me. Saint Anthony is the Catholic Saint of Finding Things, and my mother, a devout Catholic, had forever implored me to pray for what I wanted.

Well, what the hell. "I need a little break here, Saint Anthony. Can you help me find something that will help me find Susan? Gracias. And solve the RISD theft. And why not the Gardner, too. Amen."

I turn around and find myself looking at a bulletin board. Above it is a sign that says Job Opportunities. That would be like my mother, wouldn't it? If only I'd become a doctor or a lawyer. It's never too late! I scan the fliers and business cards and formal notices...one in particular catches my attention: SANTA COSTUMES AND SANTA JOBS! GOOD PAY OVER THE HOLIDAYS! KLYMAX COSTUMES FOR EVERY OCCASION—DRACULA TO DRAGNET!

I jot down the address as the young man from the alumni office comes out into the hall.

"Scuze me," I tap the costume notice. "Has this place been around long?"

"Forever," he replies

"That's awhile."

Just then, there's a sharp cracking noise outside.

The young man flinches. "What was that?"

"Dunno," I say. "Sounded like a giant pencil snapping. Anyway, thanks for your help. Ciao!"

I throw myself into the back of the Escalade.

"Fuckin-*A,* Tiny! That was the *Tits!*"

He grins, revealing a bright gold incisor and we of the Escalade blur into the stream.

"The Eagle has landed," announces Tiny, and in a couple minutes Aleda appears through a revolving door, followed by a guy who looks like he works for the Secret Service. He escorts her to the car and doesn't leave until the automatic door locks clamp down.

"Jaysus! Jaysus fucking Christ! Gimme a drink! Quick!" she bawls, and I hit the vodka button. She slugs it down and wipes her lips with the back of her hand.

"Dear God in Heaven! Spare me *ever* producing a movie again! Why did I want to do this? Why? Because I admire Isabella Stewart Gardner. Couldn't that be enough? Did I really have to make a movie about her?"

"What is it?"

"What it is, my handsome man, is a co-producer who is *fucking insane,* and a studio that is even more fucking insane. Tiny, I want to go to the Hermès Store. I need another drink. No I don't. You know, Swanson, it's not even the money. I can deal with the money. I'm good with money. I understand money. I've been financially independent since I was eighteen. What kills me is people who don't understand you get what you pay for. Don't you think you get what you pay for?"

"Well...I think that sooner or later, you pay for what you get."

Aleda takes a deep breath and brings her hands together prayerfully. "O-K. Tell me about your day."

"Right. After we dropped you off, Tiny and I drove over to the Museum School, which is next to the Museum of Fine Arts."

"And did you find what you were looking for?"

"The wheels are turning...."

Aleda takes my hand. "You've got to let your subconscious take over and work on it. The conscious mind locks up. I've got just the thing...."

Across the street from the Public Gardens, the Hermès store. Within its luxurious confines, Aleda spritzes me with *Eau d'Orange Verte* cologne from an emerald green bottle. "Isn't that heaven! My life can be turning entirely to merde, but if I can spray myself with Hermès I feel there is hope." Turning to the store manager: "Could you put together a mixed case of the cologne and moisturizer and soap?"

"Of course. I'm sure we can—"

"Wonderful. That's so kind of you," Aleda cuts him off as she cruises across the floor to examine handbags.

When she's ready to go, she suddenly grabs me by the arm. "I didn't bring my wallet," she says. My breathing becomes shallow as I guess what's coming next. "I'll give you the money as soon as we get back to the hotel."

"Sure. Not a problem."

The sweat glands in my armpits open up, beads of perspiration racing down my sides. Aleda smiles her famous smile, gives me a little peck on the cheek and tosses the orange shoulder bag she's been fondling onto the counter.

"That, too," she tells the clerk.

I hand over my Visa card. When I get it back with the slip to sign, I can't bear to look at the total and just quickly scribble my name.

"Isn't this fun!" says Aleda, squeezing my arm. "Where to now?"

CHAPTER 11

♦

Cambridge. Klymax Costumes. Riley O'Reilly. Lunch at
the Gardner Museum.

THE PLACE LOOKS LIKE A GIANT CIRCUS WAGON.
A brightly painted red and yellow sign runs the full-length
of the old, clapboard warehouse: KLYMAX.
  "A costume store?" asks Aleda skeptically.
  "Hey—it's my turn, remember?"
Klymax Costumes, just over the Charles River, in
Cambridge, is creaky and cavernous. Inside the front door, an
old man wearing red suspenders is slumped down like a
marionette on an armless wooden chair next to a glass
counter.
  "Excuse me....Do you have any Boston Police uniforms?" I
ask. He slowly lifts his head and rotates it around in our
direction.
  "All uniforms are in the basement. Go down the stairs and
keep going straight. What we have will be on the right, all
the way till the end."
  The place smells like what it is: miles of old wood and old
wool.
  "Can you believe this place?" says Aleda wide-eyed. "It's
Moth Heaven. Why are we looking for Boston Police
uniforms?"

"The Gardner was robbed by two guys posing as Boston policemen. When I was at the Museum School today, trying to get some info on your friend Madeira, I saw a help wanted ad for this place. I dunno...something just sorta clicked."

"Are you saying Madeira rented a police costume here and robbed the Gardner Museum?"

"Do you think Madeira could've robbed the Gardner?"

"Why would he? asks Aleda"

"Because he could.

"You mean it was a lark?"

"It was a lark."

"Then why hasn't it been returned?"

"Maybe he decided to keep it. Maybe it was stashed somewhere and got ruined. After all these years, if somebody stole it for ransom money, it would've turned up by now. If the issue was money, it would've surfaced."

"I think you're right," says Aleda.

"You do?" It lifted me that I'd convinced a savvy person like Aleda so quickly.

"Well, maybe not about Madeira—but the lark theory makes sense to me. Haven't we all done things, or fantasized doing them just to do it?" She looks across row upon row of woolen suits and coats. "Let's dig in!"

There are a lot of police uniforms, mostly generic, and a ton of military uniforms, everything from bright red British Revolutionary War coats to dusky, modern day camouflage. We paw through the racks until Aleda announces, "Here we go: Boston PD...One...two...four. No, five. Five Boston PD's."

I pull one out and try on the jacket for size. Huge. I try on all the jackets; a couple are about my size, 42 regular.

"Hey. Here's something!" says Aleda, and from a side pocket pulls out a fake mustache, plopping it onto her upper lip.

"OK," she says in a gruff voice, "Where's the art, mister? I know ya got it."

"Very suave. You make a ravishing transvestite."

"Did either of the robbers have a mustache?"

"I want to say, yes. I'll have to reread some stuff. Hang onto it."

"No, you keep it." She hands it to me and checks her watch. "If we're gonna have time for lunch and get back in time to pick up your kids, we better get outa here. Let's go someplace wonderful. Hey—Let's go to the café at the Gardner Museum!"

Leaving the store, I ask the old man if they keep records of their rentals.

"Of course we keep records," he answers. Then his eyes brighten up and he cackles, "Except for Boston Police uniforms! Aha-ha-ha!" and the old bastard laughs so hard he falls into a violent coughing fit, torn sails of sticky phlegm billowing up into his throat.

"Glad we could amuse you, y'old fart."

"Swanson!" Aleda glares at me.

We drive across the Charles River on the Harvard Bridge and as we make our way toward the Gardner, I notice a fabled site: " Hey—there's Fenway Park! Can we swing by it?"

As Tiny navigates the Escalade around the back of the green outfield wall, we round the corner and the statue of Ted Williams comes into view.

"I know that guy!" says Aleda.

"Ted Williams? He's dead."

"No. That guy walking by the statue. Pull over," and she shoots down the window. "Hey Riley!" she shouts. "Riley O'Reilly!"

A skinny older gent with wisps of grey hair, khaki pants and a green Celtics windbreaker turns toward us.

"Is thee-at Aleda Cwally?" he asks in a Boston accent so thick it qualifies as a foreign language.

"It's me! But what are you doing here?" she asks, sticking her hand out the window where Riley O'Reilly clasps it.

"I work secuity he-yah at Fenway," he says, gesturing back at the venerable old ball park with his thumb. "I came beeyack he-yah around a ye-ah afta yaw show closed down. I'm from Bwoston awriginilly. Got fyamly he-yah."

"That's right. I remember you were from Boston...God— how could I forget?"

"I know, huh?" smiled Riley. Evybawdy out in L.A. always sad, 'You twalk fawny."

Aleda and Riley chat for a couple minutes and he tells her, "If you evah want tickets to a Sawks game, why you just give me a cwall," and he tells her his phone number, which she punches into her phone.

"That was pretty amazing," I say, as we pull away.

"I always make it a point to be friends with security," she says.

Tiny lets us off in front of the entrance to the Isabella Stewart Gardner Museum. From the outside, nothing spectacular. The face of the building, solemn. Italianate, but conservatively so, with a slightly institutional cast. Square. A

staid building of tan brick, four-stories high, the fourth floor
the former living quarters of Gardner herself, now
administrative offices for the museum.

A frieze of St. George slaying the dragon above the main
entrance, a doorway less imposing than what's found today
on many a McMansion. Tall, plain windows on the second
and third floors, a glimpse of tile roof...the understated
nature of exterior adornment utterly belies the palazzo
wonderland waiting inside.

Passing from the dark entranceway, it hits you with the
eye-popping effect of a heavy velvet curtain rising to reveal a
sunlit Broadway stage—the light-suffused center courtyard,
gushing and sparkling with fronds and palm trees and
flowering plants laid out along carefully combed gravel paths
that surround an intricately patterned tile mosaic with the
image of Medusa in the middle.

Verdant, studded with sculpture, dappled and softened by
the light pouring in from the glass roof four stories up,
spilling down the faintly pink stucco walls, past the open,
Moorish arches of the galleries.

The rest of the world could be a chaotic hell, a confused
mess or whatever it may be—here, you are in the middle of a
Venetian Dream.

Facing us from the end of the long Spanish Cloister
bordering the center court—the dramatic blacks and whites
of *El Jaleo*, John Singer Sargent's imposing 1882 painting of
a flamenco dancer.

The museum is quiet as rocks on this weekday in
November, as Aleda and I choose a table in the café.

"It always just takes my breath away," I say.

"It gives me an appetite," says Aleda. She orders a bottle of

Château Ausone St. Émilion and the Roasted Atlantic Salmon. I—mindful that I'll be paying for this too, and not sure if Aleda will see lunch in the reimbursement equation—stick with the Polenta Milanese.

"Too bad they nixed shooting here," I say.

"The lights. They claimed the brightness would affect the art. Maybe. I also think they didn't want Hollywood people running around the place. And the issue of security. Basically, they don't need the aggravation. There was also the insurance. That alone made it impossible.

"On the other hand, we can shoot the museum interiors anytime we want on the sound stage we built in the Providence Armory, and set up shots in ways we couldn't here. And you said you live near there! I'll get a chance to see your place soon!"

A momentary panic rushes through me: She'll finally see my genteel poverty and drift away....

We pass on coffee, the desert menu, wanting time to glance into the galleries before heading back to pick up the kids. I ask for the check.

Because I have to figure the tip, I can't ignore the details and just sign as I had at Hermès. *Yowser!* The fucking bottle of wine alone was three hundred and twenty dollars! Christ! Is this going to push me over my credit limit? Oh, *Borther, capital B!*

We climb the broad stone staircase to the museum's second floor and enter the gallery known as the Dutch Room. Walking across the oxblood-colored tiles, each one an irregular little handmade loaf, I stand in front of the empty gilt frame, tall as a man, from which Rembrandt's *The Storm on the Sea of Galilee* had been cut. In my mind's eye I can see the stolen painting—Jesus in a small, storm-tossed boat, surrounded by his apostles, the sail ripped and flapping, a ferocious wave pushing the bow skyward.

I ponder the space within the frame, fuzzing out the green brocade of the wall, then turn around to look at the Rembrandt self-portrait hanging on the opposite wall.

"¿Dónde?" I ask the face that looks back at me, the face of a young Rembrandt wearing a fine, puffy cap adorned with a feather sweeping over it. It is the face of youthful uncertainty—not the face one would normally present of themselves. This was Rembrandt's first self-portrait. It had been brokered to Gardner through Berenson.

"Wonder why they didn't take him?" muses Aleda.

Here, another opportunity to counter my material shortcomings.

"They tried to. Julie told me they left him on the floor here, after trying to cut him out of the frame. She said they didn't realize he's painted on wood, not canvas."

"Morons."

"Maybe not," I shrug. "Not if they wanted you to think they were morons." Aleda pats my arm approvingly.

"The thieves stood here, in this room," I begin, "the guards out of the way, bound and gagged in the basement. They had the run of the place. In this room they cut the two Rembrandts out of their frames and the Flinck landscape and Vermeer's *The Concert.*" I walk over to the writing desk, above which the Vermeer and the Flinck frames hang, back to back, just as when they'd held canvas.

"Swanson's been doing his homework," says Aleda.

"Swanson always secretly liked homework," I say. "It gave

him a chance to use his slow but thorough mind away from the pressure of the clever and the quick."

Crossing back across the length of the room with Aleda trailing me, we pass through a narrow passage into the auditorium.

"They cut through here," I say, as we stride through the vast twilight dimness, the walls hung with huge tapestries. "Then they entered this gallery—"

"I know this room! It's where we shot the scene you saw with Marcus Drowne and the Degas. Or is it Degases?"

"I'm still not sure. But you are correct. This is the Short Gallery. In this room..." and I swing the tall wooden shutters upon which are mounted drawings in frames, "they take four Degas drawings, smashing—but carefully?—the glass frames to remove them. Then they grab the gilded bronze eagle finial off the top of this flag pole (I gesture to a seven foot pole from which hangs a silk flag bearing the insignia of Napoleon's Imperial Guard). They must have stood upon this counter and stepped onto this lectern and just popped it off. Then, cutting back through the Dutch Room, they grab the bronze Chinese drinking beaker—the Ku—which I am guessing they swiped last, to toast their success."

"A lark. Taking the eagle thing and the Chinese beaker does have that frat-boy, prankish quality. So, could two people carry all of that?" asks Aleda.

"They made two trips. Even though they were able to disable the alarms and remove a video tape that filmed them coming into the building and into some of the rooms, they didn't realize their travels were also recorded onto the hard drive of a computer that was connected to motion detectors throughout the museum. The motion detector equipment generated a paper printout, which they took, but the digital storing of their movements to a computer hard drive just didn't occur to them. Or they forgot. That's how it's known how long they were in the museum and what pathways they took.

"You said it was 1990," says Aleda. "Only uber-geeks were thinking computers back then. Everyone knew video tapes, but not computers.

"Maybe they were *artists,*" I say archly. "Imagine if they were artists and made it look messy, so investigators would think it was pulled off by the usual boobs. Two big Rembrandts, the Flinck and Vermeer...the Manet from the first floor, all rolled up inside one another probably...the Degas—I think it might be Degas, not Degases—small finial, small beaker...Yes. Get it all by the side door, then two quick trips out to the car and they're off."

Aleda glances at her watch. "I want to see Belle."

We hike upstairs to the Gothic Room, the gallery directly above the Dutch Room. Here stands the life size, full-length portrait of Isabella Stewart Gardner, black dress with a plunging neckline, a huge ruby at her throat and a double strand of pearls wrapped around her corseted waist, painted by John Singer Sargent.

"She knows," says Aleda.

"Yes," I say. "Look at her eyes. She is surprised. But not shocked. She knows it is all part of a game. She got, they got, now what?"

"Swanson. You will have to come back here alone. I have a movie to make. This—" and she pauses to breathe in the very essence of the place—"is for you." She squeezes my hand. "Come, dear—two children await."

4 PM. Soccer practice over. Tiny pulls the Escalade up to the main entrance of the Wheeler School, where Eric and Abby and a dozen other kids wait for their rides. Much waving, blowing of kisses, and loud *Byyyyye's* after which they tumble in, then it's on to Aleda's hotel.

While the kids wait in the car with Tiny, Aleda and I go up to her suite. On the back wall of the living room coat closet, she dials open a wall safe. Inside are several neat stacks of crisp paper currency.

She turns to me and holds open her hand. From my wallet I withdraw the receipt from Hermès and hand it to her.

"Where's the receipt from lunch?" she asks.

Thank God.

After reviewing them, she withdraws a number of bills from each stack and hands them to me. "Count it," she says.

I do. "Seventy-three hundred," I say.

Aleda pulls a dark green Hermès bottle out of her jacket pocket and spritzes her neck. Then she spritzes my neck, draws a deep breath and presses her cheek against mine.

"Loves it!" And she breaks into a smile known the world over.

That night, after I've finished writing and the kids have long been asleep, I pour myself some of the smooth Havana Club rum, smuggled into the country by a fellow photographer who'd taken a surfing trip to Costa Rica. I stick my hand into my pants pocket and come up with the false mustache Aleda found in the cop outfit and press it onto my upper lip.

Dipping once more into the pants pocket, I withdraw my key ring, from which dangles a fob in the shape of a flattened 8 ball. Rubbing it between my fingers I ask: "Is Susan...OK?" Gradually the answer floats to the surface: *The outlook is not good.*

"Oh, borther." I rub again and ask, "Does Madeira know anything about Susan's disappearance?" The answer pops up: *What do you think, Swanson?*

"Swanson thinks, yes. OK, let's have some fun: Does Madeira know anything about the RISD theft?....answer....*Yes!*

"OK let's get crazy now: Does Madeira know anything about the theft from the Isabella Stewart Gardner Museum?" This time I give the 8 ball a really good rub and a shake to boot, and as the imaginary bubbles clear I hear my name called out in an urgent, raspy whisper:

"Swanson."

Pale as a little ghost, Abby stands in the foyer.

"What is it, sweetheart?" My heart is pounding.

"I had a bad dream."

I go over and hold her close.

"It was only a dream, sweetheart."

"I know, but it scared me."

"Do you want to tell me about it?"

"Somebody called and said we could come and visit Auntie Susan, and we went to a house and they took us in the basement, and she was walking around but she looked like a cat, and when I went up to talk to her, her head was gone and it was just all bloody."

Abby begins crying and shaking and I hold her and tell her it will be OK. I carry her upstairs, get her back under the covers and sit next to her, stroking the top of her head until she stops crying. Suddenly she smiles.

"You look funny in a mustache."

I'd forgotten. "It's not an improvement?"

"You don't look like you."

"Well then, it's going," and I peel it off.

"That's better," she says, and yawns. I put my hand on her forehead and soon she is asleep.

I tip-toe downstairs. The runner is worn all the way through on the front edge of each step. Looks ratty as hell, to say nothing of somebody possibly hooking their foot and breaking their neck. I had to start thinking about these things now with the kids here. I wonder how much a new runner would cost...or maybe I could stitch the gapers together?

The mustache. I place it on my desk and pull up an archived *Boston Globe* article on the Internet.

It traces the theft from beginning to end, mostly based upon statements from the two guards. I find what I'm looking for—yes, the thieves' both had mustaches—but I also find something else, startling.

The fake cops gained admittance by telling the guard through the intercom that they'd come to investigate "a disturbance on the grounds"—the very phrase Susan stumbled over when she'd related the details of the RISD theft to us in the hotel restaurant.

PART TWO

CHAPTER 12

◆

Naomi Rosenthal, DCYF Bitch-Ass Extraordinaire.
Dinner at Red Stripe. Aleda goes all Angry Mommy.

I'VE JUST RETURNED FROM GROCERY SHOPPING
and realize that I've forgotten to get the kids' favorite,
Annie's Macaroni, when the doorbell rings. A woman is
standing on the front porch. In the parlance of my dear,
departed father, she is built like a brick shithouse. Her
heavily socked feet are planted in tan suede Birkenstock's.
Her thick, reddish hair is tied back like a sheaf of field grass.
Glasses. Briefcase with straps. Early thirties.

Her name, she tells me, while at the same time proffering
her business card, is "Naomi Rosenthal." She's with the
Department of Children, Youth, and Families, otherwise
known as, DCYF, and she jumps right in.

"Let's see now...Abigail is ten years old and the daughter of
deceased parents. Currently, she has been under the
guardianship of her aunt...How is her health, Mr.
Di...Di...Di Cheerio?"

"Whoa...whoa...waitaminute," I stop her. "I'm not gonna
just stand here and be interrogated."

"*Excuse me?*" Ms. Rosenthal replies, as though she's just
smelled shit, not hers.

"A phone call would've been a nice courtesy. I am in the

middle of working. Why don't we make an appointment for a time that's good for both of us."

Ignoring me, Naomi Rosenthal opens her briefcase and begins pawing at some papers. She hands me several forms in triplicate. "I'll need those filled out and in my office by next Monday. Have a nice day." And with that, she thumps off the porch and squish-squashes down the walk.

Just loud enough for her to hear, I fling out, "And you can kiss my ass, bitch."

She stops. Slowly, deliberately, with an expression of utter astonishment on her face, she turns around.

"What did you just say?"

"What do you think I just said?"

"I think you said, 'You can kiss my ass, bitch.'"

"*What?*" I shriek. "I can't believe you just said that! And you work with children? Who's your superior? I'm not going to turn *any* information over to you. You've got *serious mental problems!*"

With that, I slam shut the door. I bolt upstairs biting my fist, steal into my bedroom and howl like a hyena. Sidling into the bathroom, I splash cold water on my face and bare my teeth in the mirror.

"Swan-*soon—you hairy dawg!*"

"Have you gone completely insane?"

"Oh, shush," I say. I have just told the story of *Naomi Rosenthal, DCYF* to my editor at *Providence Monthly*, Iphigenia Melikis. "How's your fish?"

Iphigenia, a Greek-Jew of Reubenesque proportions with thick ringlets of shining black hair tumbling over her shoulders, is taking me out for a nice dinner at Red Stripe.

Eric, under threat of waterboarding should he mess up, is at home looking after Abby for a couple of hours.

"My fish is fine, but I think you like to piss people off, Swanson. I really do."

"I do not like to piss people off, Iffy. I like to live my life without people screwing with me."

"Listen to me, Swanson—those people down at DCYF can make your life hell if they want to. They could have those kids in a foster home tomorrow. Is that what you want?"

"Oh, for God's sake, Iffy. I know I messed up, but—" I stop. Aleda and Royal Madeira have just walked into the restaurant and are being seated at a booth in the corner.

"Isn't that Aleda Collie?" asks Iphigenia.

"I dunno," I say, watching them.

"It is! Hey, you guys are pals, right? I saw that photo in the *Journal* last week. How about doing an interview with her for the *Monthly*?"

"I'd rather not."

"I'll pay you well for it."

"Of course I will."

"Good. Why don't you tootle over there right now, and I'll snap a picture of you both; you can find out why she's eating here, what she's ordering….People love to read about what celebrities eat."

"Not here. She's gets peckish about being bothered in restaurants."

"Then I'll go!"

"All right. I'll do it."

"Good boy. You march right over and turn on that famous Swanson Di Chiera charm. Ha!"

"OK. But let's just give them a few minutes to get settled.

Don't wanna jump on her right away." I was curious as hell
to watch them unobserved as long as I could.

"That's unusually reasonable of you, Swanson. Maybe you
got out all of your aggression for the day on the lady from
DCYF."

"No...I feel like I still have a little left in the tank."

As we continue our dinner, I surreptitiously watch Madeira
order a bottle of champagne. Cristal. Christ—stuff was
probably over two hundred dollars a bottle here. They were
really yucking it up, Aleda putting her hand on Madeira's
arm from time to time.

"I wonder if that's her boyfriend," says Iphigenia. "Are you
jealous?"

"Why would I be jealous," I say. "We're old friends. And
I'm sure that's not her boyfriend. She has somebody out in
California."

"They look pretty chummy to me."

"Trust me, Iffy—I am *sure.*" Suddenly, Madeira leans over
close to Aleda and whispers something into her ear. Turning
her head, Aleda sees me and frowns.

"Swanson!" gushes Iphigenia. "She looked straight at you.
You get over there right now!"

I amble over to their table trying to remain calm, trying
not to smile stupidly. I want to be the dispassionate
researcher, a scientist of the pathology of sexual incongruities
and perhaps art theft and abduction as well.

"Good evening," I say, hoping to sound more like Cary
Grant and less like Alfred Hitchcock.

Aleda and Madeira look up at me. Madeira's face is
timeless. It's neither male nor female. It has a debauched,
seductive beauty.

"Swanson," says Aleda. "Give me a kiss, dearest. What are you doing in public without me? Where are the children?"

"I'm giving Eric a chance to flirt with maturity and look after things for a couple of hours." I turn to Madeira and say with an exaggerated formality: "Royal Madeira—We meet again."

He looks at me with those eyes that turn to dark mirrors the way certain sunglasses darken in the light.

"*C'est mon plaisir,*" he says in barely a whisper, as though it's a secret between the two of us.

"Who's that?" asks Aleda, looking over toward Iphigenia.

"My editor at *Providence Monthly.*"

"She has beautiful hair."

"Her skin is lovely, too."

"Is it?"

"It's the olive oil. She's Greek."

"Greek," repeats Madeira in a faraway voice.

"Anyway, just thought I'd pop over and say, Hola."

"Hola," says Aleda.

"The Greeks have such beautiful names," says Madeira. "What's hers?"

"Iphigenia."

"Iphigenia...the daughter of Agamemnon and Clytemnestra," he sighs.

"Who the hell was Clytemnestra anyway?" I ask.

Madeira's eyes gleam. "*Clit,*" he says sharply, "was the slut wife of Agamemnon. She murdered him. She was bad news, Di Chiera. Sired by Tyndareus and born of Leda—the same Leda raped by Zeus masquerading as a swan. I'm surprised that as a writer, you don't know this."

"Maybe it's more of a painterly thing," I reply weakly,

taken aback by his ferocious intelligence and, frankly, that he remembers my name.

"No. The visual artist, the writer—kith and kin, Di Chiera. Van Gogh was a wonderful writer, as evinced by his letters to Theo, his brother. Eudora Welty—quite adept with a camera, as was Lewis Carroll. As are you."

"Indeed," I say.

"Kith and kin," smiles Madeira, the limousine eyes gleaming. "You and I are kith and kin."

I look at Aleda and raise one eyebrow.

"I must get back to my table," I explain hastily. "Please enjoy your dinner. My fiancée recommends the filet of piranha."

"Your fiancée?" says Aleda, and she looks over at Iphigenia who smiles and plays air piano with her painted claws.

"*C'est mon plaisir,*" I say with a small bow and retreat.

"Well? Did you get the interview?" demands Iphigenia.

"She said she'd have to think about it." I'd been distracted and embarrassed by Madeira and fall quiet.

"What's the matter?" asks Iphigenia.

"I just remembered that I'm not as smart as I think I am."

"I hate it when that happens," she says.

The next morning there's a message on my answering machine from a Luke Bainer, at DCYF. It is "vital," says Bainer, that I return his call "immediately."

After putting the kettle on, I go to the DCYF website to see who this Bainer is. There is no "Bainer," but there is a Luke Boehner, Director of Child Welfare.

"It's a no-Bainer: you're a *Boner,* you phony piece of shit. Spell it B-o-e-h, in my book that's Bo. You want the 'Bay' sound, as in Beowulf, then reverse the o and the e. And you can kiss my ass too, muthafucka."

Late in the morning, I phone Detective Porcaro. They have no leads. Susan is a missing person. There is no evidence, even, of a crime having been committed.

"It's possible she simply walked away...into another life," says Porcaro. "These things happen. I have learned that people are surprisingly good at hiding important parts of their life, until one day—Snap! They're gone!"

"That's not Susan," I say. "For starters, she loves her job. And more than that, she loves Eric and Abby. She would never walk away from them."

"Mr. Di Chiera, I do not know the woman but I am inclined to believe you. It's just that I have *nothing* to go on."

"What about Kurt Madeira? Did you talk to him?"

"Did. Mr. Madeira is quite an interesting person."

"No kidding?"

"He and Susan Mack have known each other since college in Boston. A long time. He's very concerned."

"Do you think he had anything to do with her disappearance?"

"No reason to."

"Doesn't he strike you as somewhat odd?"

"I've met odder. He seems a very intelligent man."

"What about the stolen art? Do you think there's any connection between her disappearance and the museum robbery?"

Porcaro emits a melancholy chuckle interrupted by a sharp *Erp!* "Sorry about that....At this point, we just don't know."

Pig. "It seems like law enforcement almost regards art theft as a joke—nobody's been hurt, and it only belongs to rich people or museums, so who cares?"

"There is that," says Porcaro in a way that crystallizes for me the realization that the cops are not going to find Susan, are not going to solve the RISD theft, and sure as hell aren't going to solve the Gardner theft.

That night, Aleda phones and asks if I'll meet her for coffee in her trailer on the Benefit Street set in the morning. Early. At seven. I let the machine take it. Her voice sounds severe, angry-mommyish—and, frankly, I've had enough of that in the past couple of days, thank you very much.

At seven-fifteen, I stumble into Aleda's trailer.

"You're late," she says. She's wide-awake and pulled together.

"May I have some coffee? Please?" I ask.

"Look at you. What time did you get to bed? You have children to watch after now."

"May I have some coffee, please?"

"Swanson. I know you do not like Royal Madeira. And that is fine. No, it's not fine. Swanson, have you ever slept with a man?"

"I beg your pardon?" It was way early in the morning for this baloney.

"Don't be *beggin' my pardon*. I asked if you've ever slept with a man? Have you ever sucked dick?"

"Christ almighty, Aleda. May I have some coffee?"

"Not until you tell me if you've sucked dick. Well? Have you?"

"No."

"Have you ever thought about it? And don't lie, cause I'll

know."

"I guess. Once or twice."

"Fibber. Of course it's been more than that. You ever taste sperm? You ever shot a wad into you own mouth?"

"Christ, Aleda!"

"I'm not Christ. Have you?"

"Yes. When I was younger. When I could shoot that far. Satisfied? Jesus."

"You see my point, Swanson? You are not entirely different than Royal Madeira. If you had a brain, you would realize you have something to learn from this person. He's a strange person, Swanson. Strange is good for people like us. Do you understand? We are not the lady who dumped Poe. We are Poe! We learn from people like Royal Madeira. Are you getting it? And don't give me a smart answer. I don't want to hear any answer. Just think about what I'm saying."

"OK."

"Royal Madeira is brilliant and I need his expertise on this film. I will get along with him, whether you like him or not. I will get along with him whether I like him or not."

"Do you like him? Her?"

Aleda draws a deep breath. "Swanson—It is not a question of like. Do you understand?" Her words are bullets, fired in rapid succession. "This person has an encyclopedic knowledge of the artwork that Belle Gardner collected. This person has supervised which paintings we had reproduced— *at enormous cost*—and where Belle would have had them displayed. Do you understand? This person is an invaluable resource and we are paying this person handsomely. This, Swanson, is what is known as business."

"How the hell does...*this person* know so much about the

art that Gardner collected?" I ask.

"I believe *this person* wrote...their college thesis or something about her life and her collection. *This person* is the world's foremost authority on Belle Gardner."

"Well, dog muh cats. I didn't know that. Why did not you tell me that, señora?"

"Because it's not my job to educate you, Swanson, and don't get smart with me. I know that you believe...*this person* had something to do with the disappearance of those dear children's aunt. I also believe that you believe that *this person* had something to do with the theft from the Gardner Museum."

"And what do you believe?"

"I believe that I have a movie to shoot! And this movie must be successful. Because, Swanson, if this movie is not successful it is unlikely that I will ever get a shot at producing another. And if this is my last job, then I am up shit's creek. I have two ex-husbands to whom I pay alimony. I have a full-time personal assistant who is dependent upon me, to say nothing of a mother and father in Georgia, both of whom are in poor health and require *very expensive* care, and a brother and sister who are dependent upon me in ways I'd rather not go into. I have been offered exactly two decent acting jobs in the last five years. I am a fifty-three, soon to be fifty-four year old Hollywood actress with a limited acting range, which means I am about as desirable as a plow horse at Belmont. Do you understand me, Swanson? This film has to have wings! It has to look terrific, and Madeira is gonna help make sure it does! What else can I say?"

"Um...."

"C'est mon plaisir."

"Oh, *borther*...."

"Swanson—This film must be a success!—*It is my pleasure.*
Got it? Now, what was that shit in the restaurant last night
about that woman being your fiancée?"

CHAPTER 13

♦

Arrow Amarusso, museum guard. The Dirt Palace in
Olneyville. Abby hears something.

THE KIDS DO NOTHING BUT EAT. I have to keep the
house at least 68 degrees while they're here. Water usage is
tripling. I use the car every day now....

"I need money!" I howl, and the best shot I have of making
real money, quick, is to solve the Gardner Museum theft.
Five million smackers!

If there's a connection between the RISD Museum theft
and the Gardner theft, maybe by figuring out the RISD, it
will lead me to the Gardner. To say nothing of finding Susan.

"My God what a mess!"

The guard—I need to talk to the guard who was on duty
the night the RISD Museum was robbed. Who could forget
her name? Arrow. I dig out the contact book I'd taken from
Susan's...here it is, Arrow Amarusso, address and phone
number. I could phone her, but think it better to pay a
visit—that way, she can't avoid me and let an answering
machine or voice mail handle it. "Takes one to know one," I
mutter.

Before leaving, I go into the room behind the kitchen
where the TV is and tell Abby I'll be out for little while and
that Eric will be here.

"Tell him not to pound me," she says, her eyes glued to the set.

Eric is playing a computer game in his room.

"Your sister is downstairs watching TV. Keep an eye on her, OK? I'm leaving you in charge."

"Uh-huh. OK," says Eric. "Where're you going?"

"I'm going to talk to someone about the theft at the gallery. I'm hoping it might shed some light on what happened to your Aunt Susan."

"Oh. Hey, Swanson."

"What?"

"Do you think...well...this kid at school said it was probably true. But do you think Aunt Susan is dead?"

I freeze. *Still Life In A Doorway.*

"I don't know, Eric."

"Well, I know what you said, that you would always take care of me and Abby—"

"Abby and me."

"Abby and me...but what I'm worried about is, if she's dead and then you got killed—then what would happen?"

I thaw out slightly and sit down stiffly on the edge of his bed.

"Eric, when I was about your age, I remember telling my father I was afraid that he would die. And he said to me: 'Swanson—I don't want you to worry about that. It won't happen for a long, long time.' So, I did stop worrying about it. And it didn't happen for a long, long time. So, I'm telling you that same thing now—don't worry about me dying. It won't happen for a long, long time."

"Yeah, but, what if the same people who killed my mother and father, killed Aunt Susan, and you're next?"

This was disturbing.

"Eric—who said anyone killed your mother and father?"

"I don't know."

"Then why would you say that?"

"I don't know."

"Do you think somebody killed your mother and father?"

"I don't know."

"We can talk about it, if you want."

"No, that's OK."

"Are you sure?"

"Yeah."

A little voice is telling me, Don't push it, Swanson. I decide to bring it down. For now.

"Well, don't worry, nobody's gonna kill me, Eric."

"But how do you know?"

"Because I'm tough. I'm a writer!"

"Writers aren't tough," smiles Eric shyly, and he begins blushing.

"Of course we are!"

"How?"

"*How?* Because we have to be! Not only do we have to live in this world, but, *my god*—we have to *write* about it!"

"That's not hard."

"You don't think so? Then you try it, buddy boy. You just give it a whirl and see how easy it is. In fact, here's your assignment: I want you to write about the happiest you've ever felt."

"This is the happiest I've ever felt—playing *RuneScape*."

"Then write about it. But when I read it, I will be looking to understand *why* it's the happiest you've ever felt. And you don't have to come out and tell me why. In fact, it's better if you don't. I want to *feel* why it makes you so happy."

"I don't know if I can do that."

"I'm not giving you a time limit here. What I'm asking you to do is tough stuff. It's why us writers get to be so tough. So ya see...nobody's gonna be putting me outa commission. Got that? Now, c'mere..." and I hug him. "Don't worry about me dying, OK? Worry about doing well in school, and being good to your sister."

Eric. Driving across town I ache for him—not only losing his parents, but now thinking they were murdered. I'd always assumed that Susan had talked to him about the incident, and I remember a few years back he'd asked me about his Dad, and the electrical fire in the car had come up. He knew the circumstances of his parents' death.

So, what had turned his thoughts to thinking his parents had been murdered? Was it the violent computer games? A media saturated with killing? Just being thirteen?

I would have to monitor his behavior more closely. One more thing to worry about.

"Let me be up to this."

Arrow Amarusso lives in an apartment on Meeting Street, not more than two blocks from Woods-Gerry, where the theft occurred.

She is skinny and very pretty; a wraith art student with a heart-shaped face that resembles Royal Madeira's. Weird. And jet black hair, blunt cut just below the ears. Pouty red lipsticked mouth, big blue eyes. Wearing a black wool hat with the brim turned up and a long, fitted black wool coat with six inches of skirt sticking out the bottom, she looks like an old John Held illustration of "Betty Coed," Roaring

Twenties flapper. She is on her way out the door. I introduce myself and explain why I'm here.

"I'll talk to you, but I've gotta get going," she says, unlocking a custom-made chopper bicycle from the bent hand railing alongside the front steps. She wraps the orange chain twice around her waist and locks it.

"Where are you heading?" I ask.

"The Dirt Palace."

"Where's that?"

"Olneyville."

"I live near there, in the Armory District," I say. Olneyville is just down the hill from my house, in what's known as the Valley section of Providence. "Can I talk to you there?"

"Sure."

"Can I give you a lift? We can throw your bike in the back of my car."

"That's OK," she says and pedals off. I hop into Veronika and follow her.

Once upon a time, Providence had been one of the big engines of the Industrial Revolution; the one-time manufacturing home of such famous companies as Fruit of the Loom, Nicholson File, Brown and Sharpe, and Imperial Knife. In addition to being a tool and textile giant, it had also been the center of the costume jewelry industry. Olneyville, and its enormous brick mill buildings along the banks of the Woonasquatucket River had been a big player in all of it.

Those days are long gone now—wrenches and knives, undies and earrings, all have been out-sourced to the Far East. But most of the cavernous brick mills still stand, some vacant and awaiting arson, others occupied by collections of small businesses—machine shops, picture framers, woodworkers, used office equipment suppliers…and artists.

I park Veronika on the crunchy, broken asphalt between two mill buildings and follow Arrow through an oversized metal door peppered with dents.

The Dirt Palace is abuzz with young women painting, sculpting…welding. Arrow walks to the far end of the room where a big press is set up.

"Can you believe RISD was throwing this out?" she says.

I look at the small gold ring passing through one of her nostrils. Why do these girls do this to themselves? She has a very attractive, straight nose. It needs no adornment.

"Arrow, I'm trying to figure out who might be responsible for the RISD theft. I think whoever did it might also be responsible for Susan's disappearance."

Arrow puffs out her cheeks then lets the air out in short pocking sounds.

"I've already talked to the police," she says.

"I know. But the police…they are not giving this the attention it deserves. They are not focusing. They see it as art/RISD/money/upper-class/so what?"

"I miss Susan." She looks down to the floor, her eyes welling up. "I don't know her well, but she's always so nice to me. She hired me. I feel like if I hadn't let the robbers in, then she wouldn't have disappeared either."

"Can't blame yourself, Arrow. Nothing like this has ever happened at RISD before. You were blindsided. Just tell me what happened that night. Not thinky, just be back there."

"OK…." she crosses her arms tight against her chest. "I was drawing in my sketchbook when the doorbell rang. I asked into the intercom who is it, and they said, Providence Police. I went to the front door and opened it. It never occurred to me that they were going to rob the museum. Of course, I feel like a total idiot now."

"*It wasn't your fault.*" God, she's so skinny. I want to take her out for a meal.

"Then whose fault was it?" she pleads desperately.

"Degas...Degas's...how do you say the possessive of his name, anyhow?"

"Degas'—with an apostrophe after the s. Same way you would say...Moses. Like, his name is Moses but you would still say Moses' tablets. You wouldn't say, Moses's tablets."

"I might. 'Cozy Moses's Tablets. Take Three, and Sleep Like a Baby in the Bulrush.' Anyway, thanks for clarifying that for me. And while we're at it—what about the plural of Degas? Degas or Degases?

"Same. Degas."

"How the hell do you know this stuff."

"My mother teaches high school English."

"There you go. I could always read and write well, but I did it by ear. I fell apart when it came to diagraming a sentence. I could get the subject and the verb and, usually, the direct object. But a predicate? And a predicate *nominative?* What the hell! But moving on....The doorbell rings...."

"The doorbell rings and I ask into the intercom, who is it and they say, 'Providence Police. We got a call about a disturbance on the grounds.' So, like a moron, I go to the front door and let them in."

"A disturbance on the grounds. You're sure they said that?"

"Yes."

"OK—you let them in. It was the natural thing to do.

So—they come in. What do they look like?"

"Well—that's the really stupid thing. They have on police uniforms, but their backs are to me—like they're lookin' around for somebody. Then, as soon as I open the door, they swivel around and push me back inside and they have masks on; those cheap plastic Halloween masks that cover your whole face? One of them is like a Marilyn Monroe face and the other one looks like Archie, you know, from those Archie and Jughead comics?"

"What were they like physically? What did they sound like?"

"They didn't say a word. They spun me around and taped me up right away. One of them was pretty big. Like football player big, and the other one was, I don't know—about your size? But I can't be positive about that because they moved so quickly. I mean, I am positive about the big guy, but the other one—let's just say I got the sense he was smaller. Average. About your size."

I emit an involuntary pained noise. "And...."

"And...I hate to say it, but that's all I know. They used duct tape to tape together my wrists and ankles. They taped a green tennis ball in my mouth, and all I could think of was, *Eeeew*....did a dog have it in his mouth? People come to the lawn behind the museum and throw tennis balls for their dogs. Then they moved a chair and pushed me under the desk and taped my arms and legs to it. And that's where Susan found me."

"Did you see anything else? Hear anything else?"

"I couldn't see anything at all. I did hear them walking around in the main gallery, then going out the side door, obviously, with the drawings and pastels."

"And that was it?"

Arrow nods. I feel she's given me all she has. Time to lay off.

"Boy, these old mills are perfect for artist studios. You can't make this kind of mess in a conventional apartment. Hey—do you think I could bring my daugh—" I stall.

"You have a daughter? Sure. You can bring her down. We actually have classes for kids on the weekends. How old is she?"

"She's ten. She's not actually my daughter—she's—well, I'm taking care of the children…Susan's children."

"I didn't know she had children."

"She doesn't. She's their aunt. Their mother and father died. The girl is ten. Abby is ten."

"That's the perfect age! Here." Arrow hands me a silk-screened flyer. "This has the hours and the phone number and some of the things we offer. Did she paint your nails?"

I glance down at my hand. I'd forgotten that Abby had done my nails while she was doing hers a few days ago. They were a pale metallic pink.

"Yeah," I say.

"I used to do my Dad's, too," says Arrow.

Before returning home, I stop at Susan's house to pick up more clothing that the kids will need. I pause in the dining room and consider the liquor bottles lined up on the oak buffet. No alcohol before five P.M. was my general rule. I glance at my watch—5:02. This is good.

"Eeenie-meenie-mynee-mo….let's   go   with   the…
McClelland…from Islay." I pour a couple shots worth into a tumbler   and   inhale.   "Ahhh….Fragrance   of   oak   and

smoke…tobacco and leather…." Nothing like a single malt Scotch whiskey that's been put together by somebody who knows what they're doing. Wonderful what you can buy when you have a nice, steady salary.

I stand still and listen. It is hollow quiet. I have a bad feeling that Susan will never be savoring this Scotch again. Still, I put the bottle back in its proper place.

Swinging into the driveway I nearly plow into the big Escalade, Tiny in the driver's seat. I pull up alongside and jump out.

"What's up?"

"Dunno. She's inside."

This is a disaster! All I can think about is cat hair and tired old torn wallpaper, and the worn carpeting going up the stairs. Toilet bowls undoubtedly need to be cleaned, too. Christ—it's all over!

"Hellooo…?" I call nonchalantly, closing the front door.

I glance into the living room and dining room. Nothing. Kitchen. Nothing. Upstairs, Aleda is sitting alongside Abby on her bed, brushing her hair.

"Hey," I say, real casual. "Wuddup?"

"Nothing," says Aleda. "We're just hanging out."

"Where's Eric?" I ask.

"Over at Bressler's," says Abby.

"What's Bressler's?"

"Sammy Bressler. He's in Eric's class at school."

"He didn't tell me he was going anywhere."

Abby shrugs. "I heard something and I got scared."

"What did you hear?" I ask.

"I dunno. Like something moving outside. Like, somebody

walking on the porch or something."

"She called me," says Aleda. "She pressed redial on your dinosaur phone."

"What's a dinosaur phone?" asks Abby.

"A very old phone," says Aleda. "Your Uncle Swanson's phone has been around since dinosaurs roamed the earth."

"Now, now Aleda," I say. "My phone isn't old. An *old* phone is the kind you used to have at home growing up...on the wall. Remember? You held one piece to your ear and spoke into the part on the wall. It had a little crank on the side...."

"Hardee-har-har." Aleda gives Abby a hug and a kiss on top of her head. "I gotta go now, honey. Your Uncle Swanson is here, so you don't have *anything* to worry about."

Outside on the porch the daggers come flying. "Goddamnit Swanson—she's just a little girl. *Never* leave her alone again like that. Do you know what can happen to a child her age?"

"I told her brother—"

"Swanson—he's barely old enough to look after himself!"

"I know. I was gone longer than I thought. I had a very interesting conver—"

"Swanson!"

"What?"

"Abby is a very pretty little girl. Things can happen to very pretty little girls. I know, because I was once a very pretty little girl."

"You're still a very pretty—"

"Swanson—shut up. I know what I am, and I am comfortable with it. Well, *somewhat* comfortable with it. The point I'm making is, Abby has lost her mother and father and, probably, her aunt. She's afraid. Can you blame her?"

"Of course not. Do you really think Susan—"

"Be quiet! Now, she lives in this creepy old house with you. By the way—you gotta rip out that carpeting on the stairs. I almost tripped and broke my neck going up. My point is, when I got here tonight she was shaking and crying. You gotta get a cell phone, for starters, and get one for her too, so she can reach you."

"I really don't think—"

"Swanson! Just do it! I know you hate cell phones, but you have to do this for her. She has to know she can reach you."

"But she's only ten. She probably doesn't even know how to use one."

"Swanson. *You* don't know how to use one! She'll pick it up in about five seconds. Kids today are born knowing how to use computers and cell phones and iPads. As the ad says, *Just Do It!*"

"You're mixing Apples and Nikes."

She places her hands around my neck.

"Swanson. I have never strangled a man before, but it's beginning to sound interesting."

When my ears stopping buzzing, I ask Aleda if she thinks Abby really heard anything.

"I don't know. What about the person you rent to?"

"Could've been. I'll check."

"You've got a nice place here, Swanson. Dark, and creepy, and it needs some work, but potentially very nice. But this neighborhood…I don't know."

"That's why I could afford to buy it, Aleda. On the other side of town, it'd be triple what I paid here."

"We can talk about this another time. I gotta get back to

the hotel, take a bath, have a drink, go over the script. I have to be up at five."

"Thanks for coming over. I'm sorry for the trouble."

"Oh, Swanson, it was no trouble. Truthfully, I loved every minute of it. But fix that carpeting, will ya. Just rip it out! Otherwise, the place looks OK. Invite me over sometime. I think a man should be able to entertain a woman in his home, don't you?"

A huge burden has been lifted. She's seen how I live and still likes me.

Before heading back in, I take a stroll around the house. Nothing looks amiss. From the backyard I look up and see nothing. Only the light on in Abby's room. I ring Ina's doorbell...knock on the door. She isn't home. Maybe she's dead on the floor inside, her throat cut. Christ, that's a bad thought to have. Still, I go and get the key to her apartment and check. No dead body. Place is spotless.

Standing on the dark lawn I look out to the street. "I need more moola," I mutter. A disturbance on the grounds. What're the odds? Two phony cops, same phrase...student guard. "Duct tape!"

CHAPTER 14

♦

Briggs Pandora. Trip to Westport. Luke "Boner" from
DCYF threatens. Arrested! Jailed!

I FIND THE BRESSLER'S PHONE NUMBER in Susan's
address book and they bring Eric home. What ensues is a
painful lecture about responsibility, and specifically doing
what you say you're going to do, and never leaving your
sister alone.

"You're too old for me to spank, but I will have to punish
you if anything like this happens again. I will find
something. Do you understand me?"

Eric nods.

"Nodding is not good enough. I want you to say, 'I
understand you, Swanson.'"

"I understand you, Swanson."

"What do you understand?"

"Uh…I understand…that…um…I'm supposed to listen
to you and look after my sister."

"That is correct. But there is something else. What is that
something else?"

"Um…Listening   to   you…looking   out   for   my
sister…um…."

"Think, boy."

Suddenly, Eric's lower lip starts quivering and tears well up in his eyes.

"What's the matter?" I ask impatiently.

"I feel like you don't love me because you called me boy instead of my name." He drops his head and stands there, crying.

I hold him until his crying slows. Eric has been through so much in his short life. I hand him some Kleenex and look straight at him.

"Eric. I love you. No matter what, I will always love you. But right now, with your Aunt Susan gone and all of our lives disrupted, I need you to be smart. I need you to use your intelligence."

"I miss my Mom and Dad," he says.

"I miss them, too. So much. Your Dad was my best friend."

"Swanson."

"What?"

Eric stands back and wipes his eyes. "I can show you something that proves I am smart."

Eric wakes up his computer and brings a schematic diagram of a car onto the screen.

"This is the same car my Mom and Dad owned when they…died. Everybody always told me that they died because they couldn't get out of the car because the electrical problem that caused the fire also made the door locks jam locked. But look here," and he points to a red circle he's made on the inside panel of the driver's door. "This is a lever so you can unlock the door in case the locks won't open."

He enlarges the diagram so it's easy to see. Sure enough, there it is.

"So, wouldn't my Dad have used that lever to unlock his

door, and then pull my Mom out with him?"

A rare moment seizes me: I am speechless.

I met Ray Mendelsohn my freshman year of college in the parking lot behind the freshman dorms. He was at the helm of an honest-to-goodness hot rod with the entire engine exposed, a metal flake purple open-cockpit body and BigFat tires on the back. It turned out he'd built the thing himself, called it, "My '23 Bucket T," as it utilized the body of a 1923 Model T Ford, seriously radicalized.

Our interest in cars bonded us right away, and while I was partial to the classic European machines—Aston Martins, Jaguars, etcetera—Ray had a fascination with one-of type cars, handbuilts, and prototypes. So, it came as no surprise that he got his hands on something called a Briggs Pandora, an aluminum-clad technological marvel built in the mid-sixties by the short-lived Briggs Automobile Company of Westport Point, Massachusetts. Innovative for its time, it boasted remote keyless entry, common today, and central power door locks, also common today. On more than one occasion I had the pleasure of sweeping along winding roads with Ray beaming at the wheel, and it was nightmarish to know that his beloved Pandora had become a death chamber from which there was no escape.

But now it appeared there was an escape, unless the manual override was broken or missing, both of which were possibilities as he'd purchased the car used. Also, it was possible that this online schematic included details never incorporated into the final production vehicle.

But why would anyone want to murder Ray and Julie? For that matter, why would anyone want to abduct Susan? The only common denominator I know of is Royal Madeira. But Porcaro's talked to him and determined he's not a suspect.

"Porcaro" I say, mimicking Aleda—"Isn't that something we had for dinner?"

Coming in the door from dropping the kids off at school, the phone is ringing. Crap. It's Luke "Bainer," the guy at DCYF I was supposed to call back "immediately," last week. Well, he'll just have to wait a little bit longer; I need to locate the listing for a Peter Briggs in Westport Point, Massachusetts.

No problem there. Small town folks are still listed, still have land lines. The phone is answered by his wife. She is most congenial—enthusiastic, even. Peter isn't available at the moment, but she is sure he'd be *happy* to talk to me and, yes, he even has a Pandora stored out there and she is sure....Sounds like she has a little bit of Southern in her. Wouldn't be surprised, nice as she is.

Westport Point, Massachusetts is about thirty miles east of Providence heading toward Cape Cod, and I make it out there in about forty minutes. The door to a sprawling, shingled house is answered by Camilla Briggs, a natural beauty probably in her early sixties; trim, but nice, broad hips, thick mane of white-blonde hair.

Exceptionally friendly and welcoming. A bright, Miss America Smile. Moments later, her husband, Peter, appears on a motorized scooter. A tan Jack Russell is along for the ride at his feet.

"Fucking Lyme Disease," he growls as I follow him down a white lane of crushed shells. "Fucking doctors didn't know what it was and it got into my joints and then it was too late.

Lookit me—I'm damn near a goddamn cripple! At least I can still get it up! You met Camilla. Imagine if I couldn't? Jesus! There would be the definition of Hell!

"Hell has many definitions," I say, and tell him Ray's story.

"Surprised I never heard of the incident," says Briggs. "Usually, a case like that, they grab a lawyer and try to sue the manufacturer for a supposed defect."

"Ray bought it used. There wasn't much left after the fire. Just a shell."

"All the same," says Briggs. "You'd be surprised what they can find. Do you know what happened to the car?"

"No. Junked, I guess."

Briggs sighs at the thought of any of his beloved Pandoras coming to such an ignoble end.

"Any vehicle, of course, can develop a short, followed by a related electrical fire," he says. "Even a Pandora, although it would be highly unlikely. Would it cause the automatic locks to jam? Possibly. Would the manual override on the driver's door fail?" He stopped the scooter and looked up at me to underscore his point: "Virtually. Fucking. Impossible. I designed it myself!"

At the end of the lane are three enormous metal buildings. Inside the farthest sits a pristine Pandora, identical to Ray's. I am not prepared for the emotion that engulfs me just seeing the car. My eyes tear and my nose fills up. I apologize to Briggs and step outside to collect myself. A bright red male cardinal sits on a tree branch not ten feet away.

"I love you, Ray. I'm gonna figure this out. I'm fucking well gonna figure this out. Your son, by the way, is a smart boy—not unlike his dad….."

Back inside, I open the driver's door.

"There it is," Briggs says, pointing to the override lever set down near the bottom of the door panel. "Go ahead, get in and try it!"

I lock the door and unlock it repeatedly with the lever. Positive as can be.

"Every Pandora had one. In order to defeat it, you'd have to unscrew the handle with an Allen wrench, remove the cup trim, and then disengage the rod that travels directly to the locking cam."

"A lot of work," I say.

"A fucking lot of work," he says. "Nobody'd do it less they wanted to."

"That sounds pretty nefarious."

"Ugly nefarious," spits Briggs.

I ask him how much a Pandora had cost new.

"What do you do for a living? Mr. Di Chiera?"

I tell him I'm a writer, and he says, "Well, unless you wrote bestsellers or had a trust fund...or a rich wife who truly loved you," and smiling, he glances back toward his house and flexes his eyebrows, "you never could've afforded one! Back when they rolled out, all forty-five of them, they went for roughly ten grand apiece. That was in 1966 to 1968, the production years. In today's dollars that would probably be a hundred g's, at least."

We return to the house and I thank him for being so accommodating.

"Sure you won't stay for a drink? Camilla makes a Sazerac can't be beat."

"Love to. Another time, perhaps. Got a couple of kids I need to get back to."

He raises a hand. "Say no more. Wife has a couple

daughters from a previous marriage. Fucking world stands still when 'em little bitches bark."

I'm halfway home when it occurs to me that I should've asked him if he had a list of all the original purchasers of the car. Bet he did, if they'd cost that much.

As soon as I get in I phone him, and again, the lovely Camilla answers. She says she will convey the message to him and she is sure, enthusiastically sure, that if he has a list he'll be happy to share it with me. What is my phone number and mailing address?

What a lucky guy, to be married to such a friendly, upbeat woman. Rich, too, if I read him right. But I hardly have time to put down the phone and savor the thought, when it rings.

"Bainer" from DCYF again. Fuckit. Might as well get this over with.

"Right, Mr. Boner. Been extremely busy the last few days, and was going to get back to you...*today, actually.*"

"It's Bainer," the man corrects me, and he wants to know about—he pauses—"Abigail and Eric."

"Abigail and Eric," I repeat softly, and reach down to pet Little Guy who is swarming around my ankles. "Abby and Eric are just fine, Mr....*Bainer.*"

I feel a wet spot behind one of Little Guy's ears. Putting down the phone, I pick him up for a closer look.

Damn it! A cat-fight bite has abscessed and now burst open.

"Mr. Di Chiera? Are you listening to me?"

"Mr. Bainer, I'm gonna hafta call ya back. I've got a cat emergency."

"I'm a dog person myself," says Boehner. "But that's neither here nor there. What's important is that we address the situation with the children."

"Sir: I've got a darn infected cat wound to deal with. And if I don't, I'll have to re-finance my house to take care of the damn vet bill."

"Having financial problems, are we?"

I draw a deep breath. "I will get back to you, soon as I attend to my cat. Within the hour."

"All right then, Di Chiera. It's ten now. Call me by eleven."

"Roger Wilco. Over and out."

After applying hot, salt water compresses to the wound and smearing on some antibiotic ointment, I call back. Boehner is not discussing anything and drives straight to the point.

"Mr. Di Chiera: CPI Rosenthal will return tomorrow afternoon to interview you and the children, Abigail and Eric. She will be there at 4 PM. Good bye." And he hangs up.

My faith in humanity is restored later in the afternoon, when Camilla Briggs phones and says that her husband will be mailing me a list of all the original purchasers of the Briggs Pandora.

The next day as I prepare to pick up the children from school, the doorbell rings. It is 3:30 and CPI–Child Protective Investigator–Naomi Rosenthal stands on the porch, glaring mercilessly into my eyes.

"I'm coming in to talk to both you and the children."

I'd hoped to play ball so things didn't get screwed up, but her arriving a half hour early (To catch me off guard?) and then addressing me as though she's the Gestapo, hits a nerve.

"Frog-et it," I say.

"I must speak with Abigail and Eric."

"They are not here."

"Where are they?"

I just look at her.

CPI Rosenthal turns from me, leaves the porch and walks out to the street and gets into her car. I continue pulling it together to leave.

I'm running around with my glasses looking for their case when the doorbell rings again. I open the door and in front of me stands CPI Rosenthal, and by her side a chunky black woman, late thirties. Her head is round as a bowling ball and she wears a pair of currently fashionable eyeglasses—narrow, rectangular frames with wide stems, giving her a cross-eyed, goggled look. She is attired in something that looks like a boys' belted Buster Brown suit out of the early 1900's.

"Mr. Di Chiera," says the black woman. "You need to answer this woman's questions."

"Pourquoi?"

"Say what?" she scowls.

"Why?"

"Because if you don't, I am going to have to escort you down to the police station, and you can answer them there."

Bullied and threatened on my own doorstep? I don't think so! Leaning forward, I whisper into the woman's face: "Bite me."

BIG mistake.

I turn to step back into the foyer when I am pushed forward, hard. My sport coat is pulled down my back and inside out, immobilizing my arms. As I struggle to maintain my footing, the black woman says, "I'm arresting you for assaulting a police officer," while at the same time handcuffing my hands behind my back.

"Goddamnit!" I scream. "Why are you doing this? What's the matter with you?"

"Resisting arrest and disorderly conduct," she growls.

The black woman, known later in the arrest report as Officer Cheryl Lopes, hustles me down the porch steps.

"Why are you doing this?" I repeat over and over, as I am forced down the driveway toward the street reduced to a captured animal.

The cop's face is contorted and bursting with anger. If she could shoot me, she would. I've never seen such hatred on a face before.

"I need my glasses!" I snarl. "The front door of my house is wide open!" The woman pushes me up against the side of a plain, white sedan and opens the back door. Across the street, I see Aoibhinn's father walking their dog.

"Patrick!" I holler. "Call Al—" I'm about to give Aleda's name at the Hotel Providence, but remember she uses her alias down there. What is it?...I'm being pushed into the back of the car...."Call *Betty Schaefer* at the Hotel Providence. Tell her it's an emergency and I am being taken to the police station. *Betty Schaefer, Hotel Providence!*" Bam! I'm in and the door slams shut.

I'm nearly foaming at the mouth. The entire backseat of this unmarked patrol car is hard, molded fiberglass.

"Hey—these handcuffs are really tight," I say up against the thick plastic barrier separating me from Officer Lopes.

"Tough shit, asshole."

"*What?*"

"Don't move," she says. "They get tighter if you move."

Tighter if you move. What will the great minds think of next?

At the police station I am relieved of my wallet, belt, everything in my pockets. Shoes. "I hear you're a real piece of shit," says the intake officer, a Spanish guy in civilian clothes. "Well I just been waitin' for somebody like you to fuck up my day. Are you gonna fuck up my day?"

Nothing like standing around in stocking feet when everybody else has heavy shoes on, to make you feel powerless. I'm walked down a cement floored corridor and into my new accommodations: a metal-walled, six-by-eight foot cell painted Nonentity Aquamarine. A steel shelf three feet wide projects off the back wall. There's a fluorescent light overhead and a stainless steel sink and toilet. No toilet seat. One button on the sink releases a stream of water.

After the first hour or so, and without my watch, it's hard to tell how much time is passing. It's a sensory deprivation chamber. It's boring. There is absolutely nothing to do except think. This is the hell of captivity!

Abby and Eric. What's happening with them? Are they standing outside the school, waiting for me to pick them up?

Hopefully, Eric has taken them back inside and spoken to someone in authority, and they've figured out how to contact Aleda.

She was so right about getting them cell phones!

You are an idiot, Swanson! An immature, self-righteous, arrogant fool! I want to lecture myself out loud, but I will not allow myself to do it. Nor show any emotion. That little thing in the corner of the ceiling is a camera, and I'm sure the cell is miked, too.

No. I will not give these bastards the satisfaction of watching me sweat. I will lie here on this metal shelf and breathe and wait it out.

"Breathe," I can hear Aleda's voice, coaching me. "Just *breathe*...."

Finally, footsteps and the sound of my door being unlocked. "C'mon asshole," says the intake officer.

Mug shot taken. Wallet, shoes, etcetera returned, I'm handcuffed and placed in the back of an airless van for the ride downtown to the Garrahy Judicial Center—the same house of woe where I was divorced four years earlier.

I'm taken to an empty courtroom. A clock on the wall says it's ten of nine. Jesus!

A door behind the judge's bench opens and somebody I could've gone to college with steps to the bench. He hardly glances at me. He is not happy. He's been dragged here from home...dinner at Hemenway's...something better than this shit, that's for sure.

A door to one side of the bench opens and an Irish-looking fellow a few years younger than I and carrying a substantial beer gut approaches.

"Mr. Di Chiera?"

I nod.

"My name is Mike Fay. Miss Schaefer's attorneys have hired me to help you. I know you're pissed off, but don't say anything right now. We just want to get you out of here."

The judge reads the charges against me: "Disorderly conduct. Simple assault. Resisting arrest. How do you plead?"

"Not guilty, your Honor," says Fay.

The judge drops papers on the table in front of me. Without my glasses, I can't read them.

"It's fine. Just sign," says Fay.

Once we're out of the building, attorney Fay says, "I don't know who you are, but you're a lucky man."

"You call getting arrested, lucky?"

"Mr. Di Chiera, do you know that you could've been held in jail for seventy-two hours before being arraigned? Do you know that under these circumstances, children have virtually no chance of leaving state custody for weeks, often months?"

"Where are they?"

"The boy is at the child detention facility in Pawtucket, and the girl is at a group home in Providence. Your friend, Betty Schaefer, or I should say, her lawyers, are working to arrange for her to obtain temporary custody of them as soon as possible, within a day or two. Highly unusual."

"Then, who are you?"

"I am a criminal defense attorney, Mr. Di Chiera. Miss Schaefer, through her lawyers, arranged for me to get you out of jail and arraigned tonight. I'm a one-shot deal, so this is good-bye. Oh, they also posted your twenty thousand dollar bail."

"*Twenty thou—*"

CHAPTER 15

♦

Sly Dr. Casavant. Ass Burgers! Attorney Drury
Leyendecker.

"SWANSON—THE KIDS WILL BE FINE FOR A DAY
OR TWO. Trust me, it'll be an experience they'll remember
for the rest of their lives. It will help them. They can use it to
get into college. Did you really say, 'Bite me' to a cop?"

"I just told you, Aleda—I didn't know she was a cop. She
was dressed in street clothes, I didn't see a gun, she never
showed me a badge…."

"Big mistake on her part. Lawyers will eat her alive on that
one—although she'll lie about it. Cops lie all the time. But
judges know that. The charges will never stick."

We're sitting in Aleda's suite sipping fresh margaritas.

"What happened to your wrists?"

"The handcuffs weren't my size."

"Jesus, Swanson….I don't think saying 'Bite me' to a cop is
against the law, but she's a cop, a woman, and black. You're a
white man. You hit all the buttons at once."

"Control-Alt-Delete."

"Whatever. But let's forget about her. What's important
here are the children. My lawyers have told me the rub is
that you are not their biological uncle, and these government
people almost *have* to do something like this when there is no

blood relative."

"Do something like what—arrest people?"

"No—put the children under state care. Now here's the plan: my lawyers are shooting to get me temporary custody of the children. At the hearing, I will swear up and down that you are the finest man God ever made, and that you are perfectly suited to be the guardian of these dear children. I then—now you pay attention to these words very carefully, Mr. Swanson—*I assure the court that you will perform as their guardian in an exemplary fashion.* That you will not tell police officers to bite you or anything else. Because if you do, I will have to pay a very substantial fine, and those children will end up being abused in a foster home. Got it?"

"Got it."

"Good. Now go home and take a bath and go to bed. I'm going to do the same thing. Jesus, I knew I didn't come to Providence just to make a movie. My astrologer said something about 'life changing events,' but I was too busy to pay close attention. I shoulda listened, though I don't know what I would've done differently."

"Not seen me?"

"That wasn't gonna happen—I needed to find good seafood."

"I was just your seafood connection?"

"Swanson—we all gotta be something to somebody. Plus—I kinda love you. Now, goodnight."

It's the emptiest night of my life, being in my house without the kids, worried about how scared they must be. Knowing I'd put them there. I beat myself up good, and deserve it.

"Please come back, Susan. I don't think I'm cut out for this."

In the silence, I remember when I told her I'd never be able to handle the kids on a daily basis, and her saying, "Never underestimate what you can do."

"Sure. Look what I've done!"

Morning brings a phone message from the office of Drury Leyendecker, the lawyer Aleda has retained to represent me. I have a two o'clock appointment with a Dr. Casavant for a psychological evaluation. "No need to worry," I'm told. "This is for your benefit."

Dr. Casavant has sly features—slitty eyes with long lashes, barely visible behind the glare of his oversized, metal-rimmed eyeglasses. He's small and trim. His lips are thin and curl up at the corners when he smiles sardonically, which is often. His nose is pointy.

In a slight lisp, he asks questions about my childhood: Did I play organized sports? Did I yell at my teammates? He reads a list of words, asking me to respond to each word with the first word that comes to mind. He takes notes.

After forty-five minutes, he touches the tip of his nose with his pen and holds it there. Smiling his sardonic smile, he regards me and says, "Ass Burgers."

I smile back. "Ass Burgers," I echo.

"Not an extreme case," says Casavant. "But enough." He walks over to his desk and flips through some papers, handing a sheet to me. "This will give you the basics."

The bold print at the top of the sheet says, "Asperger's Syndrome Behaviors."

"Oh, *Asperger's.*"

"Figured you'd heard of it," says Casavant. "In my estimation you have a mild case that could flare up, from time to time, causing you to exhibit anti-social behavior." Casavant glances at his watch. "It's been a pleasure, Mr. Di Chiera. See you in court tomorrow. And," pointing to the sheet, "wouldn't hurt for you to have a look at that."

I roar all the way home, roar like I haven't since telling CPI Rosenthal that she could kiss my ass. I run upstairs to the bathroom with the sheet in my hand and sit on the toilet and read:

Asperger's Syndrome Behaviors include: Repetitive behaviors or rituals; Peculiarities in speech and language; Extensive logical/technical patterns of thought; Socially and emotionally inappropriate behavior and interpersonal interaction.

"Bite me, bitch! *Bite me!*" I bellow, forcing an explosion from my bowels that ignites another round of insane laughter. "Bite me! I got ASS BURGERS!!! I can't fuckin' help what I say! Sometimes can't help what I do! I'm a *high-functioning,* autistic sonofabitch! Jail me? Hell—I should be in the fucking Special Olympics! Miracle I can get through the day, you stupid bitch! Oooops...*ASS BURGERS!*"

The next day, back at the same courthouse where I'd been arraigned, my hilarity is ruthlessly de-twinkled and the humbling continues.

First I'm ripped a new asshole by the attorney for DCYF, who walks Judge Ursula Diggett (a few years younger than I, straight brunette hair, over-sized horn-rimmed eyeglasses and a flat-chest—bad sign in the compassion department?), through the occurrences on the day I was arrested, and that of a week earlier, when Rosenthal first visited.

Ouch! Does it ever hurt to hear those words flung back into my face in a humorless court of law. Needless to say, Judge Diggett doesn't dig it. She looks at me over the tops of her glasses like I've just laid a really dark trumpet fart.

But then, finally, the cavalry arrives! Prominent Rhode Island attorney Drury Leyendecker deftly outlines my long friendship with the children's father, and the close bond between "Uncle Swanson" and the children before their parents died; one which continues when they are under the care of their Aunt Susan, who is now a missing person.

Leyendecker then calls Dr. Casavant to the witness stand, and Casavant testifies that I indeed suffer from Asperger's Syndrome, which, as he tells the court, "…causes Mr. Di Chiera to unpredictably and against his will, say the most objectionable things, often of a vulgar nature. However,"concludes Dr. Casavant, "the particular *lineage* of Asperger's afflicting Mr. Di Chiera, confines his outbursts to authority figures, and in no way would impact his ability to care for the children."

"But, Dr. Casavant," inquires the judge, "what might be the result should Mr. Di Chiera confront an authority figure while in the presence of the children? Might not such a violent outburst have a negative effect upon Eric and Abigail?"

Dr. Casavant nods and smiles understandingly before answering. "Not an issue. In the class of Asperger's Syndrome with which Mr. Di Chiera copes, the presence of children has an antidotal, in fact, *neutralizing* effect."

Finally, Leyendecker calls Aleda to the stand. That she and I have known each other some thirty years makes quite an impression on the judge. But what Aleda says when asked to characterize me, her eyes shiny and moist, totally rocks the house.

"Swanson Di Chiera is the kindest, sweetest man I have ever known. When I first met him I thought: Here is a prince. Like most women, I always thought that someday I would have children. But—I made my choices. I put my career first and I do not regret that decision. However, without hesitation I can say that if I had decided to have children, I could not imagine a better father for those children than Swanson Di Chiera."

Wow. I look across the room and see Ms. Rosenthal, her eyes narrowed, grinding her teeth. The judge asks to see both the prosecutor and my lawyer in her chambers. When they emerge ten minutes later, the judge summons Aleda and me to step up before the bench.

"I have come to a decision," the judge intones—"a temporary decision. The children, Eric and Abigail Mendelsohn, will be returned to your care, Mr. Di Chiera. However, they will be, as will you, under the watchful eye of Miss Collie. Miss Collie, the terms of your supervision will be that you physically see the children at least three times per week, and that you speak with Mr. Di Chiera at least once daily, specifically to ask about the welfare of the children. Do you both understand?"

"Yes, your honor," we answer in unison.

"And once per week, Miss Collie, I will request that you contact the appropriate person at DCYF and relay to them the condition of the children, etcetera. A form will be provided to you for this purpose through your attorney. Do either of you have any questions?"

"No your Honor," I say.

Aleda and her attorney exchange a glance, followed by Aleda also saying, "No, your Honor."

Across the room, Ms. Rosenthal's entire corporeal self has become a black, roiling cloud.

Outside the courthouse I tell Aleda, "That was some performance in there."

"That's why I get paid the big money, darlin'."

"But it must be true—you were under oath!"

"That's for you to ponder. As for being under oath—forget it. I once had to do jury duty and I learned all about 'a jury of your peers.' All my fellow jurors cared about was getting out of there! Justice? Don't ever expect justice in a courtroom. The important thing today was getting you and the kids back together—Mr. Asperger's!" she exclaims, smiling wide, like she was back in her modeling days, pimping Lincoln Continentals.

"Isn't it the bomb?" I enthuse. "'Hi—I've got Asperger's— *go fuck yourself!*' It's fabulous! It's the greatest hide-behind affliction ever invented!"

We are free to pick up the kids immediately, and our ebullience dies as soon as Abby comes running toward us in tears. She'd been placed in a group home with fourteen other girls, and throws herself into my arms.

I glance at Aleda who has a hand on Abby's back and an expression that says, See—sometimes you have to do whatever it takes.

Next stop is outside of Providence, in Pawtucket, to pick up Eric. In some ways it breaks my heart more than seeing Abby, because Eric is forcing a stoic bravery. I hug him and he shuffles into the car. After closing the door behind him, I turn to Aleda.

"I'm so ashamed of myself for letting this happen to the kids. I feel like such a failure."

Aleda squeezes my arm. "It makes you more empathetic toward parents. You've been free for a long time, Swanson. Now you're going to have to learn self-control. Unless you find that Gardner art. Then everything will change and you can start given' people shit again. To a degree. Ain't nuthin' like money, darlin'. But until then—try and be a g'boy."

I begin to make noises about the cost to her of this little fiasco and she puts her fingers to my lips.

That night, Abby cries and cries. "Where's Aunt Susan? What happened to her? She's dead, isn't she? We'll never see her again!" Violent sobbing, and then, "I was so scared. I didn't know what happened to you. They wouldn't tell me anything!"

I hold her and rock her and promise her that nobody will ever take her away again. But even as I say the words, I am fearful. My world has changed.

When Abby finally falls asleep, I go into Eric's room. Eric, who has acted so grown up since being retrieved—now it's his turn to break down. His crying isn't quite as loud as Abby's but it's every bit as brokenhearted, and his deep sobbing brings Abby into the room.

"Is he OK?" she asks.

"Oh, he's fine," I manage. "It's just been hard on all of us, being taken away."

"They took you away, too?" asks Abby.

"Yep."

"Where did they take you?".

"Jail."

"You were in jail?" asks Eric, wiping an arm across his face. "Holy Shmoly! What was it like?"

I describe the size of the cell, the paint color, the stainless steel facilities.

"You mean they could watch you go to the bathroom?" asks Eric in disbelief.

"If they wanted to," I say. "You get a private room, but without any privacy. Go figure. Basically, it's boring, so you wanna stay out of there. There is nothing to do, and I do mean nothing. All you can do is think or sleep."

"Or drink water and pee," Eric reminds me.

"Or drink water and pee."

What I don't explain to them is how insignificant it made me feel. How deep down my pride was hurt and my self-esteem crushed. And that I am still feeling the aftershocks. That when the power wants to come down on you, you-are-fucked.

No. I cannot let them see my fear or my anger. And I don't want to try to explain it to them until I understand it myself.

The most important thing is to make them feel safe.

CHAPTER 16

◆

WaterFire. Gondola ride. Something horrifying in the river.

"SWANSON!" ABBY ZIPS ACROSS THE ROOM and leans all springy on the front of my desk. "There's a WaterFire tomorrow night and Aoibhinn has never been to one. I told her you might take us to the next one."

My enthusiasm shoots up like an arrow, then clangs against a steel sky. Suddenly, I worry about every move I make with the kids. Jail and the legal system have made me feel like a goddamn criminal. I have to shake off this paranoia.

"Sounds like a plan," I say. "Tell her we'd like her to join us. We can have dinner here, then go downtown."

The next morning, Aleda calls. "Swanson—I'm readin' the paper and they're havin' one of those fire-in-the-water things tonight."

"They are. In fact, I'm takin' the kids. Wanna come?"

"Yeeeeeessss!" she squeals. "Why don't y'all come down here and we can have a drink, then I'll take us all out to dinner at Hemenway's. It'll be one of my court-ordered observations."

A sudden snow squall swirls around us on the drive

downtown. When we get to the hotel, the kids want to play outside in the courtyard between the hotel and Grace Church. I head up to Aleda's room where there's a bottle of champagne on ice.

"Why don't you open that and pour us a coupla glasses, honey baby."

"Honey baby?"

"It's Southern, darlin'. I'm finding as I get older that I'm returning more and more to my roots."

"Does that mean we'll be ordering the poke weed *salat,* this evening, darlin'?"

"Why don't you just close that pretty mouth of yours and get busy. You Yankee boys got a lot to learn."

"No kidding. We just don't cotton well to authority."

"Fortunately, I find some rebelliousness in a man to be attractive."

"Good thing."

"I didn't say rudeness, sir. I said rebelliousness."

"Often a fine line between the two, Miss Scarlet."

As I fill the glasses, the bells of Grace Church toll.

"Come," and taking my hand, she leads us into the bedroom. She pushes back the floor length drapes with both hands in one dramatic motion and we gaze up at the steeple of Grace Church, flocked with fresh, wet snow.

"I love to look out this window and listen to the bells."

BANG! Aleda screams and I pull her to the floor. Keeping low, I peer out the bottom of the window. Snow slides down the plate glass and Eric's ruddy face smiles up from the front steps of the church. Abby and Aoibhinn start shrieking and pelting Eric with snow.

"Look at them. Look at their cheeks," says Aleda. I roll over onto my back and let a long breath whoosh out. If that didn't give me a heart attack, I was probably good for awhile.

As we come down the homestretch of dinner at Hemenway's, the fires suddenly blaze up on the river and Abby and Aoibhinn run over to the windows.

"No manners," comments Eric.

Outside, Aleda takes my arm and Eric's while the girls walk on ahead leaning into each other. Crowds line the quays and flames dance in the middle of the river, orange cinders spewing skyward. Soulful cello music resonates from speakers camouflaged amidst the stone walls banking the river.

"Doesn't the wood smell good!" says Aleda. "It's so not L.A."

"I'm thinking I'd like L.A.," I say. "The sun, the warmth, the brightness. I'm beginning to feel over the Northeast."

Below us glides a black-lacquered gondola. A couple sit on the red, tufted seats sipping champagne while the gondolier in his striped shirt and hat with a black ribbon fluttering down the back, works the long oar.

"Can we ride in that?" asks Abby excitedly.

Soon, it's us gliding along in the gondola, the heat of the fires warming our faces, the people, so many of them lovers sitting close, lining the riverwalk bathed in flickering orange light. At water level, the cello music feels as though it is emanating from within our own chests.

"Venezia" sighs Aleda, "Belle and Jack in Venezia…."

Eric is leaning to one side, letting his fingers trail in the water. I am about to say something cautionary but stop myself—leave the kid alone for five minutes.

Just then, Eric yanks his hand out of the water. "Aagh!" he

screeches.

Damnit! I should've told him to—

"Something's in the water," says Eric, recoiling.

We all look over the edge. The gondolier stops rowing. Something has bumped up against his oar, and all at once we see what it is.

"Oh my God," moans Abby.

"It's Aunt Susan!" croaks Eric.

Providence Morgue. Aleda. Me. Detective Porcaro. Dr. Melaragno, the state medical examiner. Susan's body covered by a sheet. Philip arrives with his trail-along. He unzips it and inside is a bottle of Ketel One pressed up against a bag of ice.

"Thank you, Philip. You're an angel!" gushes Aleda. "Did you get snacks for the kids and something for them to drink?"

"Uh-huh."

"What are they doing?"

"They're playing darts in a room down the hall."

"Darts! Philip—go keep an eye on them. *Darts!*"

Philip departs and Aleda pours vodka into all the waiting coffee cups.

"Here's to Susan," toasts Aleda. "To Susan," we all chime in and drink. Aleda refills the cups. "I'm not gonna leave here with this bottle," she says.

The doctor coughs and wipes a dribble of vodka off her chin. She's a midget and stands on a milk crate to view the body on the stainless steel table.

"This is what I've found: she was asphyxiated—probably carbon monoxide. A rope was tied around her waist and then around some heavy object and she was dumped, possibly in the river, but I would guess the bay. Where the rope drew blood a predator fish chewed her body, allowing it to slip free. The tide eventually brought it from the bay up the river. From the condition, I would say she's been in the water for about a week."

"But she's been missing for more than two weeks," I say.

"With tests, we'll be able to pin down exactly how long she's been in water. But I've seen drenched bodies before and from the level of adipocere I'm confident we're looking at a week, not two."

"Adipocere?" I ask.

"In the absence of oxygen, such as submersion in water, the body actually preserves itself. Fat and soft tissue turn into a soap-like substance we call adipocere. Some recovered corpses are actually referred to as 'soap mummies.'"

"Good lord," I mutter.

"They're everywhere," says Dr. Melaragno, hopping down from the milk crate. "Embalming encourages the process. So do metal coffins. Whenever oxygen is kept out, the saponification begins. In cemeteries all over the country, dig up most graves and you'll find a soap mummy."

"So then," says Detective Porcaro, "you think she was kept alive for a week—before she was killed?"

"I would say so. If you're gonna dispose of a body, probably you don't want it just laying around dead for a week before you cast it off."

"That's always been my opinion," says Aleda, followed by a little burp. "Ooops. Sorry."

Suddenly, there's a blood curdling scream from down the hall and I take off, busting through the swinging doors.

Abby is on the floor wailing and Philip is standing over her.

"What happened!" I cry.

"Eric whipped a dart into my butt!" yells Abby.

Sure enough—there's a dart sticking out of her bottom.

I look at Aoibhinn who is white as a ghost and looking very still and Irish.

"Aoibhinn—Is it like this in Ireland?" I ask.

"Well, I have a cousin, Seamus, and he once took the stomach of a dead cow and...."

CHAPTER 17

♦

Back in court. Judge Ursula Diggett. DCYF petitions
court to take Abby and Eric from Swanson's care.

MY LIFE FEELS LIKE A JACKSON POLLOCK
PAINTING—splattered all over the place. Which way to
turn next? First off, the kids—will they be all right?

"I'm fine," says Abby.

"I'm OK," mumbles Eric.

"Are you sure? It's OK if you're not OK. I mean...your
parents died and now your Aunt Susan."

"We're used to it," says Abby.

"Don't be an idiot, Abby," sneers Eric. "Nobody gets used
to...people getting murdered."

I shoot Eric a look.

"Well, what am I supposed to say?" Abby bleats.

"You guys can say anything you want. To me, to Aleda.
But I'm gonna tell you one thing right now, and I want you
to think about it before tomorrow: The people who took you
away last week are gonna be all over us. They're probably
gonna want to talk to you—"

"No!" shouts Abby. "You said we wouldn't have to see
them anymore!"

"I know. But I hadn't counted on your Aunt Susan turning
up murdered."

Abby draws her knees up to her chest where she sits on the sofa and starts crying. "No. I'm not gonna do it. I'm not gonna talk to anybody!"

I hold her, try to comfort her. She won't budge. I don't know what to say, except, "It's gonna be all right. Trust me. We're gonna get through this. Together. We have to be strong. And you have to trust me."

That night on the phone Aleda is very understanding.

"Swanson, I don't think this is the kind of stuff most parents have to face. Don't be too hard on yourself. Did Susan have a will?"

"Presumably."

"Go over to her house and go through her files. She must have some info there. Do it first thing tomorrow morning, before the shit starts hitting the fan. Call me if you need to. I'll be on the set all day."

"Aleda—I feel like I've trampled all over your life enough already. I mean, good god—you come to Providence to make a movie and now this."

"Yes—it does make the movie business look pretty dull."

The next morning, right after I drop the kids off at school, I zip over to Susan's and search through the room she used as her office.

I move quickly. I'm not doing something illegal, am I? The charges filed by the arresting officer are still pending: disorderly conduct, assaulting a police officer, resisting arrest. I have a court date next week. Satisfying as a trial might be, and suing the city for a pant load, we are going for a dismissal. Anything could be dug up in a trial. What if a different judge just doesn't like the way I part my hair? Or speak? What if I lose my temper?

"Another judge might not understand Ass Burgers. Fuck!"

Flipping through the files I locate one marked "Personal Info." Within that is a manila folder designated, "Legal Papers: Will, Power of Atty. Etc." I shove the entire file inside my shoulder bag and vamoose.

At home, I examine the papers and see that Susan has, as she'd once told me she would, designated me the executor of her will and given me power of attorney, should she become incapacitated and unable to make decisions for herself.

"Guess that sure as hell applies now."

The will is simplicity itself: all of her property is to be equally divided between Eric and Abby.

"Thank God." How else was I going to afford to raise two children? Still, I have no idea what she has in the bank, what she might have for investments, insurance, and what she owes on her mortgage.

I haven't seen the morning paper yet, and fish it out of the pyracantha prickers in front of the porch.

Splashing across the front page: MUSEUM DIRECTOR FOUND MURDERED

"Shit." Well, what can you expect from a newspaper—sensitivity? So, Susan was forty-five and the rest I know, including ...*the police have no clues.*

The phone rings. Guess who? Dear Naomi Rosenthal. I listen to her jabber into the machine: "Blah-blah-blah...call right away...blah-blah-blah...tragic death of the children's legal guardian, Susan Mack, necessitates changes...blah-blah-blah...." I turn off the volume, stick a pencil in my mouth and take a long drag. Smoke of the imagination. I look at myself in the oval mirror hanging in the foyer. I take another deep drag. I exhale. "Smoke and mirrors...."

Debating what to do next, the phone rings again. "Gee— I'm suddenly a popular guy." It's Attorney Leyendecker.

Leyendecker tells me not to phone Rosenthal—he will. Less than an hour later, he phones back and says we'll have to meet with the judge tomorrow morning, and for me to have the power-of-attorney, the will, and any other relevant papers with me. Good news, though, on the assault, resisting arrest, etc. front: He's managed to have that hearing postponed.

Next day. 10 A.M. District Court, Courtroom 4-F. Swanson Di Chiera and his attorney, Drury Leyendecker; Naomi Rosenthal from DCYF and the judge from the last hearing, Ursula Diggett.

Rosenthal pushes hard to make the case that now with Susan dead, the children should be taken away from me, "Until the matter is settled."

"What matter?" I blurt.

Immediately, Attorney Leyendecker jumps in, defending my right to keep the children, but perhaps most importantly, shutting me up so I don't nuke myself.

I listen while Leyendecker makes a convincing case for the children remaining with me, while "the court moves forward with its...blah-blah-blah...." Fortunately, the judge agrees that preserving the status quo makes the most sense.

Leaving the courthouse, a glowering Naomi Rosenthal hefts her shoulder satchel down the street. I ask Leyendecker why this goddamn woman is so out to get me.

"She's probably still pissed that you called her a bitch and told her to kiss your ass."

"But that was weeks ago!"

"Two weeks ago, Mr. Di Chiera. And it was refreshed in court last week."

"True."

"Plus, she's a man-hater."

"What the hell does that mean?"

"She's a dyke. A lezbo. She thinks men are shit anyway."

"How do you know she's a dyke? Plus, just because she's a dyke doesn't mean she's man-hater. Susan was a dyke, and she didn't hate men."

Leyendecker pauses, resplendent in his bespoke Ercolino shoes, charcoal pinstriped suit...a cream colored shirt that would've made Gatsby cry.

"Susan Mack was a lesbian, Mr. Di Chiera. There are lesbians and there are dykes. Gays and faggots. There are blacks and there are niggers. Hispanics and spics. Whites and honkies. Catch my drift?"

CHAPTER 18

♦

Swanson's water is shut off!

"WHAT ARE YOUR PLANS FOR THANKSGIVING," I ask Aleda.

"I'll be at my mother's in Dahlonega for Thanksgiving Day, then on Saturday fly to L.A. for a delayed Thanksgiving with the boyfriend. I'll return to Providence on Monday. I've had my lawyers take care of suspending my visits to the kids for the next week. What will you guys be doing?"

"The usual…dressing up as Pilgrims. Walking around the city with a blunderbuss, looking for turkeys. Plenty of those around here."

Know thine enemy. I Google Naomi Rosenthal and the first references that come up relate to her position as a DCYF Child Protective Investigator. Then I add "man-hater." No relevant hits, but fun to type in. Then I enter "dyke" and a reference actually does pop up, linking her to a Providence a cappella singing group, Fingers in The Dyke.

"Vulgar bitches. Oh, I'm sorry—I have Ass Burgers."

Going to the page *About Us,* and then *Bios,* I learn that *Naomi received her B.A. in Women's Studies from Brown University where she was also student coordinator of The Gallery at the Sarah Doyle Women's Center, as well as a co-founder of BSA—Burden of*

Sexual Assault. Besides singing with FID, her interests include kayaking and painting. She is also on the board of directors of the Providence Dog Park Association.

"She sounds like such a *nice* person," I mewl.

I'm in bed reading when Abby comes in to tell me the toilet isn't flushing. A panic shoots through me—but, no—it couldn't be. First of all, I owe less than five hundred on the water bill and it's my understanding that over six hundred owed triggers a possible cut-off, and secondly, the water was fine a couple of hours ago. No way would city employees be working on the night before Thanksgiving. Like all municipal employees, they're outa there at four-thirty sharp.

"Are we talking a number one or two?"

"What? Oh—one."

"Don't worry about it, sweetheart. I'll take care of it. Just go to bed and I'll see you in the morning."

I'm tempted to have a look, but half out of laziness and half out of fear I keep reading, finish off my nightcap in one gulp, snap off the light and go to sleep.

In the morning I go into my bathroom to pee and when I flush it goes away, but the bowl doesn't fill.

"Oh come on!" I turn on the sink faucets. A dribble runs out, then nothing. "Fucking sonofabitch!" They've turned off the water! Just to be sure, I run downstairs and try the kitchen faucets. Yup. "Sonofabitch!" Ina hasn't called yet. That's good. Since she pays me rent, I have a real responsibility to her. "Shit!"

But what the city hasn't counted on is The Swanson Self-Insurance Plan, which I created more than two years ago, when, out on my bicycle I noticed forgotten on a sidewalk the very implement Providence Water uses to turn off city water to a residence. I had no compunction about shouldering the thing and bringing it home, because what could be more dastardly than turning off somebody's water?

From a ceiling rack in the garage, I slide out the ten-foot long iron pole with a small horseshoe at the business end and a T-handle at the other, and march down the driveway to the street. Sure fucking enough: right there, where the sidewalk meets the curb in front of the house, the iron access cap to the branch to my house is clean of the dirt and crud that had encrusted it.

Popping it off, I lower the bar into the narrow hole and jiggle it around until it catches the slot on the valve and with one good twist we're back in business. But how the hell had it worked out that they'd turned off my water on the night before Thanksgiving? Somebody had to know somebody to make that shit happen. Had to be Rosenthal. Christ—was the woman certifiably insane?

My first turkey comes out pretty well, and Eric's cranberries with pickled onions and chipotle chilies comes out wonderfully. We also make some very chunky mashed potatoes. We have chocolate cake and strawberry ice cream for dessert, because that's what Abby wanted.

"I don't think the Pilgrims had chocolate cake," says Eric.

"You don't know," says Abby.

"History isn't entirely clear on that," I say. "What is known, is that strawberry ice cream and chocolate cake is a good combination."

"It's a delicious combination, if you ask me," says Abby.

A scraping of forks against plates is the universal response. I look at the kids making short work of dessert. Suddenly I see tears dropping from Abby's eyes down onto her plate.

"What's the matter with her?" asks Eric.

"Aunt Susan was like the only mother I really had," she cries.

I go sit next to her on the couch and hold her.

"I know...I know...." My heart is breaking for her. "But we'll be OK. I promise. I'll be your mother and your father, Abby. I love you so much. I love you both enough to be your Mom and Dad."

I hold her until she stops crying, then I get her some Kleenex. As she blows her nose and wipes her face, I see what a beautiful young woman she's going to be. Huge responsibilities are piling up on the horizon.

"Maybe I *should* get a blunderbuss," I muse out loud.

"When's Aleda coming back?" asks Abby.

"A few days."

"Can I take a bath if I want?"

"Of course you can. You can take a bath whenever you want. So long as you don't turn into a prune."

To insure that the child can at least have her baths, I go down to the sidewalk and throw a few coffee cans of dry cement down the access hole to the water valve, followed by a jug of water.

"Jackwads will need a backhoe to turn it off next time."

CHAPTER 19

◆

Susan's ashes. *Belle* has money crisis. Eric cooks gumbo.

THE DAY AFTER THANKSGIVING, the kids and I take a somber walk over to Jawaharjian Funeral Home on Westminster Street to pick up Susan's ashes.

At home, I remove the urn from the cardboard box. It's a pretty blue and white porcelain urn, depicting birds and trees in the Japanese style.

"Can I look inside?" asks Eric. I remove the lid.

"What do you see?" asks Abby.

"Just some grey stuff."

Abby looks into it like she's looking into a well.

"How do we know it's her?" she asks.

"We don't," I say. "We have to take their word for it."

"Where should we put…it?" asks Eric.

"Where everybody else does," I say, setting it down on the mantelpiece.

"Why does everybody put it there?" asks Eric.

"Because important things are often set upon a mantel."

"Is that because fireplaces are important?" asks Abby.

"Very smart, Abby," I say. "Fireplaces *are* important. It's how people used to heat their houses and cook their meals. It's where people today go to feel cozy and—"

"Look at pictures," Abby cuts in. "I love to sit in front of the fire and see the pictures."

"But we're still going to sprinkle Aunt Susan's ashes where our Mom and Dad are, right?" asks Eric.

"Of course we are. Your Aunt Susan wanted her ashes to be spread on Rose Island too, and we will. But let's wait until a nice day in the spring."

Aleda returns after the long weekend and I stop by the hotel for a visit.

"Did you have a good Thanksgiving?" I ask.

"No. My mother is getting older and tedious. She repeats herself endlessly. It's not her fault. My sister and brother are both pains in the ass...and my old friends down there don't feed me anymore. I know that sounds bratty, but there it is. I just feel—"

"I know," I cut in. "The older—"

"Would you please not interrupt me? It's very annoying when you do that. Thank you. I feel that I don't have the time anymore to spend around people who are just...jibber-jabbering. I think I'm getting tired of people. Now you may speak."

"How was L.A.?" I was going to add, and the boyfriend, but didn't need any more heartache.

"L.A. was L.A."

"Did you see Dan?"

"No. He was up visiting his sister in Vancouver. But I talked to him on the phone. Oh—I did see someone you know."

"You saw Gwyneth Paltrow?"

"Do you know her?" asks Aleda.

"No. But I could imagine knowing her. I think I would

like to know her."

"She's just a child," says Aleda dismissively. "I saw your friend Royal Madeira. He was at Pinot having dinner with Chester Hurling."

"Who's Chester Hurling?"

"My co-producer."

"The guy you met in Boston when we went up?"

"That's right. And guess what he was doing in Boston besides meeting me that day?

"I don't have a clue."

"Attending a trustees meeting at MIT"

"So?"

"So—that's where he went to college."

"And?"

"You know what, Swanson—you can be a real pain in the ass."

"I guess that's what happens when you suddenly have two kids."

"Hey, buddy boy—don't pull this 'I'm exhausted' thing. I've just traveled back and forth across the country, and every stop felt like work."

"Yeah, but you're a woman. Men tire more easily. You gals just kinda plow right along."

"We have to plow along because you guys are too tired. Somebody has to do it." Aleda pushes her hair back and looks around. "I'm beginning to feel peckish. I want to eat something, but I'm not going to. Well, maybe a little something. Are you hungry?"

"You know me."

"OK. I'll order up something."

"Are you going to tell me that your co-producer went to

MIT at the same time Madeira and the kids' parents and Susan were in Boston?"

"No. I mean it's possible, but not probable. I am saying there sure seems to be a Boston connection with all these people."

"But not in school at the same time as the others. Why not?"

"Because Chester is in his mid-sixties, at least, and what is Madeira—Forty?"

"Who can tell," I sigh.

"Who's with the children now?"

"Little Guy."

"*Little*—Swanson, get the hell out of here! *Now!*"

"What about my snack?"

"Take an apple out of that bowl and get out of here. Now!"

Firefly voices in the night, little creatures emerging from the side door of the Wheeler gymnasium.... "Bye....*Bye*...See ya tomorrow...Ooops, I mean *Monday!*...call me laterrrrrr....I *Promise!*...." There's Abby coming toward the car, backpack slung over one shoulder. She's beginning to act like a teenager. She will be eleven on Christmas Day—only two more years left before becoming an official teenager. "Ohmigod!Ohmigod!OMG!" Will I be able to deal with it? *"Totally!"*

"Hi, sweetie," I say, pushing open the passenger door. "How was rehearsal?"

"Good." She's landed the part of The Second Angel. "What smells?"

"A pumpkin pie. I made one for us and one for Aleda. I'm dropping hers off on the way home."

As we approach the hotel entrance Aleda is getting out of the back of the Escalade. I flash the lights to get her attention and pull up behind. I'm barely out of the car before she has me clutched in a bear hug.

"Missed me, huh?" I say. She leans back, distraught. "What's wrong?"

She shakes her head. "Come upstairs," she says, her voice hoarse.

"I've got Abby with me."

Aleda smiles and waves to Abby then turns abruptly around. "God!" she gasps. She brings her hands to her face. She collects herself. "Has she had dinner yet?"

"No."

"I'll have Philip sit with her in the restaurant."

As soon as we're alone in her suite, Aleda shrieks and crumples into a chair. In the ringing silence that follows, she sits up straight and brings her hands together prayerfully.

"Swanson—I need ten million dollars. God, Swanson. Oh, God!" she swoons.

"What the hell happened?"

"An investing group in L.A. has reneged on ten million dollars. I met with them when I was out there. I showed them the reel, they said they liked it and that five million would be in the account this week. Then, today, they called and said they can't do it."

"Why?"

Aleda shrugs. "Who knows? They said it's because they haven't been paid for some other investment, but who knows what the truth is. It's a cesspool of sharks. It happens."

"But how can they do that?"

"Because they can! I need to find ten million dollars!"

"But I thought you said they were going to send you five?"

"The deal was that Rodio would get five million up front before he came here to shoot, and five million at the completion of the film. Somehow, his people got wind that the investors pulled out, and now he wants the entire ten million up front, before he comes to Providence."

"That's terrible."

"It gets worse. If he doesn't get it, he's gonna sue us, because he's already packed on fifty pounds to have Sargent's girth—same way he did for *The Sultan of Swat.*"

"What about Hurling?"

"He's trying a few things....I've sold jewelry! I've re-mortgaged my goddamn house to make this film! I don't know what to do! What do I smell?"

I open the bag I've brought up from the car. "Here, it's for you. And Philip. It's a homemade pumpkin pie."

Aleda goes to New York City for the weekend to try and drum up financing. A few possibilities surface, but nothing definite. She returns on Sunday night and comes over to see the kids and joins us for dinner.

I'm trying hard to give our little family stability by making sure we have dinner together every night. There is music, but only classical. We've come to favor Chopin. There is nothing like the piano music of Chopin. I am trying to introduce the kids to something other than popular culture and its onslaught of forgettable music and so-called social networking that constantly threatens to swallow them whole.

We also join hands and take turns saying a little prayer

before the meal. It can be anything.

Tonight it's Eric saying, "Thank you to the East Side Market for carrying filé to sprinkle on the gumbo. It's a great recipe that Aleda gave us. Us Yankees would never have thought it up on our own."

"We Yankees," I say softly.

"We Yankees," says Eric.

"Yeah," pipes up Abby. "We Yankees are glad Aleda is here with us tonight!"

Late the next morning, Aleda phones. She's screaming. "Swanson! We have the ten million!"

CHAPTER 20

♦

At MIT to investigate Chester Hurling. Swanson's house broken into.

"HURLING MADE A DEAL WITH THE MAYOR."

"The mayor?" I ask incredulously. "Mayor Cabrini? *The Weenie?"*

"Does Providence have any other, darlin'? The Weenie wants this movie to get made in his city, and he found a way to come up with the money. That's all I know, and that's all I need to know."

But I need to know more. Providence is on the verge of bankruptcy. No way could the mayor grab ten million from city coffers. It must be some private deal.

And Hurling…I don't know a damn thing about him, other than Aleda trying to persuade me to see him in the Boston mix, with Madeira and the kids' parents.

The juices get flowing. Who is this guy, Hurling? An Internet search links him to ownership of a vineyard in Healdsburg, California, but that's about it. Nothing about MIT Board of Trustees. Clearly, it's time for some old-fashioned sleuthing.

The next morning I zoom up to Boston. First stop, the library at the Massachusetts Institute of Technology. Tzipi

Mencoff, a woman I know who once worked at a used bookstore in Providence is now a librarian at the MIT library and she lets me search the alumni database.

I quickly learn that Chester Hurling graduated with a B.A. from Boston University in 1964, and from MIT in 1970 with a degree in electrical engineering. Further drilling into committees and speeches reveal that his father, a Scottish immigrant, founded a business called Back Bay Electric. The old man was an electrician. But it gets better than that. It turns out the father parlayed his little business into a big business, so by the time Chester popped out, there was a fleet of fifteen trucks and over sixty employees.

My research also turns up an awards dinner transcript in which Hurling talks about going to jobs with his father as a boy and helping him. That his love of electricity had come from helping fish wire through walls and wire up service panels, alarm systems....

"Alarm systems," I whisper. The Gardner thieves had known all about the alarm system.

I hold my face in my hands. Had Hurling's father's company done work at the Gardner? I would have to check that out. How? It's not like I was with the FBI. I had an idea. Damn—now would be a good time to own a cell phone.

I look at my watch. If I'm quick, I have just enough time to whip over to the Gardner.

After driving around the museum a couple of times looking for a free parking place, I succumb to the big, surface parking lot across the road at the Museum of Fine Arts. Eight bucks—what a rip. The guard breaks my ten and hands me the change.

"Mordez moi," I smile. Mindful of the need to watch my mouth, I have taken to converting into French some of my more resonant phrases.

"You're welcome," replies the guard, tapping the brim of his hat.

Inside the Gardner I pull out my wallet again and pay the ten dollar admission. The woman hands me my ticket.

"Mordez moi."

An expression of shock comes over her face.

"What do you mean, saying 'bite me'?" she replies.

"I am so sorry," I apologize. "I am just learning French. *Excusez-moi.* And I have the Ass Burgers." I beat a quick path away from her. "Yeesh. Shoulda known, fancy-ass museum...oh, well...."

I make my way around the center courtyard and up the stone staircase to the Dutch Room. I walk across the tile floor and stand in front of the empty, gilt frame, tall as a man that had held Rembrandt's *Storm on the Sea of Galilee.*

"Where *are* you, sumbitch?" I whisper insistently, pulling the imagined painting into the empty frame.

I walk over to the desk by the window where the Flinck and the Vermeer had been displayed, back to back, and now only empty frames. "Where are you?" I draw a deep breath and stride across the room, sitting down on a cement bench in front of an open archway that looks out upon the courtyard.

I think about how the fake cops, once they'd been buzzed in, say to the desk guard, a 23-year-old Berklee College of Music student: *You look familiar. Isn't there a warrant out for you? Step over here and let's see some identification.*

Protesting that he is not wanted on any charges, the guard

nonetheless produces his wallet and steps out from behind the chest-level desk—and out of reach of the sole alarm button that could have summoned outside help. He is promptly handcuffed. When the guard who'd been doing his rounds appears, he too is handcuffed.

The fake cops then hustle the two guards into the basement, gag them, bind them to posts with duct tape, and for the next fifty-seven minutes, proceed to stage the biggest art theft in history.

I know the available facts of the theft, now I need to see what we're conditioned not to see. I let my mind go...sunlight streaming down through the glass roof panels...dappled greenery...ferns...ivy...pale stucco walls, faintly pink and foamy cream... drifting...letting go...letting in...breathe...*breathe*....

When I leave, I turn around and gaze upon the front of the museum.

"Your face," I murmur, and snap a few photographs.

I pick up Veronika and drive around to the side entrance of the museum, on Palace Road. This is where the robbers had parked, loaded in the art and driven away.

"Take me."

Hands barely touching the wheel, I let Veronika progress straight ahead to the end of Palace Road where I do the simplest, most automatic thing—make a right onto the busy lanes in front of the museum and follow the flow. And the flow curves through the park-like grounds of the Fenway. Coming out the other side, I continue on the path of least resistance, following the road through a neighborhood of residential apartment houses and small businesses. I cross several intersections and can go no further. I am on Yawkey

Way—right in front of the entrance to the home of the Boston Red Sox. Fenway Park. The drive, with traffic, has taken no more than five minutes.

Pondering what this might mean I suddenly realize, "Crap!" I'll have to fly to pick up the kids from school on time! And, of course, we don't have cell phones.

"Yehhhhhhhhhhht!" I yodel.

I hit the sludge of rush-hour traffic. School sports will be long over by the time I get there and I decide to drive straight home. Hopefully, they figured out a way to get there. They know where the front door key is hidden, so at least they can get in.

Rolling into the driveway the first thing I see is a police cruiser. Eric races to meet me as I get out of the car.

"Somebody broke into the house!"

"Where's your sister?"

"I think she's over at Aoibhinn's."

A police officer is standing in the foyer writing on a notepad. I introduce myself.

"Your son came home and the door was wide open, so he called us. Nothing appears to be disturbed but you might want to take a look around yourself."

"I called Aoibhinn's," says Eric. "Abby's over there."

I ask Eric to look around and see if he notices anything strange or missing. I do the same. Everything looks fine.

"Maybe you forgot to close it," says Eric.

"No. I closed it, I locked it. I remember, I tossed Little Guy in, then I shut the door and locked it. How the hell would somebody get in?"

Eric shrugged. "A key?" I call Ina who has a set. I catch her at St. Joseph's Hospital where she works in the STD clinic and no, she hasn't gone in.

"The only people who have keys are Ina and your Aunt Susan. Ina, I completely trust—she's come in before to feed Little Guy when I've been away. And, of course, your Aunt Susan...."

Maybe I hadn't turned the damn key twice around, or maybe I had left the door open. I'd been so distracted lately....But that wasn't like me. But maybe me was changing as I became like any other overwhelmed parent.

The next morning I dial *67 to block my number, then dial the number for Back Bay Electric. When a woman answers, I say I am calling from the Isabella Stewart Gardner Museum and that there seems to be a malfunction with the alarm system.

"Is the museum a client of Back Bay?" she asks.

"I believe so. I just started here, but Back Bay is written in our reference book of systems maintenance people. Maybe you could check your records to be sure?"

I'm put on hold and when she comes back she says, "Yes, the Gardner Museum is one of our accounts. We can have someone out there this afternoon."

"That sounds great! There's one other question...some of the panels I'm looking at seem to be pretty old...don't know if I can find...um...If I have questions about the older components, has Back Bay been servicing the museum for awhile?"

"Hold on...." She comes back. "Yes. For years."

"This stuff looks like it's at least twenty years old."

"That shouldn't be a problem. We've had the account

since...let's see...I'm seeing records that go back at least until the late-seventies. Back Bay has been around a long time. I wouldn't be surprised if we did the original installation."

"Gosh—neither would I. Well, thank you very much for your help. I think what I'll do is take one more look at it, and if I can't figure out the problem I'll give you a call back...."

"I need to talk to Madeira. I'd like to talk to Hurling, too."

I am watching Aleda unclip underwear she has drying in her bathroom. Ever since somebody tried to sell a pair of her panties on eBay, she hand washes her own undergarments when she stays in hotels.

"Why not use Susan's memorial service," says Aleda. "They'll both be there."

"Why would Hurling be at Susan's memorial service?"

"Because Madeira and Hurling are partners."

"What do you mean *partners?* You mean, like—"

"Like they swap spit...and do a buncha other stuff you probably don't wanna think about. They've been together for years. You should've seen them in Venice. In Paris—my god! Running around the Marais like it was Christopher Street in the mid-seventies. All leathery and fisty...."

I am dumbounded, moving quickly toward being pissed. It's a novel feeling to be having toward Aleda.

"Aleda—why didn't you tell me this before?"

"Because Hurling is the big money behind the film and I didn't want that jeopardized. Now that I can see we're gonna make it, I don't feel any need to protect him."

"Wow!"

"Yeah. Wow, Swanson! Grow up. It's a tough world."

"I know. But—"

"Don't but me, Swanson. You wanna win?"

It's really good I don't smoke anymore, otherwise, I would light up a fistful of cigarettes at once.

"You have a stunning way of clarifying one's thinking, Al. I was raised to be a good kid...polite. It's taken me awhile to get in touch with my deeper, more shallow qualities."

"It's not shallow, Swanson. It's called going after what you want. I'm getting what I want. Don't you wanna get what you want? Don't you want to be *Swanson the Magnificent?*"

CHAPTER 21

♦

When Swanson and Aleda first met. NYC. Kennedy
Airport. Stormville. Swanson naked in boat. Aleda
excited about ISG.

*SWANSON THE MAGNIFICENT....*I had just completed
my freshman year of college and through a friend's father,
landed a summer job in the research department of a Wall
Street brokerage house.

I found an inexpensive place to live in an NYU dorm and
had two brand new Brooks Brothers suits: a khaki one and
one that was drab olive green. I could walk to and from work
at my office on lower Broadway in the Equitable Building
across from Trinity Church, and got paid one hundred and
twenty-eight dollars every Friday, cash. Walking home up
Broadway after work in the slanting red-gold sunlight, the
smell of Sabrett hotdogs and tobacco, sweat and perfume and
window reflections and honking and crazies was the happiest
I've ever felt in my life.

One afternoon, I was sitting at my desk reading the *Wall
Street Journal* when the phone rang. It was Dan Evans, whom
I'd met in Washington Square Park when he came up and
bummed a Marlboro off me. He'd been cruising me, but not
being gay that went right over my head. Dan worked for
ABC. He was ten years older than me, and a VP in their

famous sports department, helping to produce "The Wide World of Sports." When he figured out I wasn't gay, it didn't matter. Dan was a person first, and we became fast friends.

"I was wondering if you could do me a favor. I'm supposed to pick up Aleda at Kennedy tonight, but I've just been booked to Miami for a water ski championship tomorrow— the production supervisor who was supposed to be there has a family emergency. I was wondering if you wouldn't mind picking her up—if you're not busy doing something else. You can use my car."

Busy doing something else? What—using my meal plan card to have dinner in the NYU cafeteria? This was the stuff of which dreams were made! Ever since meeting Aleda through Dan at an ABC function at Lincoln Center, I'd fantasized about somehow getting closer to her. Now, a miracle had occurred, and all I had to say was—

"Sure, Dan. I can do that."

Dan had an old, red Triumph TR-3 that he kept in a parking garage on a Hudson River pier and I drove with the directions in one hand, and shifted with the other. Long Island…Rockaway Boulevard…"Christ Almighty!" the car heaved over vast undulations in the road, taxis and airport limousines careening by on either side.

I pulled up to the TWA terminal at seven exactly. The sky was turning Technicolor shades of robin's egg blue and putti pink. The Triumph was aglow. My hands were rosy and I hustled inside.

There she was, striding down the carpeted Arrival corridor. She had an enormous blue and white duffel bag hanging off her shoulder. She was surrounded by an entourage. I realized the man walking next to her was the singer, Tony Bennett, and the group of beefy, Mafia-looking guys belonged to him.

I waited till I caught her eye and then smiled tentatively and waved, just a little. Would she even remember what I looked like?

"Hi!" she gushed—but she didn't say my name. Did she remember my name?

Aleda gave Tony a big hug and then they peeled off in separate directions.

"Dan couldn't come," I began. "He had to—"

"Could you take this please?" and she dipped her shoulder down so the bag slid into my hands. "I feel like a pack animal." She was wearing a khaki jump suit, belted at the waist and a Panama hat.

I threw her bag into the jump seat and we roared off, joining the artery of tail lights flowing toward Manhattan, a very juicy red corpuscle amidst all the others under a full moon.

"I'm so glad to be back! Alaska is freezing, even in July! And the clothes they made me wear were so *ugly*. I don't know why anyone would want to model, except for the money. Take the next exit!" she commanded, her face bright in a circle of blonde flames. "Here!"

Suddenly, we're heading away from Manhattan. We drive into the night, along the Henry Hudson Parkway into cool, dark countryside. Ahead is a highway sign: STORMVILLE.

"Get off here," she says, and digs a bottle out of her bag.

"Take a swig."

It was like swallowing grain alcohol with little globby things in it.

"What is it?" I coughed.

"I don't know—an Eskimo gave it to me." Then she took a

belt. *"WOOOOOOOOOO–WEEEEEEEE!!!"*

"Is there something in there besides alcohol?"

"Tadpoles!" she shrieked.

We flew up one side of a mountain and down the other, the car's lights swinging wildly through the trees.

"Here!" she yelped.

I overshot, screeched to a stop, whirred backwards and turned down a gravel lane bounded by trees entangled by vines of honeysuckle...a white-fenced paddock came into view...then a barn...then the lake...then the white clapboard farmhouse with the porch light on. The front door was lapis blue.

"Where are we?"

"Maison Cha-Cha!"

"Say what?"

"Chavchavadze's country house."

I knew from Dan, that Nicholas Chavchavadze was the director of Aleda's first film, which was now in post-production. Who knew she was on the cusp of becoming an overnight major movie star?

A black housekeeper named Jessie told "Miss Aleda," that she'd pull something together for dinner.

"I need to walk," said Aleda, and she lead us down to the lake where a wooden speedboat chafed against the dock.

Next, she wanted to go water skiing.

"Where's...Nicholas?" I asked, trying to sound nonchalant.

"Rome."

The water was black...it was cold...the house was comfy and warm...there would be dinner smells....Aleda stripped down to her bra and panties and climbed into the boat. She was a big girl: well-formed shoulders, strong hips and legs. I stripped down to my tightie-whities. I should've bought those striped boxer shorts at Brooks Brothers when I'd bought the two suits.

"Look at you..." she purred.

"*Swanson the Magnificent,*" I said, figuring this was as good a time as any to remind her what my name was.

She turned the key on the dash and the motor roared to life.

"*Swanson the Magnificent* goes first," she announced, and leaned the skis toward me.

Swanson the Magnificent had only water skied once before in his life, and he was probably ten at the time. Rrrrruuuuum! She takes off and I go straight up. A fuckin' natural! But then my legs begin splaying and I'm fighting to bring them together, but I can't and I slam face first into the water, still holding onto the stupid line as though I'd miraculously rise up. Finally, before I'm drawn and quartered, I let go.

Far in the distance I can see the green light on the nose of the boat. Was Aleda even aware I'd gone down? Suddenly, I'm enveloped by a looming, amorphous presence that's alive and hissing!

Gigantic wings are beating against my face and I start screaming. The swan's long bill bites into my neck and shoulders. "*Fuck! Fuck! Fuck!*" we're shrieking together.

I'm thrashing, I go underwater, I feel the big, webbed feet pushing down against my head. I grab a narrow ankle and feel it snap. I come up for air and the thing is going for my eyes! I flail my arms, punching it in the chest as the long neck whips back like a cobra. The bill's about to strike me when there's a thud against the bird's side and it paddles sullenly away, trailing its broken leg.

"Are you all right?" Aleda huffs, tossing down the oar she'd used to strike the swan.

She pulls me over the side and I flop down on the bottom of the boat, panting like a sled dog. The water runs off my eyelashes and I see Aleda and the full moon behind her head and the sky blasting stars out of a blue-black background. In the struggle I'd lost my underwear and saw that my scared penis had retracted into an acorn.

"Oh, look at you...just look at you," Aleda says. "Bless your heart."

I felt like I was ready to be diapered.

From Chavchavadze's closet she picks out a soft, cream-colored shirt. Black silk trousers and black leather slippers complete the ensemble. I ferry all of this back to my room.

Showered, dressed and ready to go downstairs, there is a knock at my door. It's Aleda holding a pearl necklace. Her eyes are dewy. Her whole manner is velvety.

"Would you help me with this, please?"

She turns around and I hold the two ends of the clasp. I stare down into her bosom and inhale the perfume off her neck. Kiss her, you fool! Kiss her ear! Kiss her neck! I stalled-stalled-stalled and finally joined the two ends of the clasp.

"There," I said.

She turns to me. "Thank you," she says dreamily. Another chance! And I just stand there gazing into her eyes. When my chance had passed she took control: "Let's go have dinner. I'm starvin'!"

We ate quail and drank champagne.

"Nick's clothes fit you perfectly," she says. "How old are you?"

"Nineteen."

"We're the same age. Do you like college? What are you

studying?"

"Political Science. I'm thinking of going to law school."

"Oh."

By the way she said, "Oh," I knew I no longer wanted to be a lawyer.

"Actually, I'm not sure what I want to do," I said.

"Have you ever thought of writing?"

"Not really."

"You should. You look like a writer."

That's when I decided to become a writer.

After dinner I took out a fresh, tight pack of Camels and offered her one.

"I don't smoke," she said and stood up. "I'm going to bed. Will you come visit me in about fifteen minutes?"

In my room I looked at my penis. Would it come to life? Should I change into the pajamas and bathrobe Jessie had laid out for me, or enter fully dressed? I decided to compromise: I took off the jacket and the shoes.

Aleda was already in bed, wearing pajamas. She had on preppy horn-rimmed glasses and was reading a book. "Come sit here," she said, patting the bed. "I'm learning all about Isabella Stewart Gardner."

"Never heard of her," I mumble.

"She's fascinating!" Aleda exclaims sitting upright. "You have to learn about her! I can't wait to visit her house in Boston. When she died, she had it turned into a museum. She had it built herself and modeled it after a Venetian palazzo, but turned outside in—so that the beautiful arched openings of the rooms, instead of looking outside to dreary Boston, look inside to a courtyard in the center filled with trees and fountains and light coming in from a glass roof.

"She collected Rembrandts and Titians and was friends with John Singer Sargent, who painted portraits of her, and Henry James, who fictionalized her. You really *need* to be interested in her. She was friends with the leading artists and writers of her day."

"I'll check her out," I said dismissingly. I didn't want to talk about books; I wanted to be desired by Aleda in the realm of the narrow and physical.

"I think a movie about Isabella Stewart Gardner would be amazing!" she said.

"Why not ask your boyfriend to make one?" I crabbed.

Instantly, Aleda's enthusiasm died. She looked back into her book. "Good night," she said.

I slinked back to my room and shut the door. "You blew it." I felt deeply bad. She'd tried to engage me in a friendly, real way, and I'd behaved like any panting male.

Right after coffee in the morning, Aleda was ready to go and we drove directly into Manhattan. Outside her apartment building I handed off her bag to the doorman.

We shared a polite kiss. Her expression was kind.

"Don't try so hard," she said to me. Then she turned and was gone.

My God...we were only nineteen years old then. Still teenagers! And like most teenagers, I was an imposter. But not Aleda. At nineteen she had a portfolio. And who would think that in a few more months, a black and white film about some high schoolers in a dusty little Texas town was going to catapult her into mega-stardom?

CHAPTER 22

◆

DCYF accuses Swanson of writing smut. Swanson fears
Rosenthal broke into his house. Aleda has a gun.

I HAVEN'T SPOKEN TO DETECTIVE PORCARO IN
OVER TWO WEEKS. I'll call him. Maybe he has
something.

All Porcaro has is a mouthful of matzo and peanut butter,
his jaw nearly glued shut. He brings up the incident of a
detective who'd been shot dead last week with his own gun
at police headquarters while interrogating a suspected
murderer.

"Does that mean the detective squad shuts down?" I ask.

"Heebruz a brubber," mumbles Porcaro through the goo in
his mouth.

"Well Susan was a *mother* to two children!" I scream,
slamming down the phone. Taking a deep breath, I call
Porcaro back. "And she was a fucking tax-paying, property-
owning citizen of Providence, paying your fucking salary and
your gold-plated health benefits, and your fucking pension!"
and I slam the phone down again.

Immediately, the phone rings back. Assuming it's Porcaro,
I pick up before letting the machine cut in. Christ—It's
Naomi Fucking Rosenthal! Switching quickly to a Spanish
accent I blurt, "No speaky ingleash," and hang up. "Bitch ass

shit!" The phone rings again and I let her blabber into the machine about needing this, requiring that, and blah-blah-blah. "Oh, shut up! SHUT UP! Fucking dyke-ass bad breath social workers....Gonna hafta drop a fucking *bomb* on them!"

Next morning I receive a summons saying that I am to appear back in family court tomorrow before a Judge Milly Mudge. "What the hell kind of name is that?!" I call attorney Leyendecker and speak to his secretary. Leyendecker has broken his leg skiing at Mont Tremblant, in Canada, and is in a hospital up there.

"Fucking Great!" I scream, pressing the mute button, but not hard enough.

"I understand your frustration, Mr. Di Chiera. Shall I connect you with Attorney Monterey? She's familiar with this case."

"Please," I say. "And I'm sorry for the outburst."

"That's all right, Mr. Di Chiera. We understand situations can get emotional at times. Hold please. Thank you."

Eugenia Monterey sounds like she will be just fine. She'll meet me outside the courtroom tomorrow. "And just so you know," says attorney Monterey, "Judge Mudge wears her heart on her sleeve where women and children are concerned."

"What does that mean?" I ask.

"It means you've got custody of children, but you're not a woman."

"And...."

"And, given that it's Judge Mudge, you'd be better off if you were a woman."

"Yeah—wouldn't everybody."

One thing about Leyendecker, Beguelin & Bedward, LLP—they know their judges—they also have a pretty good eye for associates. Leyendecker's pinch hitter is a dead ringer for the actress Marisa Berenson, when she was young and luscious. Interestingly, Marisa Berenson is the great-grandniece of Bernard Berenson, who'd procured European art for Isabella Gardner.

At the polar opposite end of the desirability scale, at least IMHO, is Naomi Rosenthal, who bubbles up out of the mire and tells the judge that the state is petitioning for custody of the children, as DCYF has uncovered evidence that I had at one time written pornography for *Gallery, Penthouse* and associated magazines.

"Your honor," says Ms. Rosenthal, "our investigation has determined that regularly, between the years 1982 and 1987, and sporadically for some years thereafter, Mr. Di Chiera wrote for these magazines and, quite possibly, others of this ilk. Indications are that he likely produced the worst kind of filth imaginable, rendering Mr. Di Chiera completely unfit to care for children within his home. Or any place else, for that matter."

Judge Milly Mudge looks down at me from her perch with that judge-patented "I believe I be smellin' bad shit" expression.

"Your Honor," I say, "I hardly know where to begin. I—"

Judge Milly Mudge's eyebrows meet in the middle as she cuts me off. "Mr. Di Chiera—is the allegation substantially true?"

"What allegation?"

"That you wrote for the...*magazines* Ms. Rosenthal just

described."

"Is it a crime to write for those magazines?" I reply.

"Mr. Di Chiera: please answer my question—otherwise, I will be forced to fine you for contempt of court."

"You honor—this is completely surreal."

"Five hundred dollars."

"*Woyt?*"

"One thousand dollars," smiles Judge Milly Mudge. "Do I hear fifteen hundred? Fifteen hundred?"

"Yes," I say, gritting my teeth. "I have written for the magazines that Ms. Rosenthal mentioned."

Turning to Ms. Rosenthal, Judge Milly Mudge inquires: "And do you have any examples of Mr. Di Chiera's magazine writing, Ms. Rosenthal?"

"At the present moment—no," stammers Ms. Rosenthal. "However, I am certain that within a short period of time we shall be able to obtain some examples for you."

"Fine," says the judge. "Please notify me when it's in your possession and we will resolve this matter." With that, she bangs down her gavel.

"Good luck digging up any of that shit!" I mumble to myself. Thank God that crap was published before everything was created and stored on computers. It would take her forever to find that stuff—the worst of it anyway.

Eric tries out for the basketball team and makes the squad. Aleda and I go to his first game and Aleda takes photos with her iPhone.

A woman sits down on the bleacher next to me, and when I scooch over closer to Aleda, I knock her purse to the floor. Reaching down to pick it up, I glimpse the handle of a pistol inside. Aleda's busy taking pictures of Eric with his teammates and never notices.

I didn't know that Aleda carried a firearm, but I'm not surprised. She's been assaulted, stalked and encountered all kinds of weirdness during her long tour in the spotlight.

They win by eight points! Eric's face is flushed and grinning. He'd made two baskets, and I get a glimpse of him amongst his whooping comrades and see the boy-Eric is fast slipping away.

Something doesn't look right.

I get up from my writing desk and cross the room to the massive bookshelf where I store copies of various publications in which my work has appeared. The row of *Penthouse* magazines and others looks shorter. My first paranoid thought is that, somehow, Rosenthal has gotten ahold of them. The day I came home late from the Gardner...the front door open...But there was no sign of forced entry. Does she know how to pick a lock? Christ All Mighty—this is not good. I phone Aleda and share my fears.

"I don't know, Swanson...She works for the state. That would be a pretty ballsy move."

"I agree. But you have to consider two things: one, she went to Brown, so she has a superiority complex, and two, she's dyke, so she has a persecution complex. And there's a third...I called her a bitch and told her she could kiss my ass."

"I hate to say it, Swanson, but you are making a case. Still, I'm not entirely convinced. It could be Eric. Check under his bed. He is at that age...same as my brother's son, Jimmy, when he started yankin' the choke."

"*Yankin' the choke?....*"

The next morning, right after I drop the kids off at school, I rush home and scour Eric's room. Zero whacking material.

"Maybe he took them to a friend's house," says Aleda.

"No...no," I moan. "It's that fucking bitch, Rosenthal. How else would she know I once wrote porn? And she told the court she was optimistic about being able to produce some of the stuff. How else was she gonna get it?" There's silence. "Hello? Aleda? Are you still there?"

"Yeah. I was just thinking...Maybe you did leave the door open, and maybe you misplaced those magazines a long time ago and just forgot....Ask Eric if he took them to a friend's house."

"Aleda, kids today don't need those magazines. Those old photos are Little Bo-Peep compared to the raunch they can access on the Internet."

"You men....Look, I gotta go. I have my first scene with Rodio tomorrow. I'm so nervous. He's such a great actor."

"When did he get in?"

"Last night. I gotta go, love."

"Be confident, Aleda. Break a leg."

I dig out the phonebook and look for a Naomi Rosenthal or even an N Rosenthal. Nothing. Phonebooks have become all but useless. I check online. Nothing there, either.

I'm hyperventilating. I don't even know what I'm going to do if I find her name and address anyway.

"Burn her house down? Kill her? Gotta get a grip here, man. OK. Just think logically....There are three keys: mine, Ina's and Susan's. I have mine, Ina has hers and Susan's...where is Susan's?" If it was a key, it was Susan's. Would Rosenthal somehow have access to Susan's house? "Of course not— she's not the police." On the other hand, she sure didn't have any problem luring that police officer out of her cave to maul me.

"Rosenthal, Susan, and bears! Oh, no!"

I ask Eric if he knows where Susan kept spare keys and stuff like that.

"Well, I know she kept a bunch of keys in the kitchen drawer underneath the blender."

I buzz straight over to Susan's and find the bowl of keys, some loose and some on key rings. I dump them on the kitchen table and pull out my key and begin looking for a match. I try them all, and nothing. I look around the kitchen and glance into the dining room and living room. I would have to decide what to do with all of her belongings and then sell the house, I guess.

"Thank God. Money," I whisper.

When I get back home and see Eric, the first thing he says is, "I remember that Aunt Susan had a little round thing on your key that said, 'Swanson.'"

"Did she keep it in the bowl with the rest of the keys?"

"Yeah."

CHAPTER 23

◆

Swanson spies on Rosenthal and Powder. Susan's
memorial service at RISD. University Club. Rosenthal
nailed! Clue on face of Gardner Museum.

THE NEXT DAY, I RECEIVE A SUMMONS to appear
back in court on Friday, three days away. Naomi Shitbitch
must be ready with her smut evidence.

"The noose tightens," I declare, staring out the window.
"Must take action."

I stake out the building downtown where DCYF has its
offices. At precisely 4:30 PM the building disgorges, and five
minutes later, Rosenthal emerges with her laptop case slung
across her shoulders. She disappears into the parking garage
across the street and drives out a few minutes later in...a
yellow *Jaguar.*

"Yeow!" Sure ain't the grey Dodge Aries state car she shows
up in as Ms. Rosenthal, CPI. I follow her through downtown
and over to the East Side, where she pulls up in front of a
handsome, white clapboard two-car garage. The door slides
up and she drives in. She comes out of the garage and enters
the back door of a very impressive colonial house with a
Preservation Society plaque on the front: Marion Morrison
House, Built 1765.

Within a minute, another vehicle rolls up in front of the

garage. What emerges after the Lexus SUV is tucked away, is a decidedly older woman—stocky, mannish, short silver hair—in a business suit.

Rosenthal meets her at the back door, and they kiss.

"Honey, I'm home," I murmur softly...."The twat thickens...." Too bad Rosenthal couldn't be flashed back in time to when this house was built. She'd be put in stocks and have rotten fruit thrown at her...or perhaps a tasteful burning at the stake.

They step inside and as I drive away I think: It's possible these women knew Susan. Don't lesbians and gays in the same town tend to know each other? Go to clubs, belong to reading groups? *Kayak?* And I remember Rosenthal's bio on that singing group website—that she'd been involved with an art gallery at Brown.

"What if Rosenthal *did* know Susan?" I blurt in a panicky voice over the phone to Aleda. "What if Susan, for some reason, gave the bitch a key to her house? Why would she? Could there have been some hanky-panky going on?"

"*Hanky-panky.* You're cute, Swanson. I haven't heard that expression for years!"

"Glad I can amuse you. But what if Rosenthal does have a key to Susan's, and what if she went in and swiped the key to my house—which had my damn name on it—and then let herself into my house and stole the damn *Penthouses* and other magazines I had stories in?"

"I'll tell you this," says Aleda. "If she was playing winky-wanky with Susan, and Miss Silverhair Business Suit and she are partners—better, *long-term* partners—and Miss Silverhair isn't knowledgeable of it, then Ms. Rosenthal's fanny could be ripe for the fryer."

"Eeew....I likes the sizzling sound of that. So—what do I do?"

"You do what anyone who's pissed off does—you set a trap! In this case, a Venus Flytrap! A real pussy-popper!"

"Jesus, Aleda!"

"Hey, I'm psyched! We got the money, Rodio's here, and I can still act. You need a win, Swanson. Come up with something good, would ya?"

I do some online sleuthing at the Providence Tax Assessor's Database and learn that the fancy, historic house Rosenthal lives in is owned by one Paget Cutler. Further Googling and noodling identifies her as the daughter of one Clement Dorrance Cutler of Manchester-by-the-Sea, Massachusetts. Paget Cutler (nickname, "Powder"), a graduate of Mount Holyoke College and Yale Law School, is an attorney with Textron Corporation of Providence, Rhode Island, a conglomerate that manufactures everything from helicopters to golf carts. Further sleuthing reveals previous employment in New York City for the legal department of Pfizer Pharmaceuticals, and prior homes in both Manhattan and East Hampton. On the New York Social Diary website, I find a 2001 party photograph with "Powder's" arm around Ms. Rosenthal's waist.

This is terrific—the long-term relationship Aleda alluded to. But what if my whole Rosenthal/Susan hunch is totally off base?

"You won't be any more fucked than you are already, my friend."

I concoct my plan; it's bold, if not bizarre, but the stakes are high: I am the only person who loves Abby and Eric like a mother and father—and there ain't no substitute for that.

My plan has to unfold tomorrow, as the day after that is Friday, when I'm due back in court to no doubt get eviscerated by Rosenthal with her evidence that I am a depraved pornographer, unfit for human consumption.

I phone Aleda with my idea and she howls. "Swanson...you're a sick man. I'm on board! But only because the woman is a first-class bitch and has to be put away. After this, you have to start behaving yourself—and I'm not kidding."

I bring Eric down from his bedroom and explain the plan. When I'm finished, he's grinning from ear to ear.

"Tomorrow," I intone solemnly, "your life will change forever. Tomorrow, Eric, you will begin to understand what it means to be a man. For tomorrow—you will do what is necessary."

"I am ready," he replies gamely, snapping off a smart salute.

Tomorrow is going to be a big day, all right, beginning with Susan's memorial service at eleven in the morning.

"Don't rain but it pours."

RISD conducts Susan's memorial service in the Grand Gallery of the museum, a big open room with hardwood floors and enormous paintings hung floor-to-ceiling. There are prayers and affectionate reminiscences by several colleagues and school dignitaries.

But that comes to an end with an absolutely shocking performance by the lesbian a capella group, Fingers in the Dyke, singing one of Susan's favorite songs (according to them) *We Don't Need Nobody Cept Us,* followed by a real uppercut to the sensibilities, *Men Used to Take Out the Trash,*

Now They Iz the Trash, leaving many a jaw resting on the floor. What this piece has to do with the moment at hand is anybody's guess, and at the song's conclusion, group member Naomi Rosenthal looks directly at me and smirks.

It is all I can do to stop myself from crooning my new tune, *You'll Be Sorry, Bitch Ass!* I feel a tingling glee, knowing what is in store for Ms. Rosenthal, who is clearly a psychopath.

"She is, right?" I ask Aleda.

"Oh, yeah."

When the service is over, the college hosts a reception right across the street at the swank University Club. Cabot Greenough himself, Chairman of the RISD Board of Trustees posts himself at the door and stops Fingers in the Dyke from entering the club.

"Good man," I say, shaking Greenough's hand as we pass through.

"Have you *ever?*" he snorts.

"Never," I say. "They should all be incarcerated."

"I've always wanted to come here," I tell Aleda, as she and the kids and I enter the main dining room. The maître d' leads us over to the choice table in front of the pretty little panes of a large bay window that looks out upon the busy intersection at the heart of the RISD campus: a picturesque view of students passing to and fro with their portfolios and projects, the grassy knoll "beach" where the kids sun themselves, and the perfectly white First Baptist Church in America with its soaring steeple.

But all of this pales against the knowledge that soon, Royal Madeira and Chester Hurling will be joining us.

They're the gay version of the rich CEO and his trophy wife. Hurling is a good fifteen years older than Madeira, built large and well over six feet tall. Could've been a retired fullback, twenty-thirty pounds over playing weight. Roundish head, full cheeks and a thick mustache. Wine is poured and after offering a toast to Susan, Aleda kicks things off.

"So, Chester—I spotted you two at Pinot over Thanksgiving."

"That so," says Hurling. "Why didn't you come over?"

"I didn't wanna disturb you. You looked thick as thieves."

When Aleda says that, I nearly choke on my wine.

"How long have you two known each other?" I cough.

"We go back a long ways. Years," says Hurling. He exudes a real sullenness, not happy at all to be where he is.

"We grew up together," says Madeira wryly. "I was working on a series of baseball drawings of the Red Sox, and Chester was working for his father, updating all the electricals at the park."

"Really?" I say. "I grew up watching the Red Sox on TV. I love Fenway Park. My father took me once. Your father was an electrician?"

"Yeah," replies Hurling.

"Chester is being modest," says Madeira. "His family owns the biggest electrical outfit in Massachusetts. Tell the baseball fan what you were doing, Chester."

Hurling casts a dark glance at Madeira before replying. "We switched them over to the fancier graphics you see all the time now on the big billboards in the outfield. Fenway's a relic, and the electrical system was completely antiquated. Had to replace everything. Customize."

"Chester's father came over from Scotland," says Madeira. "He began working for Boston Electric and then he started his own business. Chester actually went to MIT—though you'd never know it. I always told him he would've been happier at Michigan State."

"So that means you can fix things? Electric things?" asks Aleda.

"Yup," answers Hurling. "I could rewire that entire white elephant you have out there in Bel Air. But I wouldn't. Too damn much hard work. I saw how hard my old man worked, even after he had fifty others working for him. I got the hell out of Dodge and headed west to make my fortune, and here I am—three wineries and a tech start-up later—a Hollywood movie producer!"

This grown-up conversation is boring as dust to Abby and Eric. When the main course is finished, I allow them to be excused. RISD and its environs is their backyard, and my only request is that they return in a half hour. I was already anticipating the show to be put on later.

"So then," I say, "you were working for your Dad at Fenway and Royal was...drawing the action?"

"Something like that," says Hurling.

"Actually, I was looking for a bathroom, and you were coming out of some tunnel," says Madeira.

"How romantic!" gushes Aleda. "Was Chester all hot and sweaty in his overhauls?"

"You were at the Museum School?" I ask Madeira. "Is that when you and Susan got to know each other?"

"Indeed," he replies.

"Did you ever meet the kids' parents—Susan's sister Julie, and her husband, Ray?"

"I did, actually," says Madeira. "They seemed like fine people."

"Did you know Susan in Boston?" I ask, turning to Hurling. "And Ray and Julie?"

"Not sure," he replies, examining the chunk of Chateaubriand at the end of his fork.

"Maybe you met Julie doing electrical work at the Gardner—"

"Can't remember," says Hurling, cutting me off. "Might've met them through Royal. Did I?"

"Possibly," replies Madeira. "I honestly don't remember."

I drain my wine glass. I once had a girlfriend who told me that whenever somebody answers a question using the word "honestly," they're lying. She'd certainly been correct in my case.

"Well, in any event, here we are," I say. "Brought together by dear Susan and a movie about the amazing Isabella Stewart Gardner."

"Oh, she wasn't all that amazing," says Madeira. "She was rich—but, in her case, that was no accomplishment. She was born rich and married richer. She was probably unfaithful to her husband. Really, she was just a well-dressed thief—running through Europe, plundering and pillaging their art and dragging it back here. Fact is, the woman was nothing more than a rich Victorian *kunta,* who wanted to impress people with her art collection. It probably gave her a sexual thrill. In fact, it probably—"

Suddenly, we hear the heart stopping screech of a car slamming on its brakes and I dash from the table.

The car is gone. There is nothing in the street, not even a squirrel, much less my worst nightmare. I'm sweating and panting. Aleda appears at the door.

"Swanson. Is everything OK?"

"I think so," I huff. "I don't see anything."

We look this way and that for the kids. A man with a walking stick and a bowler stops in front of us. He wears a black patch over one eye. His skin looks molten, as though once badly burned.

"Do you know why colon cancer is the thing today?" he asks us, in a tone that promises he has something to say on the subject.

"Pray tell," asks Aleda.

"Because, young lady—and because you are a lady, I know you'll excuse my bluntness: It's because men, and women too, are stuck in offices all day and can't take a good shit when they have to. A *good* shit takes *at least* ten minutes, and requires absolute privacy!"

"There they are," I say. They're up on a terrace, clambering over the soft curves of a Henry Moore sculpture, and come running when I call them.

"Ah, the golden children!" exclaims the man. "I have something they should know about...."

"Another time, old sport. C'mon inside you guys."

When the luncheon is over, Aleda takes Abby to leave her with Philip, who will look after her for the rest of the afternoon, and I race home with Eric.

"OK, amigo, I'll call Ms. Rosenthal. When she gets on, tell her that you're worried and could she come over and talk to you now. Now! It has to be *now!* Tell her I've gone out and won't be back for at least an hour. We're gonna get her out of our hair. Fo-ev-uh."

"Good!" says Eric. "I don't wanna go live in some foster home."

"Don't worry—that's never gonna happen. That's why we're gonna do this. But remember—you must insist that you can't tell her the problem over the phone. She must come here so you can tell her in person. Maybe you have something you need to show her. Yeah—tell her you have something you have to show her, but you can't possibly describe it over the phone."

"Like maybe a dungeon in the basement, where you take us and whip us!"

"There ya go. Something that will get her *reeeealy* nutty. Something I could get thrown in jail for."

"Got it. I'm ready."

"OK. Here we go," and I dial the number and hand Eric the phone.

The kid is fabulous. Rosenthal does her best to wangle out of him what the problem is, and he parries each of her jabs.

"I have to *show* you," whines Eric, sounding like he's about to cry. When the phone call is over, I pat him on the head.

"Good job, my man! I'm gonna have to talk to Aleda about getting you a screen test. You're a natural. Speaking of Aleda...." Good timing. The big Escalade is just now rolling into the driveway, pulling right up in front of the garage, in which Veronika is safely tucked out of sight.

Eric retreats to the kitchen pantry, under express orders to not make a sound. I stand behind the bookcase, and through a break in a shelf of books, train the video camera on the big sofa in the living room. When the doorbell rings, Aleda answers it.

Ms. Rosenthal recognizes Aleda immediately and falls quite atwitter. Aleda confesses that she's heard I'm having difficulty with the children, so she's stopped by to see for herself.

Rosenthal tells Aleda about Eric's phone call.

"That's troubling," says Aleda. "Well, Swanson told me he had to take them for their annual physicals, and they wouldn't be back for a couple of hours…BTW…your hair is *gorgeous!* Do you always wear it up like that? Bet it looks *fabulous* down! You know, I was about to pour myself a martini. Can I pour one for you? Today's been *très* heavy— wouldn't you say? *Loved* your songs at the service today.

In about twenty minutes, when Ms. Rosenthal's blouse is off, brassiere history (kinda nice tits, I have to admit), and one leg slung over the back of the couch and Aleda's hands everywhere, I pull a string attached to a piece of paper taped to the pantry wall.

Seconds later, Eric appears at the entrance to the living room. "Ms. Rosenthal!" he shrieks. "What are you doing!???"

With the camera continuing to run and Aleda standing behind me sipping her martini, I begin the interrogation:

"We agree, of course, that the children are no longer an issue. Am I correct, Ms. Rosenthal? *Naomi?*"

Naomi Rosenthal's visage might as well have been manufactured from clay.

"Not an issue. The court will be notified immediately that DCYF withdraws any and all complaints."

"I do like the sound of that *Naomi*. I do indeedy do. And now to the matter of Susan Mack, the children's former guardian and your former lover. I am correct, am I not,

Naomi? That the two of you were lovers?"

"Yes."

"How long?"

"Recently. Only a few times."

"And you never encountered the children?"

"We met in her office."

"You mean, that's where you had your...trysts."

"Yes. I feel like I'm in court."

"Oh, you are most certainly in court—the personal court of Judge Swanson Di Chiera. And I most definitely smell shit. Now, *fermez la bouche*. Speak only to answer my questions. How did you get the key to Susan Mack's house?"

"She gave it to me."

"Why would she give you the key to her house?"

"We were going to play. A game. She wanted to come home from work and find me there."

"Like a wife...or a partner."

"Yes. I guess so."

"But it never worked out."

"No. She disappeared before we could."

"Do you know who abducted her?"

"Of course not! I would have gone to the police."

"Did you talk to the police about Susan? Do they know about you?"

"No."

I look at Aleda then back to Rosenthal. "That will be all, Naomi. You may go now. I never want to hear from you again, or see you, unless I request it. Is that clear?"

"Yes."

"Say, *Yes Sir, Mr. Di Chiera—a man among men. A living god!*"

Rosenthal looks at me with pure, utter hatred, then glances at Aleda.

Aleda shrugs. "He has Asperger's."

"Yes. I have Ass Burgers! Now say it, bitch."

"Yes Sir, Mr. Di Chiera—a man among men. A living god."

"Now beat it. Oh, and leave my key on that table beneath the mirror—the key you stole from Susan Mack's house, correct? That you used to break into my house and steal my possessions. Correct?"

"Correct. But I don't have the key with me."

"Fine. Mail it back to me with the magazines and a handwritten letter of apology. Now get the hell out of here, and I never, *ever* want to see your fucked-upness again."

I close the front door. "Bitch didn't know you have to turn the key twice to lock it. Oddball lock saved the fucking day."

"Holy shit, Swanson!" beams Aleda. "You're almost as scary as I am! Success can't be far behind."

"It's my Asperger's Syndrome. Loves it! I can be a self-centered megalomaniac, prone to anti-social behavior. I can say whatever I want and blame it on Asperger's. *C'mere baby—I gots sunt'n for ya.*"

"Yeah, you got sunt'n for me, all right. Hand over that video card so I can get outa here. I have a movie to finish."

"*Waaah.*"

"Stop whining. I'll put it in my safe where it will be—safe. Then, when all of this is over, I'll destroy it. Now c'mon—fork it over so I can go."

I pop the card out of the camera and hand it to her. "My first movie—and Aleda Collie, starring."

"Oh, don't sulk. Someday, we'll make a movie together. I

promise. You write the script and I'll star in it. Isn't there a part for me in the gay football player story? Dan said one of the team owners is a woman. I could own a football team. I could hang around in the locker room!"

"Would you really do the part?"

"I can't make any promises. I'd read it. But first I have a film to finish here in Providence. And it's gotta make money or else the only locker room I'll be hangin' out in will be at the Y—right below my room."

"Hey—do you think Eric was traumatized?"

Aleda love-taps me a couple times on the side of my face.

"Oh, Sweetie…like you said—he's seen it all and more on his computer."

"But this was real life."

"No. This was acting. And we all played are parts exceptionally well. Go talk to him. I'm sure he's fine. Oh, and remember: if you are smart—and I know that you are— this is the end of your anti-social behavior. Start making friends, Swanson. Start being friendly and respecting people, accepting people. You can be a gentleman and still be true to yourself. Ciao, handsome."

I trudge upstairs feeling wasted, but good. Cleansed. "I feel *free!*"

I lean into Eric's room. He's seated in front of his computer clicking away at *RuneScape.* "Cover my back," squawks another boy's voice out of the speakers.

"Wuddup?" I ask.

"Hmm," says Eric. "Are they gone?"

"They're gone."

"That was pretty cool."

"What?"

"You know. Do girls really like to do that?"

"Some. Apparently."

"Why?"

"Jesus, Eric. Why does anyone do anything?"

"Yeah, but...why would a woman want to, you know, with another woman?"

"Because, to them, it must feel good. I mean, you know why people have sex, don't you?"

"To have babies. But two women can't have a baby. I know that much."

"Right. But mostly people have sex because it feels good. And do you know why it feels good?"

"Because....I don't know."

"So we'll do it. Nature doesn't care about anything other than reproduction. Remember that when you are tempted to have sex."

"I'm not gonna have sex!"

"Wouldn't that be cool. But I'm afraid it's in the cards. Eventually."

"Noooooo...*No!*"

I go back downstairs and drop into my desk chair. Searching for something mindless to do, I download pictures from my camera to the computer. I look at the thumbnails. There are photos of Little Guy stretched out on the couch like he's flying, and photos of Abby and Eric sledding, and the photos I'd snapped of the Gardner Museum last week. I double click on one of the photos and let my eyes wash over the front of the building.

There's the main entrance, and above it the frieze of St.

George killing the Dragon. Above that is a decorative medallion of some sort, and further up, the name of the museum and date of construction. Above that is the fourth floor where Gardner herself had lived, and the bay window from which she would've looked out over the Fenway.

My eyes run back down the front of the building to the medallion above the entrance. It's a crest of some sort, a shield, a coat of arms. I enlarge the photo to see more detail. Beneath the shield is a ribbon of words, a motto: *C'est Mon Plaisir.* Christ All Mighty! Is this not Royal Madeira's favorite phrase? I remember that night in the restaurant when I went over to the table where he sat with Aleda, him looking up at me and whispering the words, as if it was a secret between us.

Then comes the real jolt. Above the motto, in the middle of the shield is the weathered image of an eagle.

I click to the Gardner website and call up the objects from the theft. I find the photograph of the eagle finial, stolen from atop the flagpole bearing the silk flag of Napoleon's Imperial Guard. I click back to the image in the shield. It is the same eagle, the wings fanned outward from the body, held open like a feathery cape. A phoenix, rising in magnificence from its own ashes. Symbol of immortality.

"C'est mon plaisir," I whisper, transfixed.

CHAPTER 24

◆

Race to Fenway Park in purloined Veyron. Arrested again!

"IT'S A BIG GAME!" I say, explaining my discovery to Aleda. "You know he sees Gardner as a thief, so he's only stolen from another thief: *C'est mon plaisir* meets *C'est mon plaisir*. And he grabs the eagle finial—the phoenix, the symbol of immortality—as a way of saying the power has been transferred. Napoleon, Isabella Stewart Gardner, now Royal Madeira. Supreme possession and control freaks!"

"God, you're handsome when you get excited."

"Really?"

"You're hair gets wavy."

"That's weird. So, what do you think?"

"I think you could be onto something."

As promised, I take the kids out to the country to Big John's Christmas Tree Farm, where we spend the better part of an hour trudging through snow until we find the perfect tree.

That night, Aleda phones.

"Swanson, I think you really hit upon something with the possession aspect of Belle Gardner. After her baby boy died, Belle was all about possession. She scoured Europe for art.

She hired Berenson to find art for her and verify its authenticity. Fenway Court is built with pieces of stone and columns ferried out of Europe and—Are you there, Swanson?"

"I am. We hunted down a Christmas tree today. I'm just a little tired."

"Well, if you want to get rich, you're gonna have to get untired."

"OK. I'm untired."

"Good. Can you imagine what it was like to live at Fenway Court? I mean, to be there alone; no party going on, no guests? There's a scene we're shooting in the studio tomorrow. It may help you. You have to come. Bring Abby and Eric."

It is one of those still, December evenings that smells like it's going to snow. Eric and Abby and I walk the several blocks from home over to the gargantuan Cranston Street Armory.

We check in with the guard at the gate and Aleda meets us halfway across the parking lot. Approaching the building's entrance, Eric says, "Hey—there's the car we saw in that driveway that day."

"Chester's toy," says Aleda.

It's the exotic, blue and grey Bugatti Veyron we saw parked in Madeira's driveway a few weeks earlier. The keys are dangling from the ignition. Now isn't such insouciance the ultimate symbol of wealth?

This is going to be an intimate scene. Only Gardner. The film company is down to a skeleton crew. No extras, no other actors. The children have never been inside the Armory before and are awed at the sheer size of the place and the majesty of what Hollywood artisans can accomplish. The cutaway of the Gardner Museum, revealing the galleries and the art is so realistic they could sell tickets.

"It looks like a huge dollhouse," says Abby.

"That's exactly what I thought when I saw it for the first time," I tell her.

In the darkness behind the cameras, we take our seats.

The year is 1922, two years before Gardner's death. The scene being shot is at night. Her residence on the fourth floor, a couple of cloisters and a gallery are lit by candlelight. Moonlight pours through the glass roof, softly illuminating the pinkish-white walls that frame the galleries all the way down to the center court.

The birdcage elevator whirls down from her apartments and stops at the third floor. Gardner steps out. She is eighty-two years old.

She walks slowly, regally into the Gothic Room. She stands before the famous full-length portrait of herself, painted by John Singer Sargent in 1888, when she was forty-eight years old.

A long strand of pearls loops twice around the waist of her black dress, a ruby hanging from the center of each loop. An enormous ruby glows at her throat, the neckline plunges. She is dressed tonight exactly as she appears in the painting.

Gazing at the portrait, she runs her hands slowly up and down her body, stroking her neck, her breasts and her hips.

In the decaying, sensual silence I wonder: What are the children thinking? And I smile. Aleda's presence has been such a trip. Not surprising that the children love her.

"Cut! Break!" The director, Beep Gamble, shatters the

illusion. House lights are brought up and we all look at each other. The kids slide off their chairs and Aleda and I walk outside for air.

"Anybody for a cigarette?" I ask.

"No kidding, huh? Isn't Fanning amazing. No wonder she has two Oscars and everybody loves her."

"She sure brings it out. Possession. Sex. Immortality. The deep, dark recesses of ourselves." I gaze over to the Bugatti. "Cars can be sexy," I muse.

"Mustangs always made me wet," says Aleda."

"I creamed for the first Jaguar XKE's. They were such dainty beasts."

Aleda folds her arms tightly across her chest. "Chester and Royal are flying to Rome tomorrow."

"Rome?"

"I think it has something to do with the ten million Chester managed to come up with. He said they'll be back for the Wrap."

"Unless they get hijacked," I quip.

Aleda shakes her head. "They won't. They're going on a Bombardier."

"What the hell's that?"

"Private jet. Stephen Spielberg has one. It's the top private jet now."

"They're going on Spielberg's jet?"

"No." Aleda pauses. "I think it belongs to some sheikh."

"OK...But why would some sheikh have anything to do with the money? I thought it came through the mayor?"

"Swanson—why wouldn't the mayor be able to get money from a sheikh? Or anybody else?" Aleda was obviously agitated now. "Influential people know other influential people. You know that."

"Sure, look at you—you know me."

"Swanson—Just before you got here, I heard them say they're going to pick up something and then leave from Boston."

I'm beginning to get the gist. "What time tomorrow?" I ask.

"Probably early," says Aleda, her voice papery.

"I wonder which one they're taking."

Aleda shrugs. "Probably not the flag thingy," she says with a weak smile. "They wouldn't take all of them, would they?"

"No. Not for a piddley ten million." I look at the sky. I look at the Veyron.

"I know what to do," I say. "Please wait right here and let me get the kids."

"OK," says Aleda. "But is this gonna hurt?"

It was a line she'd made famous in her television show, *The Dish and the Spoon,* when she and her sidekick were about to embark on a perilous adventure. Like every other guy watching, I'd wanted to be that sidekick. Now, by some miracle I'd gotten flashed into the part and I stick faithfully to the script.

"Naaah..."

In a minute I return with Abby and Eric, and taking Aleda's hand, lead all of us quickly down the steps into the parking lot. Hustling over to Hurling's Veyron, I open the passenger door.

"This is me, getting ready to self-destruct," says Aleda. "But I've always come back—right?"

I give her a kiss on the cheek. "You're a regular phoenix, darlin'. Get in. You kids, right after her."

Recalling an article I'd read in *Road and Track* magazine, I reach below the front of the driver's seat and find the hyperspace key. I turn it. A purple LED lights up in the speedometer. It blinks quickly and then turns into the word, *Sì*, Italian for Yes. I am now cleared to take the vehicle up to its maximum speed of two hundred fifty-three miles per hour. I turn the main key switch, press the start button and the engine snorts and fires up—I might just as well have slapped a sleeping wildebeest on the ass.

The security guard appears at my window.

"You're not Mr. Hurling."

"No. I am not," I say. "He asked us to pick up some Altoids for him." Then I goose it.

Pulling onto 95, I glance at the fuel gauge. "Thank God it's almost full. This thing gets about ten miles per gallon—and half that at top speed."

"We don't need to do top speed, do we?" asks Aleda.

Abby turns on the radio. It sounds like the entire Metropolitan Opera has just squeezed in with us.

"Wow!" says Eric, leaning over to look at the speedometer. "We're doing a hundred and thirty miles per hour."

"Yeah-*huh!*" I grin. "It feels like sixty. This thing is great!"

"Abby—how much do you weigh?" asks Aleda.

"I dunno."

"I can hardly tell you're sittin' on me."

"Where're we going?" asks Eric.

"I think your Uncle Swanson wants it to be a surprise," says Aleda.

"Be surprised no longer. Aleda, sweetheart, call your friend—the guard with the funny name at Fenway Park. Ask him to meet us at the entrance on Yawkey Way in…fifteen minutes."

"What should I tell him?"

"Tell him it's important."

I punch the accelerator and a couple seconds later the Veyron hits two hundred miles an hour, automatically lowering itself closer to the ground and pinning everyone back.

"Shit Swanson!" yelps Aleda.

"Wahooo!" yells Eric. Abby has her hand in her mouth.

From a pure physics point of view, the cars we're passing really are standing still.

Approaching Boston, Eric figures out how to operate the GPS and vectors us in to Fenway Park.

"This is it," I say, pulling into the quiet shadows of Yawkey Way.

"This is where the paintings are?" asks Aleda.

"Yup."

Just then, the huge cast-iron gate swings open and there stands Riley O'Reilly.

"Well, isn't this jawst the best Christmas present!" declares Riley, giving Aleda a big hug. "And who might these tykes be—Aleda's Little Helpers?"

"Yes, they are, Riley," and she introduces Abby and Eric who shyly shake Riley's hand.

"Hoo-wee!" hoots Riley. Steam's rising off the rear of the Veyron where the monster engine is making pinging and popping sounds while four electric fans work to cool her down. "What the heck is this ding-dang thing? Oh, nevuh mind. Knowin' you, Aleda, it's some don thing built specially fuh the movies!" Then Riley turns serious. "But thyat's not why yaw he-yah, is it? This ain't a movie thing, is it?" and he glances at me as he says that.

"No it's not, Riley," I say. "We believe there's stolen art hidden somewhere in the park. Do you remember the theft from the Isabella Stewart Gardner Museum?"

"Kyant say thyat I do," says Riley.

"Most people don't. Anyway, I believe the art is stashed somewhere in Fenway, probably in a...room...a tunnel...maybe that carries electrical lines. Under the stadium there must be all sorts of passageways where the electrical lines run to the scoreboard and the lights."

We disappear into the vast understructure of the stadium, where in a few months' time, thousands of fans will pour through the gates to see their beloved Red Sox.

"Can I see the field?" asks Eric.

"Me, too," says Abby.

I know we don't have much time. A car like Hurling's Bugatti must have LoJack or some other type of satellite homing device.

"Stick with us," I tell them. "We'll come back again."

Riley takes us to his office where a color-coded map hangs on the wall. It looks like the New York subway system, and it shows all of the stadium's underground tunnels.

"Who'd know where to begin?" wonders Aleda.

"An electrician," I reply.

"I gawt one a them. Gawt a nephew, my brother's boy. He wax for the big electrical outfit in Bastin. Byack Byay Electric."

"Hurling's company," I say.

"Why thee-ats the name of the fee-amly thyat owns her. Yep. Hurlin'."

"Could you get him over here?" I ask.

"Oh shuwah. Wait—*you mean tonight?*"

"Yeah. Like now."

"Oh, no…no….He'd be home with his wife and baby. I wouldn't wanna bawthuh him nyow. Maybe—"

Aleda opens her purse and pulls out a wad of hundreds and hands them to Riley. Then she whips out her cell phone. "What's his number?"

Teddy O'Reilly is tall and skinny with a brush top and arrives with tomato sauce at the corners of his mouth. Aleda hands him three one hundred dollar bills.

"We want to see where the electricity starts and how it gets to the field," I say. "There must be a room, a tunnel. We must be talking about some heavy stuff, right?"

"No question," says Teddy. After tracing his finger over the map in Riley's office he says, "OK. Follow me."

Teddy O'Reilly leads us to a concession stand, behind which is a heavy steel door. I'm tingling all over. I've figured it out. Breathe…*Breathe….*

Riley has passkeys to all the doors. Inside is a room of big breaker handles and switches. It's the control room for every light in the stadium. Inside this room is another door that obviously leads to all of the cabling. It's locked with a padlock the size of a fist. Riley starts trying keys.

"Never been in this room befwah," he complains. "None a these keys ah fittin'."

"Goddamnit!" I growl.

"Well, it must come out somewhere…Right?" asks Aleda. We all look at her.

"My guess," says Teddy, "is that if there's another access

point, it will be at the end of the line. And that would probably be out near center field, beneath the big video screen."

I look at the panel and the breaker handles. There are four big handles below a sign that says Stadium Lights. I throw all four and we head back out and up to the field.

Under a dusting of snow crystals and beneath the bright lights, it really is a diamond. We make our way down the aisle between the box seats, step over the wall and onto the field.

"I dreamed of playing here," I say. Then we hear sirens.

"What the heck?" says Riley.

"Somebody probably saw the lights," says Aleda. "We'll head out there and you go see what it is, Riley." She puts a hand on his arm. "Stall'em if ya can, would ya?"

Riley smiles at her. "Aleda, you make me feel like we're in a movie together."

We reach the bullpen when two Boston police officers appear in the stands behind home plate. One of them has a bullhorn.

"Stop immediately," commands the crackily, amplified voice.

"What's goin' on?" asks Teddy.

"They're phonies. C'mon," I urge, and we slip over the wall, quickly followed by Abby and Eric. Beneath the enormous video display, we find what we're looking for—a metal hatch in the ground.

The hatch, like a manhole cover, requires a pry bar to open it. While we're trying to figure out what we can use, the police officers arrive. And they are real. So are their guns.

"What in God's name were you thinking of?!" thunders Hurling.

Aleda and I are sitting like misbehaved children on a scarred wooden bench at Boston Police Headquarters. Eric and Abby are sprawled in a corner on the floor half asleep, an empty pizza box and cans of Coke at their feet.

I motion to Hurling to come closer. "They have to leave," I say, referring to the two detectives. "And could they look after the children, too?"

Hurling opens his wallet and hands the cops a hundred each. "We need some privacy," he tells them. "Take the kids, too. And keep an eye on them."

I look at Aleda and draw a deep breath: "OK—here's the deal...."

I tell Hurling everything that I've put together about the RISD and Gardner thefts. I leave out the murder of Susan. I don't want to think I'm with a murderer at the moment. By the time I'm finished, he looks like he's going to explode.

"This is fantastic!" he says, looking back and forth from me to Aleda. "This is our next movie! It'll be the sequel to *Belle!*"

No charges are filed. Tiny is waiting outside the police station in the Escalade to take us back to Providence.

I turn to Hurling. "If you're not transporting stolen Gardner art—or RISD art, for that matter—to trade for money to finish the film, then why are you and Madeira going to Rome?"

"Mr. Di Chiera, no matter what I tell you, you won't believe me, so what's the point?"

"Try me," I say.

Hurling looks at me steadily, and says, "Royal and I are going to Rome to get married."

I snort. "C'mon. You're supposed to be back in two days for the Wrap. What's the rush? How about New Year's—that would be romantic."

"True enough, Di Chiera—but it's not every day the Pope has the time to perform a wedding ceremony."

"Are you telling me that you and Madeira are going to Rome to be married by the Pope?"

"You see, Mr. Di Chiera?" smiles Hurling in a pitying way. "I told you that you wouldn't believe me."

"But married by the *Pope?* C'mon...."

"Mr. Di Chiera, I can assure you that in *my* imagination, such a thing is as plausible as your preposterous tale. Now, would you like to accept your free pass, and head back home with the children, or do you need more trouble with that social service agency and the State of Rhode Island? Life can be good if you don't fight it, Mr. Di Chiera."

I look at the children, nearly asleep in the big back seat, and Aleda watching me from the inside. Without saying anything more, I climb in and we drive away.

CHAPTER 25

♦

Wrap Party for *Belle*. Aleda returns to L.A.

I MEET WITH ATTORNEY MONTEREY TO DISCUSS SUSAN'S ESTATE. I need some cash right away—to buy Christmas and Hanukkah presents for the kids. To feed and clothe them.

Eugenia Monterey tells me that the will must be probated. That could take some time, a couple of months probably. Until then, to cover expenses for the children and play Santa, she has a check cut from the law firm's account. Now that's class.

I phone Aleda and thank her again for hooking me up with Leyendecker's firm, and I apologize for the abortive trip to Fenway Park.

"Swanson—you did what you thought was right. And maybe you were right. But it no longer matters. If the art was stashed at the ball park, it's gone now. We survived that car ride. Oh my god!....Swanson, I have three days to wrap up filming here."

"Are you going to make it?"

"Yes."

"Is there anything I can do to be helpful?"

"Stay out of trouble. The Wrap party is Friday night. Will you bring the kids?"

"Of course."

"There'll be a lot of people," says Aleda. "Chester and Royal will be back—if they haven't run off with all the art!" she laughs weakly. "Rodio will still be here...and Georgette. Her last big scene is on Friday....And Gash is coming in on Thursday."

"Well, I better get to work," I say. "See you Friday night." Then I hang up the phone and just stand there.

On the night of the Wrap, the kids and I return to the Cranston Street Armory. Almost immediately, we run into Madeira and Hurling.

"You came back," I say.

Madeira holds out his left hand. On the ring finger, he sports a huge ruby.

"Would you like to kiss it, Di Chiera?"

In the crepuscular light of a make-believe world, Georgette Fanning as Gardner, swathed in white drapery exactly as Sargent had painted her in 1922, is borne by gondola chair down into the lush center courtyard of Fenway Court. There she sits, alone amidst the sculpture, the mosaics, the flowers and fountains. Slowly, she raises her head and gazes up to the arched openings of the galleries. And as she looks from one to another, a light comes up in this gallery and that one, each filled with remembered moments of her life. Then, very gradually the lights dim and all is extinguished save one last spot, pale as moonlight, lingering, fading on Gardner. Then she too, is gone.

The pulse of dark silence is broken by Beep Gamble's voice, clear and reverent: "That, lovelies, is a wrap."

Up come the lights and the entire crew, fellow actors, technicians, spectators…everyone bursts into applause. Fanning, tears streaming down her face, stands and bows. Within minutes, the set is swarming with film people and waiters from the caterer. A band breaks into music and the champagne flows.

The explosion of people and music and movement is overwhelming. Suddenly, Aleda is in front of us, and by her side stands a tall, well-built, and devilishly handsome… Hun!

"Wasn't that amazing!" gushes Aleda. But the kids and I can't take our eyes off the manly hunk of man standing in front of us. Finally, Aleda says: "This is Kurt Gashwantner."

"Just call me Gash," the man says, the words tumbling out of his mouth like boulders, a crack breaking across the broad planes of his granite face.

"Your name is Gash?" asks Abby timidly, while at the same time moving a smidgen behind me.

"Wow! Look at the size of your shoes!" says Eric. "They must be like size twenty or something."

Gash tries to smile in a friendly way.

"Eric," I say, "it's not polite to notice somebody's shoe size. At least not out loud. Plus—I don't think they're any bigger than…sixteens."

The kids wander around and sample all of the food on the buffet tables. Everything feels strange now and I just want to get away. I look around for the kids and Aleda.

Aleda finds me first, and she's pretty sloshed.

"Swanson! Swanson! C'mere…." She pulls me over to a corner of the set, to a copy of the famous fourteenth century Farnese Sarcophagus, around which, in relief, dance satyrs, erotes, and maenads in Bacchanalian revelry.

"Here, siddown," she says. "Swanson...*Swanson The Magnificent.* Chester's serious about making a movie sequel to *Belle.* You inspired him with your tale in the Boston police station."

"Gee—I'm glad I could be of some use."

"Get off it, will ya. They came back. I know you wanted them to be running off with the art. It made sense. But it didn't go that way. But listen, Swanson, it gets better. A lot better. Hurling wants you to write the script! Isn't that fantastic! He said he wants you to come out to L.A., and he wants to hook you up with a couple other writers who have experience—"

"Whoa. Whoa...hold on," I protest. "I have a novel I'm trying to finish, and two kids who go to school here—"

"Swanson! You can finish your book in L.A. And there are schools in L.A.—Oakwood...Harvard Westlake...friends of mines kids go and they're every bit as good as Hogwarts or whatever it is here."

"Wheeler."

"Big wheeler-dealer whoop! Well, *Swanson The Magnificent,* do what you wanna do. If you do ever get out to L.A., give me a call and we'll do lunch." And with that, Aleda stands up and sweeps herself away.

"Ah, women...." The voice comes from just behind my right shoulder, and I turn to face Royal Madeira. "They're strange creatures, you know. Barely human."

"You would know," I say.

Madeira smiles, relishing my comment as though he's been waiting for it. Hoping for it.

"Yes. I would," he answers. "It was *such a fucking relief* to shed that female identity and become who I was all along. Who do you think you've been all along, Di Chiera? Have you realized your...ambitions? Have you become you? Or do you feel as though the world controls you? That you have been cast off onto the sea of life, your sails flapping, your direction determined by whatever winds (and he looks off in the direction Aleda has flown) happen to be blowing?"

"I feel chilly. That's how I feel," and go off in search of Abby and Eric.

I find them, listening to Beep Gamble who's happily lit and holding forth on the second floor of the set, in the recreation of the Dutch Room. They're sitting in front of Madeira's magnificent copy of Rembrandt's, *Storm on the Sea of Galilee.*

"You look like a little Vermeer-eeer girl to me," Gamble hiccups to Abby. "It's your high, round forehead and that little chinny chin-chin of yours."

"And who do I look like?" asks Eric.

"You? You look like-*ike.*" He hiccups. "So sorry....You could be a young Hemingway!"

"What did he paint? Are any of them here?" asks Eric.

"He was a writer," I cut in. "All right, you two. Time to go." I walk over to Beep and shake his hand. "It's been a pleasure. You've been very kind to all of us."

"Di Chiera—" Grabbing ahold of the Rembrandt's frame to pull himself up, Gamble brings it crashing down, popping one of his hands straight through Jesus.

"Ooops...my ba-ad! Imagine if this was the real thing. I'd be wo-*orkin'* the rest of my life to pay it off. Di Chiera...couldn't have done it withoutcha. No kidding. You kept Aleda busy—thas the most impor-*ort*...important thing. Bon voyage now, voyagers."

"Bon voyage…Bon voyage…Bon voyage…." we call back, and climb down the stairs to the main area and make our way toward the door.

"But where's Aleda?" asks Abby. "Aren't we going to say good-bye to her?"

"She's with Gash the Giant, dummy," says Eric. "Holy Shmoly! They say that guys with big feet have big you-know-whats. His must be the size of a….cucumber!"

"Eric, you're sick!" says Abby. "There she is!" Catching sight of Aleda, Abby runs across the room toward her. Aleda spreads out her arms and gathers her up, lifting her off her feet.

When Aleda finally lets go of Abby, she holds open her arms to Eric and hugs him tight. When she lets him go, Abby says, "Aren't you gonna hug Swanson?"

Aleda opens her arms and we hug. But it doesn't feel real.

Aleda gets a tap on the shoulder. It's Gash.

"Somebody wants to talk to you," he says.

Aleda looks at all of us and barely audibly mouths, "I love you." Then she turns and flies away.

On Christmas Eve, just before dinner the phone rings. It's Aleda.

"Hi Swanson. What are you doing?"

"Tearing lettuce. What are you doing?"

"Flying over the Rockies."

"That's nice. How do they look?"

"Rocky. Listen. I'm sorry I got peckish with you. I just—" The line went silent.

"Aleda. Are you there? Is…*Gash* there with you?"

"I'm here. No. He left earlier. Um…I'm sorry for throwing a nutty. I realize you've got a life in Providence, and you know what is best for you."

"I don't know that I know what's best for me. I mean, it takes me awhile to digest things. I'm not quick on my feet, the way you are."

"Well, let me tell you, quick on your feet is not always the best way to be. Anyway. I just wanted to call you."

"I'm glad you did."

"How are the kids? Do you think they'll miss me."

"They're fine. And if they don't miss you, I'll beat them till they do."

"Thanks. I'd appreciate that. Listen. I'm gonna send you some books. Maybe they'll help with your Gardner theft research."

"Thank you."

"What are you doing for Christmas?"

"Opening presents. Then we might go sledding. It's snowing here. What are you doing?"

"Going to Belize. Francis Coppola has a place there. A resort."

"Nice….Gash goin' with you?"

"Yeah."

"He seems like a nice guy—in size extra-large."

"Yeah—he's OK. I gotta go. Give my love to the children and…take some for yourself, too."

"Love to you, too. Thanks for calling."

"As long as I'm talking, I'm not eating. I think I put on ten pounds in Providence."

"That Belize sun will toast it up nice. You'll look great. Ciao."

I hang up. "Belize…Francis Coppola…what a life…."

But I have a different reality in front of me: two children who deserve some happy Christmas memories. So, I smile and laugh and make myself have fun with them, even though I am broken-hearted and worried about many things. This, I now realize, is what parents do.

PART THREE

CHAPTER 26

♦

Arrow hired to look after Abby and Eric.

JUST AFTER THE FIRST OF THE YEAR, I return from grocery shopping and find a FedEx package on the porch. It contains several books pertaining to Isabella Stewart Gardner. There is also a notebook Aleda has kept over the years.

How touching it is to find, in Aleda's hand, her Gardner musings that began way back during the summer we first met.

....ISG Not pretty—maybe a blessing? If I was not pretty (in conventional sense—blonde American), would I be more interesting? Maybe work harder to learn things. Have to be smarter, not rely on looks....

There's a note sticking out of one of the books: *Swanson, Maybe this material will help you figure out the Theft and Get Rich! xoxo Aleda.*

Does money beget money? Well, at least in this case there seems to be a little rub-off. A few days after receiving Aleda's care package, my agent calls and informs me that I've been offered a ten thousand dollar film option on my first novel, the one about relay operators for the deaf. Not that I have any expectations—very few optioned books ever make it into film—but it's a nice chunk of unexpected change that's mine to keep no matter what, especially as Susan's will is still tied up in probate.

About the Gardner theft, I am feeling mudflat low. With the daily excitement of Aleda gone, and my certainty about Madeira and Hurling's connection deflated, the very thought of it is depresses me. Who was I to think I had any special insights? Plus, I'm busy as hell with the kids, and working like a banshee to finish my football novel.

My agent feels the film interest in my first novel is ammunition to help her sell the one I'm working on now. She also thinks the time might finally be ripe for a story about two gay, professional football players.

No more illusions. I have to focus on what is real, what is in front of me.

On an ass-bite cold night, I zip into Whole Foods to pick up a few things. It's impossible to keep enough food in the house.

At the check-out line I run into Arrow Amarusso. She has two oranges, one cellophane package of 365 pasta, and a pound of Pleasant Morning Buzz coffee in her basket. Her eyes are burning bright and she wants to know about Abby and Eric.

"The kids are generally fine, but Abby seems kinda bored lately, and she and her best friend have been bickering. How are you? How's life at the Dirt Palace?"

"A hive of activity, as they say. If Abby's bored, maybe she'd like to come down and try one of our classes."

And that's how Abby ends up spending Saturday mornings down at the Dirt Palace, making art with Arrow and Jen and Tamara and the rest of the "Ladies of the Dirt."

"Careful!" I caution, as Abby tumbles out of the car. She can't wait to disappear into the old mill building. I'm proud of Abby and fond of these young women who are helping her. I want Abby to grow up inquisitive and confident, and skilled. Most of all, I want Abby and Eric to have an enthusiasm for life. I decide to park the car and stick my head inside.

A hive of activity, indeed. Young women and girls drawing, painting, sculpting, printing posters. Pink, blue, and white hair. Tattoos. Lots of tattoos. Well, I'll draw the line there. And piercings. They're out, too. Abby's ears are already pierced, and that was going to be it—Finito, Benito!

"Hey, Arrow."

"Hey, Mr. Di Chiera. How are you?"

"Doing well. And you."

Arrow says she's fine, but still looks so thin to me. Under her make-up, her face looks a little broken-out.

"I'm finished with school," she says. "I could get my diploma now, but I'm going to wait till June and get it with the rest of my friends. Hey, Abby's doing great!"

"She lives for this place," I tell her.

"Excuse me, just a sec." Arrow crosses the room, where Abby and two other girls are getting ready to guillotine a hand with the big blade of a paper cutter. Watching Arrow show them how to use the device properly, a thought returns—Abby needs a woman's presence in her life—outside of the structure of school or even this.

Before I leave, I ask Arrow, "Would you be interested in a small, part-time job?"

"Such as?"

"Such as, picking up Eric and Abby a day or two each week from school and spending a couple hours with her. I'll throw dinner into the bargain too...."

I'm smiling driving home. She accepted the offer.

"Give Swanson ten thousand bucks, watch ten thousand bucks evaporate."

Ah, well, story of my stupid life. But this will be money well-spent. How can you go wrong investing in children?

I am at my desk when I hear tires crunching over the snow in the driveway. It's Arrow, bringing the kids home from school for the first time.

All in one motion, Abby pushes open the front door, drops her backpack and kicks off her boots. "C'mon, I'll show you my room!"

Arrow waves to me from the foyer and then follows Abby, who's already halfway up the stairs. Eric comes in behind them and closes the front door.

I give him a knowing look. "Grrrl power, duuude."

"Whatever," he grumbles.

Guessing that Arrow has vegetarian leanings (Abby has recently declared she's no longer eating meat), I mine a recipe for Tempeh Stroganoff from a macrobiotic cookbook I haven't opened in more than twenty years. I start Eric off slicing onions. They haven't invented salivary glands yet that can resist the smell of onions sautéing in a little olive oil.

Abby doesn't leave Arrow's side for a moment, except to brighten the surroundings. She and Eric lay a fire in the fireplace and Abby lights the candles on the dining room table. Abby looks at Arrow as if she's a fairy tale princess, and that every word she speaks is wise and beautiful.

"Where were you from, before Providence?" I ask.

"Well, my father lives in Oregon now, and my mother's in Maine. But I actually grew up in Gloucester, Massachusetts."

"Have we ever been there?" Abby asks me.

"I don't think so, unless you went with your Aunt Susan."

"No. We haven't been there says Eric. But I think that's where the movie, *The Perfect Storm,* was supposed to take place. I mean, where the boat originally left from, before the perfect storm."

"You're right," says Arrow. "Luckily, my art teacher at Gloucester High School, Mr. McAdam, told me about RISD and encouraged me to apply. I got in and here I am!"

After dinner, Abby and I walk Arrow out to her car.

"You should give her a key to the house, shouldn't you?" asks Abby.

"Good thinking," I say, and take the house key off my key ring and hand it to her.

"And I'll show you how to do the special lock thing," Abby tells her. "You have to turn it twice to lock it. But it's really easy."

CHAPTER 27

♦

Swanson discovers Hurling owned a Pandora.

THE MANILA ENVELOPE ARRIVES IN THE MORNING MAIL, return address: P. V. Briggs, P.O Box 110, Westport Point, MA 02791. There's a letter inside from Peter Briggs, typed on an actual typewriter upon engraved Briggs Pandora Automobile Co. letterhead, apologizing for the delay in furnishing the names of the original purchasers of the forty-five Pandoras. Camilla, his wife...riding accident...Charleston, SC...but she's all right now...etc.

I put the letter aside and scan the list. My eyeballs freeze. Halfway down the first page is the name, Chester A. Hurling.

Has to be the same Chester Hurling. I phone Aleda out in L.A. She's in the middle of doing "ADR's."

"Additional Dialogue Recording. It's the stuff that got knocked out by an airplane flying overhead, a bus passing by...or for whatever reason didn't record well. Or, something we might decide to add."

I ask her if Chester's middle initial is A, although I don't really have to. After all, how many Chester Hurlings could there be with an address in Boston, Massachusetts? Part of it is just an excuse to talk to her.

"Yes, it is," she says, "Chester A. I remember seeing it on some document. We've got documents up the wazoo. We've also got a terrific movie on our hands. I really think we do."

I tell her about the Pandora.

"So, you're going back to investigating them?"

"Got to, with this info. He never said anything about knowing Ray when I asked him at Susan's memorial service."

"Maybe he didn't sell it to your friend. Maybe he sold it to somebody else and that person sold it to Ray. Or maybe he had somebody else sell it for him, and he never met Ray. Or, maybe it wasn't even the same car."

No, Aleda. It's just too much of a coincidence."

"Well, as I said before, proceed carefully. Keep your head down and your ears back."

"Sounds like something Gash would say."

"Gotta go."

Now, why did I have to say that?

Where to begin? Is this stupid? So what if Hurling sold his Pandora to Ray. What was I trying to prove? That he had something to do with the disaster? Was I about to embark upon a real time-waster, when I have a novel to finish as fast as I can?

I feel nervous and stumped and way over my head. How would I even approach this?

"CRAP!" I yell at the top of my lungs. *"CRAP!"*

Aleda demands that we get cell phones and insists on paying for them, so now we all have cell phones. But I hardly ever use mine. I'm resisting on moral grounds. I tell people

I'm a "late adopter." I like that. It makes me chuckle inside.

"Chuckling inside is important," I tell Eric one night. "The ability to amuse oneself can save oneself."

"That sounds like something a writer would say," says Eric.

"Well, *duhhh....*"

Aleda calls. "How do y'all like your cell phones? You don't have to tell me about the kids—I know they love theirs. What about you? Do you ever use it?"

"Yes, I used it yesterday. I was outside shoveling snow, and I kept hearing *boop...boop.* Finally, I realized that every time I bent over to shovel I was taking a photo of the inside of my pants pocket."

"Jesus, Swanson. You are funny."

"Someday, maybe I'll have a show of photos of the inside my pants pockets."

"I know," sighs Aleda. "All I want is to be able to make a phone call where everybody can hear each other. I just want a good connection. Do you miss me?"

"No."

"Liar. Tell me you miss me."

"I miss you."

"You sound so robotic."

"It's the cell phone in my pants. It's taking over my life."

"Well, take it out of your pants. I read somewhere that it can make you sterile. Though, in your case, that could be a good thing. You have two children now."

"Still, there's always the dream."

"Better keep it in your pants, Swanson. Gotta go. Byyye."

I click off and look at a photo of Julie and Ray and the kids. I think about Susan. Jesus. The police investigation into her death is comatose. I haven't talked to them in weeks, and the last time I did, they still didn't have any clues. I recall hearing somewhere that most murders go unsolved. I lean over my desk and put my head in my hands.

CHAPTER 28

♦

Swanson runs into Madeira and Hurling at public
hearing in Providence. Arrow and artist friends testify
against gentrification.

MAN, PROVIDENCE IS DEPRESSING THIS TIME OF
YEAR. T.S. Eliot might have said April is the cruelest
month but obviously he never passed a year in Rhode Island.
Here, cruelty really defines itself starting in February.

Cold-Cold-Cold. Grey-Grey-Grey. This year is no
exception, and with a phone call from the law offices of
Leyendecker, Beguelin & Bedward, LLP, it becomes
incalculably worse. On the line is not attorney Eugenia
Monterey, who's been handling Susan's will as it wends
through probate, but Drury Leyendecker himself.

"How's your leg?" I ask, recalling his skiing accident.

"Forget about my leg," says Leyendecker. "You need to
come down to my office, ASAP."

At his office of cream and mahogany in the Turk's Head
Building, Leyendecker cuts to the chase. "Di Chiera, the
estate of Susan Mack has no money. The fact is, she's in
debt—even though she's dead. That's not your worry. But
you won't be seeing a dime, nor will the kids. The woman
didn't file income taxes for the past ten years." He takes off
his glasses and looks directly at me. "Everything she owns

belongs to Uncle Sam."

The damned mantra never seems to change: "I need money!"

The most immediate route to cash is Iphigenia Melikis, my editor at *Providence Monthly*. At least I can level with her.

"Iffy, I need work. Do you have a story that needs to be written? Photos? I'll take anything."

She asks if I would be interested in covering a meeting down in Olneyville, and developing an article around it? "The Transformation of Olneyville," as she puts it. I know what she's talking about and say, yes.

"But you haven't let me finish," Iphigenia protests.

"I don't have to, dear. It's all about *adaptive re-use;* converting old mills into upscale yuppie housing and little metallic offices for techno-nerds. *Start-ups. Mixed-use*, running the artists and the old-timers out. Hello SoHo, good bye funk. Goodbye art, Hello Starbucks."

"Well. It sounds like you've already gotten this written," says Iffy.

"Pending any last minute changes in the course of human events, yes."

The night of the presentation, I take Abby along with me. Eric has a photography club meeting at school and I never ask Arrow to give up her Friday nights.

We're fated to see Arrow anyway. Getting out of the car, Abby spots her across the parking lot and takes off in her direction. The Ladies of the Dirt Palace have more than a passing interest in tonight's meeting.

It's held in the Bridgham Middle-School cafeteria—

polished linoleum squares, bright overhead lighting. Metal folding chairs are set up and there's a table with stainless steel coffee urns and boxes of donuts. Abby asks if she can sit with Arrow. I say that's fine, and she hugs me around the waist, then she says, "You're not wearing green."

"So?"

"It's Saint Patrick's Day!"

Turning to scoot back across the room, Abby abruptly halts and says, "Oh. Look."

Sitting in the audience at the front of the room are Royal Madeira and Chester Hurling. Weird. What the hell are they doing here? I sit down in the last row, where I can take in all the action. I notice that Madeira has a balding spot radiating out from the crown of his head, making him somehow more human. Abby has snuggled deep into a group of young women from the Dirt Palace and a bunch of other raggle-taggle urbanland creatures.

The first forty-five minutes of the meeting are consumed by a Power Point presentation given by a representative of the developers, Straffer Brothers, showing how wonderful their project is: illustrated people walking illustrated dogs along the illustrated banks of an illustrated Woonasquatucket River flowing through an illustrated Olneyville. All of it an illustrated Nirvana. The next forty minutes are chewed up by the six members of the Providence Plan Commission heaping praise upon the project—your basic display of architects and political insiders creating work and influence for each other.

"Le dung, it is deep," I murmur.

Finally, almost two hours after the meeting has begun and the professional windbags have sucked nearly every molecule of oxygen from the room and you can hardly remember your own name, the meeting is opened to public comment—but wait!—not before the chairman of the commission cautions that each speaker will be limited to a maximum of two minutes. *My God!* I scribble, *Not only do they smother the citizenry under their bullshit, but then shoot in the head those who are still breathing!*

But I have underestimated the kids. Patiently and politely they have waited for the face-sphincters to close. Now, one by one, they take their turn at the microphone and, to a person, are articulate and passionate.

For almost an hour the young artists including Arrow, speak out about how the development will displace them; how they will never be able to afford what the developers consider affordable rents.

"Providence boasts about how it's a city of the arts," says a skinny young man holding a poster by his side. "The mayor and all of the politicians never miss an opportunity to ballyhoo *The Providence Art Scene.* Well, what kind of art scene will exist if artists can't afford to live here? We don't need a Wal-Mart or a Home Depot or a Whole Foods in Olneyville. We need what we already have: affordable space to live and make work." He then holds up a beautiful silk screened poster. "Do you like this? Well, here's what's going to happen if you approve Straffer Brother's project," and he rips the poster in two.

The developer's representatives and commission members wait with dough-faces for the storm to pass, and I see that the kids are ultimately just as screwed as the raccoons, frogs, ducks, and myriad other creatures that live along the untamed banks of the Woonasquatucket River. All the wild creatures with their hearts beating pure are gonna be run off.

When the farce ends, I make my way across the room toward Abby, purposely merging into Hurling and Madeira.

"So...what brings you two gourmets to this charming, middle school cafeteria?" I inquire.

"We heard they make a mean fruit cup," quips Madeira.

"We own one of the buildings Straffer wants to buy to put their project together," says Hurling. "Thought we'd come and see what they had in mind."

"And?"

"Looks fantastic. They've done similar projects in Baltimore, and Baltimore loves them."

"What about the kids?"

"Eh..." and Hurling shrugs his shoulders. "They've had a good run of cheap rent. It's time to move on. They'll find someplace else."

Abby sidles up to me and I place my hand protectively against the side of her head. Business people really do see the world differently. Growth to them is something that happens on the outside.

This is my chance and I take my shot: "Say, Chester—you never mentioned that you knew my old pal, Ray Mendelsohn—Abby's father?"

His expression tightens and I know that I have something.

"Didn't I?" he says. "Thought it must've come up."

"You sold him a car, Chester. That gorgeous old Pandora."

"Right....How was that?" he asks, turning to Madeira.

"Ray had seen the car," says Madeira vaguely, smoothing out the road for his thoughts. "You know Ray was a car nut. He'd seen it when Chester and I first got together. He said something like, 'If you ever decide to get rid of it, let me know. So, when Chester said he was going to sell it, I told him to contact Ray."

"I gave him a good deal on it, too," says Hurling. "That I recall."

"Basically, gave it to him," sniffs Madeira.

Abby sees Arrow and asks if she can leave for a minute. I am glad of it and turn my gaze back on Hurling.

"But Chester—there was a very bad electrical problem with that car."

"No problems when I owned it." I can see Hurling has regained his composure. This encounter has been mined for what I can get, and I have gotten something.

Madeira has been regarding me with his glossy mirror eyes, and now his gaze falls upon the slender book I hold shut in my hand, one of the Gardner biographies Aleda sent. Never go anywhere without something to read is my motto.

"That's an interesting volume," he observes. "Not one you come across every day."

"Probably not," I reply

"A bit on the fawning side. But Isabella-useful in its own way."

"Don't tell me you're reconsidering my offer to work on a sequel to *Belle?*" asks Hurling. But before I can answer, Madeira jumps in.

"No, Chester—his standards are much too high for that. I'm afraid Mr. Di Chiera is still hoping to collect the five million dollar reward for finding the stolen Gardner art. You know, Di Chiera, five million is really crap for recovering art that's worth a hundred times that. Maybe more."

"It's OK. I'm a writer. I'm used to crap."

Hurling snorts, amused.

"It is true," muses Madeira, "that the artist usually gets the short end of it. Rembrandt...Vermeer...so many of them died broke. And writers...poor Guy de Maupassant—without a franc, syphilitic...licking the walls of an insane asylum...."

"Spoke with Aleda," breaks in Hurling. "She mentioned the bad turn with that estate business. I want you to know that my offer of developing a screenplay still stands. Of course, I do have some suggestions to make it a bit more credible. There'd be upfront money, of course. May ease the crunch."

"I appreciate that Chester. I really do. But for now, I think we'll be fine." Inside I'm thinking, What is the matter with me? Just saying Yes will instantly solve my money problems. If not for myself, don't I owe this to the children?

Madeira lifts his chin and strokes his neck with the back of his hand.

"Di Chiera...given your interest in all of this Gardner stuff, I'd like to invite you up to our summer house. It has some history. We'll be up there soon—a little shakedown cruise before the season begins. Come up for lunch. Give me your email address and we'll set it up...."

When Hurling and Madeira walk away, Arrow comes up with Abby.

"I'm leaving for Oregon tomorrow," says Arrow. "My father isn't doing very well, and my stepmother bought me a plane ticket."

Arrow mentioned awhile back that her father had been having some sort of health problems.

"I'm sorry to hear that. Do they know what's wrong with him?"

"The doctors still aren't sure. His joints ache, he's tired, and he's having trouble breathing."

"Hmm....It's good you're going. Do you need a lift to the airport or any—"

"No. I'm all set."

A week later, I receive an email from Madeira with directions to their summer house. "Why not come up next Saturday for lunch? The drive will take a couple of hours—but you should find it worth the trouble."

"This could be interesting." The house is on Eastern Point, in Gloucester, Massachusetts, a place mentioned in early research I'd done on Gardner, and in one of the books Aleda sent. And isn't it funny that Arrow said she'd grown up in Gloucester?

Did any of this mean anything, or was it just the coincidental reality of living in the concentrated northeast?

CHAPTER 29

♦

Swanson bones up on Eastern Point in Gloucester. Learns about Isabella Gardner and Piatt Andrew.

IF YOU WERE ALEDA, YOU WOULD SAY, "EVERYTHING MEANS SOMETHING; WE'RE JUST NOT ALWAYS ALERT TO THE SIGNS."

Look at your life, and look at Aleda's: who's more successful?

If this Gloucester coincidence means something, prepare for your visit by revisting the material that mentions Gardner on Eastern Point....

After her husband died in 1898, Isabella Gardner continued to make new friends, many of them artists, scholars, politicians and others who appreciated her eccentricities and wherewithal to indulge them. Among these were a group who summered on a small peninsula off Gloucester, Massachusetts called Eastern Point.

One of the most prominent residents of Eastern Point was a fellow named Abram Piatt Andrew. A strikingly handsome young economics professor at Harvard, he quickly dropped the Jewish-sounding Abram when he moved East from the Midwest, becoming instead, A. Piatt Andrew.

Piatt Andrew and Henry Sleeper, an interior decorator, and others built homes on Eastern Point: people with names like

Cecilia Beaux, Caroline Sinkler, and Joanna Davidge. Their rambling, shingled manses, with sweeping porches and ocean views had names: Beauport. The Ramparts. Green Alley. Red Roof and Wrong Roof. The family of poet T.S. Eliot had a spacious summer house on Eastern Point. But it was to the home built in 1902 by A. Piatt Andrew, Red Roof, that the most celebrated came, including a student of Piatt Andrew's at Harvard who would later become known simply by his initials, FDR.

Piatt Andrew's most frequent guest was Isabella Stewart Gardner. Andrew was some thirty-three years younger than Gardner; only thirty years old when he and Gardner met in 1903, and she, sixty-three. But for the next twenty-one years, until her death, Gardner and Andrew would be very close friends. Any hint of a romance, in the conventional sense, would be just that, as Piatt Andrew and his pal, Henry Davis Sleeper, were young gay blades of the refined variety found in those circles at that time. And the seclusion of Eastern Point was just the place for them to carry on, far enough from the prigs of Boston, yet close enough to plug into work and the cultural life of the city.

So there it was, I muse. The old rich lady and the young gay men. Isabella had her own room at Red Roof, called Her Room. Piatt Andrew went on to found the volunteer ambulance corps during World War One known as The American Field Service, and Gardner donated money for ambulances. Andrew kept marching further, being appointed Assistant Secretary of the Treasury and eventually becoming a Congressman. He and Gardner and their circle shared a love of art and music and literature—with the freedom and privacy money can buy, to be...themselves.

During these years, Isabella also became a die-hard Red Sox fan, wearing a headband to Boston Symphony Hall that proclaimed, *Oh You Red Sox,* when the team won the 1918 World Series.

"So—she must've made it to Fenway Park," I mumble to myself. Then I check online. Yep. Fenway, open in 1912, is the oldest park in the majors. "Ysabella" as Piatt Andrew called her, had a dozen years to root for the Sox at Fenway before the game was over.

"Ysabella...." I turn to look out the window at the falling snow. The aroma of dinner cooking wafts in from the kitchen, where Eric is busy preparing chili.

"Ysabella...." A girlish, Español-way to call Isabella. I bet the first time Piatt Andrew laid eyes on the big, dramatic John Singer Sargent painting of the flamenco dancer, *El Jaleo,* at the end of the Spanish Cloister at Fenway Court, he knew how Isabella saw herself. He knew he could touch her with "Ysabella." Oh, the handsome, well-put-together Piatt Andrew fawning over her, enlivening her life. A joy for him to be in her palace of art, a joy for her to be in the company of such a witty, intelligent, *interesting* young man as he. It worked for both of them. It was good they found each other. Straight men are too busy with their own wives or hunting down younger women to be interested in an old lady like Isabella Stewart Gardner. But gay men, with their sensitivity toward art and design...who can see women as people because they are not thinking about screwing them...these young men could appreciate "Ysabella," learn from her. And she could learn from them, all the while luxuriating in the attentions of attractive young males who were "safe."

CHAPTER 30

♦

A visit to historic house, Red Roof, on Eastern Point.

ON THE COOL AND DRIZZLY MORNING OF APRIL FIRST, I fire up Veronika and drive the two hours to Gloucester, Massachusetts.

Following Madeira's directions, I take the main road through town, past the busy part of the inner harbor until things thin out. Just before the road curves away from the water, I stay straight and continue along the water, passing between two stone gate posts marked, "Private Road." To my right is the bowl of Gloucester harbor. There are whitecaps on the water.

I quickly realize that the private road is the beginning of Eastern Point, and I feel the thrill of seeing something for the first time that, heretofore, has only existed for one in a book. Madeira said to look for the fourth house on the right, with a stone wall in front of it.

The first clue to where I might be going comes when I pass Beauport, the fanciful turreted chateau built by the interior designer, Henry Davis Sleeper. A McMansion comes up next, totally out of place with its surroundings of old trees, old homes, and natural beauty. But it is the next house that takes my breath away—or rather, what I tinglingly know the next house is going to be.

Here is the stone wall, but much higher than I'd envisioned, a good eight feet high, completely blocking from view what is behind it. Pulling Veronika off the road and onto the grass in front of the wall, I see the small, hand-carved wooden sign above an entrance door built into the wall: "Red Roof."

Two garage doors are built into the wall, as well as another wooden door marked "Service." Peering through spindles at the top of the wooden door beneath the Red Roof sign, I press down on the latch and enter the long front yard and open my umbrella. How strange and lovely that there is no driveway leading to the house. The closest one can get with a vehicle would be to pull into one of the garages and enter the front lawn through a door off the garage.

I step along the small flagstones. The house is so pretty, and much larger than the few photographs I'd seen would lead one to believe. It's a Cape Cod style *villa*—very large and white with a steeply sloping red shingle roof and a third floor dormer on the front and red shutters framing all the windows. Approaching the front door, I pass beneath a bower of woven branches and ring the bell. A life size statue of a handmaiden, painted in pink flesh tones with bare arms and a green toga stands off to my right, her pretty head tilted to the side in an attitude of gentle supplication and welcome.

The black inside door opens and for a moment, Madeira stands indistinct behind the screen door and regards me, before giving it a little push.

"Di Chiera," he declares formally. "Welcome to Red Roof."

I step into a large foyer. An impressive fireplace, high enough to walk into, is built into one wall. Above the fireplace hangs an oil portrait of Hurling and Madeira.

Joined by Hurling, we take lunch in a lovely white dining room trimmed in seafoam green overlooking Gloucester Harbor. The table is set with Majolica plates of the same shade of green.

"Of course, you've learned something about this house in your research," says Madeira.

"I have," I reply. "And it is even more beautiful than I had imagined."

"It is a work of art," says Madeira. "Chester bought it for me—for us—a few years back. The family had neglected it, didn't appreciate it. A squabbling tribe of impecunious Andrew descendants who had...*descended,* would be the best way to put it. Selling off pieces of furniture to pay the taxes. Can you imagine? When I heard that and took a drive by, I realized it had to be saved from the Philistines. Piatt would have wept to have seen the way they'd let it go. Peeling paint...in need of a new red roof. Rotting wood."

I look out the picture window in front of which the dining table is placed, to the fieldstone terraces, stepped down to the water. In one corner, just overlooking the harbor, is a swimming pool built discreetly into the rock. The window becomes streaked with rain which has picked up again.

"Your friend, Isabella Stewart Gardner was entertained down there," says Madeira, and I recall a photo of Gardner and Piatt Andrew sitting on a stone seat between two statuettes; funny little men in top hats, perhaps leprechauns, that are still in place. And there are other photographs on these terraces I have seen in the books: photographs of John Singer Sargent...John D. Rockefeller, Jr....Mary and Bernard Berenson....the Japanese scholar Okakura Kakuzo, who authored *The Book of Tea.*

"FDR visited here," says Madeira. "He was a student of Piatt Andrew's at Harvard.

"I know," I say.

"How is your turkey breast?" asks Madeira.

"Perfect."

"You know," says Madeira, "I can see why Aleda finds you attractive. You're a *real* man, yet you have a feminine, sensitive side. I must say, your hair is silvering wonderfully. You are a very handsome man. Are you sure there's not a smidgen of gay in you?"

"Perhaps. But if there is, I repress it."

Hurling excuses himself and disappears from the room.

"And you have a sense of humor too," smiles Madeira. "Women like that. You know—of course you do—that you and I are alike in many ways."

"I do know that," I say.

"And it's not just our love of art."

I gaze out the window at the whitecaps, remember standing on a pier at the Newport Naval Base waiting for my father's ship to return from a six month Mediterranean cruise. I remember sitting in the car with my mother on a drizzly Newport afternoon, eating fried clams from a paper bag and looking at the boats in the harbor, listening to the halyards chiming against the masts.

"It's the money thing," says Madeira, turning also to look out the window. "I know about St. George's...your aunt who worked in the kitchen. Don't blame Aleda for telling me. She cares about you. She wants you to succeed. Our past can hold us back, Di Chiera. You cannot help who you were, Di Chiera—only who you are.

"I know you don't like me. But you don't know me. You

know some *things* about me. But you don't know me. Your friend, Ray Mendelsohn knew me."

"What do you mean?"

"What do you think I mean?"

"That he knew you when you were a woman?"

"He knew me when he *thought* I was a woman. He picked me up in a bar in Cambridge one night. We went back to my place and made love."

"So, you're telling me he was unfaithful to Julie?"

"Not at all. I believe he was very faithful to Julie. This was before he met Julie. No, Ray was unfaithful to himself. He knew, just before we started having sex, that I was also a man."

"Did he tell you that?"

"He didn't have to."

"Well—so what?" I say.

"So what nothing, I suppose. Except, after being with him, I decided I wanted to end my charade. I'd already met Chester, whom I knew was gay, and yet was strangely attracted to me. He was a big, strapping he-man, Chester. He thought if he was attracted to me, he couldn't possibly be gay. I was a beautiful woman. But what he was seeing was the boy in me. Di Chiera, I am one of those who was born with what they call indeterminate genitalia. So the delivering physician just pushed everything that looked male inside, and made me female. I was brought up as a girl, but always felt that I was really a boy. Chester loves it. I'm a man with a cunt. What could be better! Would you like to see? Me?"

I turn my hands outward and shrug, as if to say, "If you want me to."

Madeira takes down his pants, exposing a vagina with a small penis grown above it. "Pretty nifty, hmm? I have a penis where most women simply have a clitoris. I really can go fuck myself!"

He steps up to me.

"Go ahead—touch it."

I look at it and remember how Aleda said I had something to learn from Madeira. That strange is good for people like us.

"For God's sake, Swanson. Do what you feel like doing. You're not going to get *arrested*."

At that, he pushes his little penis against my lips and I take it in my mouth. He puts his hand on the back my head and begins pulling out and pushing back into me.

"Oh, for God's sake, Di Chiera. I can feel your brain working! Just let go!"

It's like having a smooth piece of okra moving in and out of my mouth and I push him out.

"What's wrong?" demands Madeira.

"Don't like it."

"But you took it."

"I was curious."

"You're a prick, Di Chiera."

"No. I'm just being faithful to myself."

Madeira glares at me then fastens his pants. He sits down, lights a cigarette, takes a couple drags and pours himself more wine, corraling his anger and circling, circling.

"You asked Aleda once if sentimentality held you back," he kicks. "Sentimentality keeps you locked in yourself. A sentimentalist is always grappling with the past. It prevents the seeing of reality.

"You want to solve the Gardner theft, and I am telling you, you cannot do it as vision-clouded sentimentalist. You must look at all your knowledge as a realist; think about all you know of the theft and then wipe away any prejudice. Any! As a realist, you can begin to actually see others. It will even help your writing, Di Chiera, which is your best shot at making a fortune, not solving the stupid Gardner theft."

Hurling ambles in, hands stuffed into his pants pockets, looking vaguely forlorn.

"Watch this, Di Chiera." Madeira reaches behind the drapery, and the large plate glass window separating us from the rain and the terraces drops straight down and out of view. Raindrops begin hitting the sill, the breeze lifting the table cloth.

His hand again disappears behind the drapery and raises the window back into place.

"I have to lie down now. Chester can entertain you for the nonce." With that, he abruptly leaves the room.

"Blood sugar drop," says Hurling. "It hits him like that sometimes after a meal."

"His grandmother and grandfather worked for Piatt Andrew," says Hurling. "They lived right here in this house. They worked sometimes for Sleeper too, down the line there at Beauport."

"Yes. I've read about Beauport," I say.

"You passed it two doors down, on the way here. Owned by a historical society now. They give tours. You should take it sometime. Very interesting. Anyhow, Royal's grandparents started working for Piatt Andrew when they were only kids really, and continued working for the family after Andrew's death. He heard all the tales from his grandfather about the Andrew family and the Sleepers, and how tough it was to be servants in those days. His grandparents really were on call twenty-four hours a day. But they didn't have any education and were happy for the work. They were Portuguese immigrants, from the Açores."

Really?" I remark. "My grandparents, on my mother's side, came to the U.S. from the Açores."

"Lots of Portuguese in New England. Maybe you're related. I am not kidding! Açores are islands—everybody marries a cousin. Royal's father was Portuguese—his real name was Medeiros—and he left Royal's mother, Roya, who was Iranian, before Royal was even born. The mother was a mess herself, took off with the Fuller Brush man, ended up dead in a head-on collision out west. The grandparents raised him.

"When he got to Boston and met me—God! And I thought I was actually normal and attracted to a woman!— he began thinking of changing to being what he felt like: a man. After graduating he decided to become who he really was. Thus was born, Royal Madeira. He had Medeiros changed to Madeira because it sounded more elegant.

"A few years ago, this place came up for sale and I bought it. We both felt it was poetic justice that he should become lord of the manor where once his grandparents had toiled. Shame his grandparents never lived to see it."

"Easy to understand his intense Gardner interest now," I say.

"His grandparents knew her. Cooked her meals when she visited…did her laundry…drove her to and from the train station. By the time Royal was ten, he'd heard all the stories, seen the photographs. Here…." Hurling crosses the room, returning with a framed black and white photograph that I recognize immediately from one of the books on Gardner.

"I know this one," I say.

"Yes. But this is the original. Look at the sharpness—you can actually see Gardner's face. She wasn't what you'd call a beauty."

"Then again, she was probably seventy when this was taken."

"Well then...she didn't age well," sniffs Hurling. "But let's forget about all this for a moment," he says, switching gears. "How about reconsidering my screenplay offer? I really think a movie about the Gardner theft has excellent commercial potential. Not your original theory, of course, but coming up with some exciting theory about what happened. I'll pay you well, Di Chiera, get you and the kids set up in L.A. I've spoken with Aleda about this, and she's all for it."

"I don't know....I've been so busy with the kids and trying to finish a novel I started awhile ago. The idea of uprooting...I don't know. On the other hand, maybe a dramatic change is just what we need. Get the hell out of Providence—out of the northeast altogether."

"There's the spirit!" says Hurling. "That's what I did. Well, except for this summer place. God, I love L.A....the weather. Sure as shit don't miss New England in the winter. When do you plan on having that novel finished?"

"I've given myself a deadline of May first."

"You're almost there! How about this: forget about my offer until you finish your novel. But soon as you do, give it serious consideration. Think of it as a reward for finishing. It'll be summer, the kids will be out of school. We could get you settled out there and the kids enrolled in school for

September."

"It is tempting, Chester. God knows the Gardner theft still intrigues me. Doesn't Royal have any good ideas about what might have happened? Or even yourself? Who do you think robbed the Gardner Museum? Or the RISD Museum, for that matter? Any good ideas about who killed Susan?"

"I wish I did know who would do such a thing," replies Hurling sadly. "As for the RISD Museum theft. No. Of course, many have speculated upon the Gardner theft. Personally—I go with the theory that there was an Irish IRA connection—you know, Whitey Bulger and his bunch—and the stuff is stashed in the mountains of Ireland somewhere. Or maybe they were mishandled and found their way to Davy Jones's Locker. It's a mystery."

I still don't trust Hurling. On some level, I trust Madeira, but this guy; he's truly dangerous because all he has is money. But is this just my uneasy relationship with money kicking in, especially the old kind I associate with the people I'd known in prep school? But there was the Pandora and not coming clean about knowing Ray. Maybe rich people are just natural liars, they have so much to hide.

"I would favor a script with the Irish connection," continues Hurling. "People just can't get enough of the damn Irish. All you got to do is feed people either the Irish, the Holocaust, the Civil War, or the Mafia. And doctors and lawyers. And dogs. Maybe you could cobble something together where, say, an Irish lawyer steals the stuff and sells it to an Italian Civil War buff who's married to the daughter of a Holocaust survivor who lives in Dublin with a lesbian member of the Irish Republican Army. Lesbians...very big these days. Eclipsing gay men for the spotlight. Maybe we could get Ellen Degeneres to star. Or that Heche gal. But I don't know if she's still a lesbian. She keeps switching. And a Jack Russell. We'll need a Jack Russell."

Suddenly the sun comes out. A few minutes later, Madeira reappears.

"Di Chiera," he announces, "you have been through too much these past few months, and I do admire your interest in La Belle Gardner. Come." Taking me by the hand, he leads me upstairs to the Her Room, where Isabella Gardner stayed on her frequent visits, and a mouse ran over her nose one night in bed.

It's nothing spectacular. A simple room with small windows that overlooks the harbor, and a door to an adjoining, smaller bedroom. In some way, it reminds me of my bedroom in Newport, when I was a boy. The thought makes me laugh.

"That was my reaction too, when I first came up here," says Madeira. "Nothing much to it, really."

We go back downstairs and outside to the terraces, where on a stone and mortar ledge, Madeira places a cushion on the wet stone and asks me to sit.

"There. You are sitting precisely where Piatt sat for his famous portrait with Isabella, you know the one! Look at the little leprechauns," and he gestures to the small statues in hats, flanking me on the wall behind the ledge, just as they had been a hundred years ago....

Standing in the foyer by the front door, Madeira and Hurling make it plain they won't be accompanying me on my walk across the long stretch of front lawn. There is a simple thank you, and good-bye.

Yet, as I pick my way almost daintily across the wet lawn I hear no door close behind me. I can feel them and the house itself, watching me.

Slipping into Veronika and performing a U-turn, I steal a quick glance toward the house. All that's visible is a trace of red roof.

"Bye-bye little house," I whisper. This is what my mother said when I was a child, as we pulled away from our house for a day trip, or longer.

God! If my mother could have seen me today! But I fight all desire to analyze it, compare it, anything. We know so little, our minds should be that much more open.

CHAPTER 31

◆

Rose Island off Newport with Susan's ashes. Explore an
old U.S Navy explosives magazine.

ON A SUNNY DAY IN MID-APRIL, WE TAKE A
LAUNCH OUT TO ROSE ISLAND TO SPRINKLE
SUSAN'S ASHES. We're picked up at the same pier where
Ray and Julie kept the Pandora, and where on that fateful
night it burst into flames.

Rose Island is an irregularly-shaped couple of acres,
depending upon the tide, sitting in Newport Harbor. A
lighthouse stands at one end, there's a stretch of pebbly
beach, and the rest is covered with bramble and wild rosa
rugosa. A foundation dedicated to restoring the historic
lighthouse acquired the island from the U.S. Navy, who'd
used it during and for awhile after World War II, to store
explosives.

In a light breeze we stand upon the terrace behind the
lighthouse, say a prayer and shake Susan's remains into the
water below.

"What are we gonna do with that?" asks Eric, looking at
the urn.

With one hand supporting it from the bottom, I hold it
out over the railing.

"Both of you put a hand on the side...OK.

One…two…three!" And down it goes, smashing to bits on the rocks, the next wave in pulling at it, redistributing the shards of blue and white porcelain and the ceremony is complete.

We have a good half hour to kill before the launch returns. Abby runs down to the beach to explore and Eric hikes around the lighthouse, his old home, which is locked. Abby has little recollection of the place, having been barely one year old when Ray and Julie moved out here. But Eric, four when they'd first arrived, has distinct memories.

I wander aimlessly in the sunshine, which feels so good after the winter. And the sea air is refreshing. Life is beginning anew, and I draw it in.

Distributed throughout the island are vegetation-camouflaged bunkers or "magazines" as the Navy called them, where they'd stored explosives, some of which had been used to pack the torpedoes for which the Newport Naval Base had been famous. They were even more overgrown now, covered with bramble and barely visible.

"What're you lookin' at?" asks Eric, coming up behind me.

"Nothing. Just remembering coming here when you were little. Visiting with your Mom and Dad."

"You and Dad ever go in the magazines?"

"Hey, that's good. You remember what they're called. I bet most kids your age only think magazines are something with pages in them. Naah. We never went inside. When the Navy removed all their explosives and sold the island, they sealed them shut."

"My Dad used to go in one."

"Really?" I distinctly remember Ray telling me that they were all sealed.

"Yup. That one right over there," says Eric, pointing to the one closest to the lighthouse. "I never went in, but he did. Hey, maybe we can get in now," and he starts over toward it.

I follow, and sure enough the heavy steel door isn't open, but it looks like it could be opened. I pull on the handle and it budges just a smidgen.

"Here," says Eric, picking up a rusty piece of iron. "Maybe we can get it with this," and he works it into the crack. I grab the end of it and pull, and am able to pry the door open a foot, and then it stops against bramble. I yank some of it away and we get the door open another foot, enough to step inside.

The first thing I notice is how dry and comfortable it is. Well, of course; if it was built by the military to store explosives, you can bet it was a precisely controlled environment. In fact, on the wall was a setup that measured temperature and humidity.

"You could live in here," says Eric.

The temperature gauge reads 68 degrees Fahrenheit, and the relative humidity is 50 percent. Nothing like military-grade instruments to still be working after sixty years.

"Did your Dad keep stuff in here? I mean like lawn furniture or wine. It would be perfect for wine."

"I dunno. I mean...I don't remember him going in here a lot. I never went in."

"He never took you in here?"

"Nope."

"Was there a lock on it?"

"I think I remember a lock. Like one of those big locks with those things stacked...."

"A padlock." I laugh. "Yeah, well, who knows. Maybe he

found pirate treasure and kept it all in here."

"Then where is it now?" asks Eric.

I hear an air horn. It's the launch.

I don't want to be having the thoughts I'm having. I want to be looking at what's in front of me: a novel I've promised to my agent by the first of May and two kids to look after. Arrow isn't due back until the end of the month. It turns out that her father is afflicted with Lyme Disease, the same tick-borne illness that brought down Peter Briggs. Now that treatment has begun, she wants to stay out there with him until she sees improvement.

"But this *is* in front of me! Imagine Ray hadn't been your best friend. Imagine you knew only the facts of his life: Goes to school across the street from the Gardner Museum. Wife works at Gardner when it's robbed. Moves to island where climate controlled magazines are perfect place to store art. Then, suddenly, he and his wife burn to death in a freak accident. He also counts among his acquaintances Royal Madeira and Chester Hurling."

Hurling, the electrical engineer, sets up the Pandora to short-out and catch fire, but first disables the manual door release. But why would he want to kill Ray and Julie? So that he and Madeira can have all of the art?

But how would they know Ray had the art? Did they all rob the museum together? But why would Ray have all the art? Because he had the perfect place to store it? But why wouldn't I have met Madeira and Hurling before, if they were all so tight?

There are just too many ragged pieces to this story. Too many to even pitch it to my biggest champion, Aleda.

"Push it from your mind, Swanson. Push it from your mind! Look at what's in front of you; what's *really* in front of you."

Not easy. That damn Gardner bug has bitten me good. And then there's Susan's murder. Who the hell would've killed her, and why?

Aleda phones just after Easter. The premier of *Belle* is slated for Providence at the end of May—the Saturday of Memorial Day Weekend.

"Are you happy with it?" I ask

"Swanson—I'm scared to death! I see all the shortcomings. But people say it's wonderful. Test audiences have been good to rave and…." She goes on and on and I keep my mouth shut and listen—something I'm trying to get better at.

CHAPTER 32

♦

Aleda returns to Providence for premiere of *Belle*. Arrow
discloses a secret.

ALEDA ROARS INTO TOWN, TAKING THE SAME
ROOMS AT THE HOTEL PROVIDENCE.

"I'm here! I'm here" she yelps over the phone. "The
windows are open and the air smells...*funky,
actually*...and—hold it...." I hear the bells of Grace Church
donging in the background—"right on time! Come down!
Bring the kids and we'll order up some dinner."

I have to tell her that we've already had dinner, and Abby is
on a sleepover and Eric has gone over to his new friend,
Guillermo's house to play pool.

"Well," says Aleda, crestfallen. "Can't *you* come down for a
little while?"

It's strange to be back in Aleda's suite. The Callery pear
trees in the courtyard below are in full bloom, the delicate
white blossoms giving off their incongruously rank odor of
stinky sneakers.

Aleda looks refreshed from the California sunshine, her skin
glowing and her eyes bright and clear.

"Hello, friend," she whispers. She smells good, like
someplace else. I am outliving Providence, and holding

Aleda makes me realize it more than ever. Twenty-five years is a long time to stay in one place—at least for what I want out of life.

"Have some champagne," she says. We toast to the success of *Belle* and then *swaff.* Aleda pours more and says, "You look exhausted. Isn't that nanny supposed to be taking care of the kids?"

"She's been away most of the last month, looking after her father in Oregon. I meant to ask you—could you swing a pass for her, for the opening? She hasn't said anything, but I'm sure she'd be thrilled to go. I mean, if you can't it's OK."

"Sure I can," says Aleda. "But just tell me one thing—"

"The answer is, no."

"Good. Not that I could necessarily blame you."

"I've made enough mistakes in my life. The last thing I need to do is kick up a dalliance with a young woman. There's so much I want to do. If there's gonna be another woman in my life, I want her to be my partner—not somebody I have to educate and watch grow up. I've been there."

"My, Swanson—maybe it's getting so smart that's made you exhausted."

"Working to finish my book has knocked me out. And worrying over the kids, and scaring up freelance work, and not wanting to live here anymore, but not knowing where to go. I'm trying to see life with less sentimentality and more how it is." I pause and then add, "I had a very interesting visit with your friends, the misters Hurling and Madeira."

"Ye-es," stammers Aleda. "I spoke with Chester and he mentioned that they'd seen you. Swanson, I've only tried to help. I think Royal Madeira is a very strange and smart person. I'm sorry if I—"

I reach over and pat her leg. Aleda Collie is one hundred percent human being to me now, no longer a famous anything.

"Not to worry, sweetheart. You've done nothing but help me. I remind myself of that old joke: 'Where were you when God handed out the brains?' I guess I was daydreaming. Now I'm scavenging to see if anybody dropped some."

"Swanson, You're good man….How are the kids? Are they doing any therapy?"

"No."

"It can help."

"I keep a close eye on them. They seem to be fine. Now, if anything ever happened to me…I think that could be a problem."

"Well, if anything ever did happen to you—I'd take them."

"Please—don't ever let them believe that, Aleda. They'd have me dead in a week."

"I want to take Abby shopping for a dress to wear to the premier."

"I'm sure she would love that. I'll snag a tux for Eric."

I shift in the chair and the cell phone in my jeans pocket goes *boop*. We laugh. Then the room falls silent.

Finally, I venture: "So when's Götterdämmerung coming in? Will he be landing his own chopper on top of the hotel? Parachuting down out of an F-15?"

"He's not coming."

Tizzy is the word in the Swanson household. Mid-morning, Aleda arrives in a familiar Escalade with Tiny at the helm to take Abby dress hunting.

"Swanson, a car will be here to pick you guys up tomorrow night. Somebody will call and let you know what time. I have to arrive with Chester. I'll see you inside the theatre."

After Abby disappears with Aleda, Eric and I drive across town to have him fitted out in his first tuxedo.

"Wow! Look at this one!" exclaims Eric, pulling out a jacket in electric blue with sequins on the lapels.

"Dream on, Liberace. We're looking for something in basic black."

"Why?"

"Why? Because it's distinguished and sophisticated—like us."

Abby's dancing around the house in her new dress, a blue satin affair with a scooped neckline and silver belt around the waist and silver shoes to match. A turquoise Alex and Ani bracelet dangles from one of her skinny wrists. Arrow arrives in something or other befitting a young feminist artist in Providence—lots of colors and cut in different angles and all sorta tied together. Chopsticks holding up her hair. Eric lets his tuxedo rest on its hanger until the last moment, and I sit at my desk in a tuxedo I'd bought in college that still fits, listening with foggy satisfaction to the chatter of voices.

I gaze into the living room, re-living the memory of Aleda and Rosenthal...God, if nothing else ever happens in my life....I scan the bookcase, old skin-magazines with their cheesy smut, back where they belong...the photographs on the wall...the sliver of space where I'd slid the big black portfolio of drawings I'd removed from Susan's house before Porcaro went through the place. Recalling the contents, I suddenly jerk forward, as though awakened from a nap. I cross the room and untie the thick black string that holds the portfolio shut.

The nude drawings come out first, then the smaller landscapes, and then the sketches of the house—three, big, charcoals—and I lay them out on the living room floor. Arrow passes through the foyer on her way into the kitchen and comes over to have a look.

"I know that house," she says. "It's in Gloucester."

"Red Roof," I say. "I was invited up there for lunch while you were out in Oregon."

"Isn't it amazing?"

"It's a beautiful place," I say. "And with an amazing history." Made even more amazing now. Why had Susan been there?

"Did they show you the secret rooms?" asks Arrow.

"What secret rooms?"

"They didn't show you the secret rooms?"

"No. They didn't show me any secret rooms. What are you talking about?"

"The guy who built Red Roof was very weird, and he had secret rooms built into the house. There's a bench-like seat in the front room, and the top flips up and there's a staircase inside that takes you down to a library that overlooks the harbor. And on the second floor, there's a bathroom with a secret door behind the tub that leads into another room."

"Are you sure we're talking about the same house?" I ask.

Arrow gestured to the drawing on the floor. "Yeah. Red Roof. Two houses down from Beauport. Right?"

"Right. But how do you know about secret rooms?"

"When I was in grade school, there was a girl in my class whose family owned it. One year she had a birthday party at the house and she showed us the secret rooms. And there are terraces behind the house with secret passageways and one leads into the house by opening a stone."

"What was your friend's name?"

"Her first name was Alice, and her last name was something like Deery or Doorly...something like that. But I don't think they live there anymore. I remember my father telling me he heard they'd sold it just after I left for RISD. Maybe to the people you visited."

"The person I visited up there was probably a professor of yours, Royal Madeira."

"Really?"

"Is it possible your friend's family sold it to him? Did he ever mention that he owned it?"

"No. I mean, I only had Mr. Madeira one year, in Freshman Foundation. I don't think he knew I was from Gloucester. I never really talked to him, except in class."

I look down at the drawings of Red Roof, one a view of the front with that high, sloping roof with a single, large dormer window in the middle, and two of the back of the house with the stone terraces layered down to the water.

"You say there's a way into the house from back here?" I say, touching the terraces.

"Uh-huh."

At a quarter past five, a black stretch limousine pulls into the driveway and who's at the helm—Tiny! Looking very sharp with a freshly trimmed beard, hair pulled back in a braid and wearing a black suit complete with vest and a red stickpin in the lapel.

"Yeah. I do this sometimes. Weddings...funerals...

whatever they need. I like to drive."

Abby and Arrow are ready to roll. But where's Eric?

"In his room, I think," says Arrow.

I take the now uncarpeted stairs by twos and find Eric in his room, trying to tie his black bow tie.

"I'm sorry. I forgot to come up and help you with this."

"I almost had it, but this side keeps slipping through."

On Eric's desk is a sheet printed out from the Internet, describing how to tie a bow tie, complete with illustrations.

"Gee, Eric. Wish I'd had something like this the first time I had to tie a bow tie."

"You mean you're saying computers are good?"

"I've never said computers are bad. I'm just not a big fan of playing games that last half your life on computers." I stand behind Eric, taking the ends of the tie in either hand. "It's actually really simple. Think of it as tying a shoelace around your neck."

"And this is smarter than playing computer games—tying a shoelace around your neck?"

CHAPTER 33

♦

Premiere of *Belle*. Celebs, media. A hurried journey in the night.

SPOTLIGHTS CRISSCROSS THE SKY and the marquee bulbs of the vintage Columbus Theater chase each other in rapid-fire around the proclamation: TONIGHT! WORLD PREMIER OF *BELLE* STARRING GEORGETTE FANNING, OSCAR RODIO AND ALEDA COLLIE. The red carpet is rolled out, the limos lined up and I sit in the back of ours with Abby and Eric and Arrow, waiting to make our entrance.

This is it. Tiny opens the door and the camera flashes splatter blinding brilliance. Reporters and photographers from all over the world lean over the mauve velvet ropes.

"Why do they wanna take our picture?" asks Eric.

"Because we just got out of a limousine. You might be the Prince of Pretzelvania!"

Aleda is waiting for us in the gold leafed, chandeliered lobby.

"Aleda," I say urgently. "This could be the night of nights!"

"I'm hopin', darlin'."

"I need to *tell* you something."

"You may," she says, batting her eyelashes.

"Ah! You look absolutely beautiful! Stunning!"

"Thank you. Now—what do you need to *tell* me?"

"It's not that simple."

"Make it."

"OK." I take a deep breath and push off onto the thinnest of ice: "I have a very good hunch where the Gardner art is, and probably the RISD art, too."

"Swanson—haven't we trodden this ground before. Is it trod or trodden?"

"I think either is fine. But this time—"

Aleda interrupts me. "Well look at *you*, Abby. You are *beautiful!*"

"Arrow helped me with my makeup," says Abby.

Makeup? I'm horrified. When had they put on makeup?

"And Eric—you are such a *handsome young man!*"

Aleda then positions Eric to escort both his sister and Arrow into the theater. Slipping her arm inside mine, she announces, "We may proceed now."

The enormous old movie house is packed to capacity. The owner, Victor Kasarjian, looks every inch the impresario in his splendid cutaway, beaming his strong seventy-five year old Armenian smile. Tonight is a galaxy away from the porn he'd been showing to keep the single screen Columbus limping along when I'd first moved to Providence.

We take our seats beneath the enormous vaulted ceiling, colorfully painted with gamboling Greek Muses, while the various moguls and dignitaries flow in. The Mayor of Providence, Paul "The Weenie" Cabrini, is seated in the aisle across from us, yucking it up with Madeira and Hurling.

In the row just in front of us sits Governor Lincoln Chafee and his wife, an old-money Danforth as well as being his cousin; Teddy Kennedy's son, former Senator Patrick

Kennedy and his new wife are next to them. It's a sea of the rich and connected, along with critics from television and various media around the world. Is that Martine Croxall from the BBC World News over there? Doe-eyed, heart-shaped face, mouth mobile as she relates the world's tragi-comic events in her lovely British accent. Late at night, I try to will her to stand up from behind the news desk.

"Would you like to meet her?" asks Aleda, catching me staring.

"Who?" I reply.

As the lights dim, I turn to whisper into Aleda's ear. I want to tell her about the plan that is fast hatching in my head. But when my nose touches the curve of her ear and I catch the scent of Hermès *Eau d'Orange Verte,* I realize how long she's dreamed of this moment and I press my cheekbone solidly against the side of hers.

She smiles at me—I glimpse what she looked like as a girl—gives me a smooch, the curtains part and off we go....

Belle tells the story of a feisty young woman "of privilege," who tries to live as freely and meaningfully as she can within the social strictures of her time.

Finding Jack Gardner is a godsend; he not only has the money to help further her interests, but is more open-minded than the majority of his wealthy set. Not a libertine mind you, but wise enough and loving enough to see that Isabella is driven to find and acquire great art as well as cultivate those who sometimes create it.

She makes his life interesting, and he is smart enough and rich enough to allow her to do so.

From the heart-wrenching disappointment of losing her

only child, to her reincarnation as the reigning "celebutante" of her day, she travels the world, studying and collecting. And in the end, she builds her Fenway Court, supervising every detail of construction, every placement of each work of art.

Georgette Fanning is magnificent as Gardner throughout her lifetime. Rodio (who arrives halfway through the screening to much applause), brooding and luminescent as the painter, John Singer Sargent, and Aleda, a cheerful comrade-in-arms as Julia Gardner, Isabella's sister-in-law, who welcomes her to Boston amidst the disapproval of so many society matrons, remaining her lifelong friend.

Then, after decades of activity, Isabella is old. Eighty-two and frail, living alone in Fenway Court. Sargent arrives with a bouquet of her favorite flower, violets, and paints one final portrait of her: a watercolor of Isabella swathed in white linen, her pale face looking out. And as he paints, the image of her dissolves into the scene I'd watched shot of her in the courtyard looking up at the galleries, this one lit then another. An image of *The Storm* appears…fades…*The Concert*…fades…*Europa*…fades…finally back to Gardner and desaturation until the entire screen becomes the light yellow-white of the wings of a cabbage moth.

Then, Sargent's voice: "Belle died two years later. She could be difficult, but mostly, she was very generous. She helped many people. She loved art and she loved artists."

The white color of the screen pulses once, then Belle's voice: *"C'est mon plaisir…*It is my pleasure."

As the credits roll, so does the standing ovation. Aleda takes the stage, along with Hurling and Rodio and Georgette Fanning, and the film's director, Beep Gamble.

Hell—I can talk to her tomorrow about stolen art. Tonight is hers.

The first floor lobby and the sweeping mezzanine swarm with waiters bearing trays of hors d'oeuvres and champagne. In the maelstrom of silk and satin, I snatch a passing flute from a silver tray and am about to *swaff* when Arrow comes up to me, the blood drained from her face.

"Good lord, what is it?" I ask.

"My stepmother just called. My father's had a stroke and he's in the hospital."

"Will he be OK?"

"She doesn't know yet. The doctors are still with him. She thinks he might be in a coma."

I hug her tight. As I do, I feel a tap on my shoulder.

"Could I have me one of those?" asks Aleda.

"Arrow just found out her father's had a stroke."

"I've gotta go back out there, but it's Memorial Day Weekend...."

"Don't worry," says Aleda. "I can get you out of here. You can have my ticket to L.A. tomorrow, and I have a friend who can fly you up to—where is it?"

"Oregon. He's in a little town in Oregon called Waldport, on the coast."

"Not a problem. My friend can land in a cow pasture if he has to."

The script has gone off course and I know I have to act.

"Um...." Both Aleda and Arrow look at me. "Really? Did I say 'um' that loudly?" I ask.

"Yes," says Aleda. "You did. That was a very loud um. Let me guess—you want to talk about you-know-what?"

"Oui."

"Does it have to be now?"

"Oui."

Aleda turns to Arrow. "Would you please excuse us for a moment?"

"No," I say hurriedly. "We need her."

"For what?" asks Aleda. Arrow looks at me, even more confused.

"I know where the art is—and Arrow has the map."

"Where is it?" asks Aleda. "And she has the map?"

Suddenly Madeira is upon us.

"Aleda! Divine Aleda!"

"C'est Mon Plaisir," she replies. "It would have been impossible without you, Royal."

"A wonder," I say, raising my glass to both Aleda and Madeira. I swaff, then notice that Arrow has opened her mouth and is about to say something to Madeira. Maybe she's going to ask him a question about Red Roof. In a panic, I let my champagne glass drop on her exposed toes.

"I'm so sorry!" Bending over to look at her foot I whisper to her pointedly, "Say nothing." Then in a loud voice, "I can't believe I did that. Let's sit down over here so I can have a look at it," and I lead her to a chair on the side of the room, glancing quickly at Aleda as I do, hoping she'll pick up on the ruse.

"Excuse me," Aleda says to Madeira, and she follows us. "Swanson—what the hell—"

"Here is what the hell: Madeira and Hurling own Red Roof, out on Eastern Point in Gloucester, Massachusetts. Did you know that?"

"The house that Piatt Andrew built, that Gardner visited

many times. No, I did not know that Hurling and Madeira own it."

"Well they do. Now, Arrow grew up in Gloucester and visited the house when she was a kid. This afternoon, I was looking at some sketches Susan did of Red Roof, and Arrow recognized the place and said it has secret rooms. When I was out there, neither Hurling nor Madeira mentioned any secret rooms. I think the art—the Gardner art and the RISD art is in one of those secret rooms."

"Oh, Swanson," groans Aleda.

"I know...I know...And now Arrow is heading out to Oregon tomorrow."

"And she knows where the secret rooms are?" asks Aleda looking at Arrow, who nods.

"And she knows a secret way of getting into the house by moving a stone," I say.

"Guh. Sounds like some gothic horror story," says Aleda. "OK. So we have to go out there tonight. Do you have a...*plan?*"

"As a matter of fact—" Suddenly I freeze. "Where are the kids?"

"They said they wanted to look around backstage," says Arrow.

"OK. I'll go find them. Arrow—you come with me. Aleda—Get the limo ready. The one with Tiny driving. We'll meet you out front."

Arrow and I find the kids backstage fooling around in an ancient dressing room.

"OK kids. We have to do some very important acting. We have to drive somewhere with Aleda. If anybody asks anything, both of you just say you feel sick and want to go home. Got it?"

"But—"

I cut Abby off. "Abby—you have to do this. You both have to do this. No questions. You're sick, got it?"

"Oohhh…I feel like I'm gonna barf," groans Abby, swooning with one hand on her stomach. "I wanna go ho-oooome…."

"Perfect! Now just follow me."

I lead the children and Arrow through the theater and outside, where Aleda is waiting for us beneath the marquee. Just as we're all about to pile into the limo, Hurling comes rushing up to Aleda.

"Dear—Where are you going?"

"The kids are sick," I say.

"They went back to the caterer's truck and wolfed down a pound of foie gras," says Aleda. "We're just gonna take them home. I'll be back as soon as they're settled."

In the car, I lean forward.

"Tiny—get on 95 North." As we pull away, I try not to notice Hurling returning to the lobby as Madeira stands inside and watches.

"Do you think they have any idea where we're going?" asks Aleda.

"Naaah," I answer. But who believes it?

CHAPTER 34

♦

Mayhem and momentous discoveries.

GLOUCESTER LOOKS DIFFERENT IN THE DARK and with the trees and foliage leafed out. Fortunately, Arrow knows exactly how to navigate through the town and get us out to Eastern Point.

"Here we are," I murmur, recognizing the stone gateposts and the Private Road sign that takes us along the water.

"This is fabulous!" says Aleda, looking out at the trees overhanging the road, the absence of any other vehicles and the looming presence of shadowy mansions.

"That's Beauport," I say, as we pass Henry Davis Sleeper's fantasy chateau close to the road.

"Incredible," murmurs Aleda, then: "What's *that?*" she gasps at the McMansion that rises up next.

"It used to be where a beautiful, old shingle-style summer house called, Wrong Roof stood, owned by a southern belle with the wonderful name, Caroline Sinkler. But it burned to the ground in a fire a few years ago, on Super Bowl Sunday, and the owners built this monstrosity."

"Swanson does do his homework," says Aleda. "God, I wish we could've included everything in *Belle*, but something had to go and this whole Eastern Point stuff got dropped."

"Madeira didn't have had anything to do with that, did

he?" I ask. "Or Hurling?....OK, slow down," I caution Tiny. The road is country dark except for a dim streetlight that is well-behind us now.

"But where's Red Roof?" asks Aleda. "If that was where Wrong Roof used to be, then Red Roof should be...."

"Here. Pull over and stop," I say, and Tiny eases the limo onto the broad swath of grass.

"What's this?" asks Aleda, looking out the window at the dark stone wall.

I point to the wooden door built into the wall with the hand-carved sign above it.

"Red Roof," says Aleda.

"I was surprised too, when I came out here last month. It's the one house you can't see from the road. Tiny—at the end of this road is a lighthouse. You can drive out there and wait. Or find someplace nearby that's discreet. I don't want to draw any attention. When we're ready to leave, I'll phone you and you can pick us up right back here. Kids, I want you to stay with Tiny."

"Not!" says Abby. "We're coming. I wanna see the secret rooms."

"Yeah," says Eric. "I'm not gonna miss any secret rooms."

"No," I say. "I don't—"

Too late. They push open the door and jump out into the chilly night.

"They're kids," says Tiny. "Who can blame 'em. Be unnatural if they didn't wanna go."

"I know...but this...never mind." I don't want to scare anyone. "OK, Tiny—I'll call you when we're ready to go."

"You got it."

Aleda stands beneath the Red Roof sign and presses down

on the door latch.

"It's locked," she says.

A few feet away, Eric tugs at the handle of the service door.

"This one's locked too."

"Follow me," and I lead us along the grass strip in front of the wall until coming to the driveway to the next house down the road. There, the wall in front of Red Roof ends. Around the corner is an embankment of low scrub and trees, and the front lawn of Red Roof visible just beyond. I'd noticed this when I'd crossed the lawn, after my visit.

I lead the way up the embankment until we stand on the front lawn. Red Roof has a serene glow in the moonlight, while at the same time its red shingles and red shutters give it a sense of gaiety.

"It's so pretty," says Aleda. "And the roof really is red."

Silhouettes in the moonlight, we steal across the wide expanse of the front lawn and swing around to the back of the house, where the terraced patios connected by open passageways lead down to the sea.

Aleda stops on the first, and largest patio and draws a deep breath.

"We are standing where Isabella stood. And John Singer Sargent."

"Yes," I say. "And FDR, too."

"It's magic. This place is magic," says Aleda.

I turn to Arrow.

"OK. Where's the secret entrance into the house?"

"Down this way," she says, and we follow her across the patio and down several stone steps to a passageway closed off by a wooden door a good four inches thick, fitted with heavy iron hinges. Arrow pushes the door open and we follow her through another passageway, open to the sky, and down more steps to a smaller patio.

"It's a maze," says Aleda, as Arrow pushes open another heavy wooden door up ahead. "But why all the doors?"

"Piatt Andrew was creating rooms," I say. "You pass from one outdoor room into another."

Indeed, here we stand in yet another patio, below which are more stone stairs leading down to another passageway that opens to yet another terrace with the swimming pool that overlooks the ocean. I grab the back of Eric's jacket.

"No," I say.

"But I want to go down and look at the pool."

"Not why we're here. OK Arrow—now what?"

"We go up these stairs," she says, standing at the foot of a narrow stone stairway, at the top of which is another heavy wooden door.

"Spooky," says Aleda. "I love it!"

At the top of the stairway, Arrow pushes open the door and we enter a storage room for lawn chairs and pool equipment. There are two kayaks at the far end of the room.

"OK," says Arrow. "We're actually right near the foundation of the back of the house. It's hard to see. It's really dark in here."

"I have some matches," says Eric.

"What are you doing with matches?" I ask.

"I dunno. I found them."

"Give them to Arrow, please."

Arrow strikes one of the matches and touches the stone wall in front of her. "I can't believe I remember exactly where this is. Watch this."

Reaching up to a narrow cleft in the stone in front of her,

Arrow's fingers find something. As they tense, she pushes against the stone and it slowly swings inward, a massive stone door about five feet high. In front of us is pitch black darkness.

"It's the basement of the house," says Arrow. She lights another match and the flame almost touches a string hanging from a ceiling fixture. She pulls the string and we stand in a dank part of the basement, illuminated by the single bulb.

"Well, that's one solution to locking yourself out of the house," says Aleda.

"This is very creepy," says Abby.

"Is the little baby scared?" sneers Eric, and just as he says it, there's a loud squeak. *"Ahhh!"* yells Eric and he jumps nearly a foot into the air.

Eric has stepped on a stuffed dog toy made to look like a quail. Abby picks it up and throws it at him. "Get scared, little baby!"

"All right. Knock it off," I say, and I look at Arrow. "Lead the way."

"Wait," says Aleda. "There's a painting over there."

I peer into the dim distance and see something in a frame standing on top of an old linen chest. I walk over to it and see that it's a painting of a bear. A brass plate affixed to the bottom of the frame says, "Romulus."

"Just a bad painting of a bear named Romulus. Let's keep going."

Arrow leads us to a narrow wooden staircase that takes us up to a door that opens into a closet. Pushing aside some coats and jackets, she opens another door that lets us into the main foyer of the house.

"Trust me—this is just the beginning," she says, flipping a

switch lighting up wall sconces around the room.

Directly in front of us is the gigantic stone fireplace, above which hangs the portrait of Hurling and Madeira. On either side of the fireplace are built-in settees. Arrow lifts the leather cushioned seat of one, revealing a staircase down.

"Cool!" exclaims Eric.

"Let's go!" says Aleda, any worries far behind her now.

Into the seat we all climb, down the stairs to a corridor beneath the house. I walk smack into a mirror that looks like a continuation of the corridor.

"Careful," warns Arrow. "This place has lots of illusions."

Aleda stops. "Look at this!" she marvels. It's a small room with an ornate pipe organ in it.

"This is the Blue Light Room," says Arrow. "There are circles of thick blue glass in the ceiling that during the day admit natural light. You can hear this organ all the way across the harbor."

"Yes," I say. "I came across this in my reading. Piatt Andrew would play his organ, this organ no doubt, and across the harbor, John Hammond, an inventor who did pioneering work with radio signals, sonar, and torpedo guidance systems, would play the organ he had in his castle. He and Piatt Andrew would play a sort of cross-harbor dueling organ duet."

Across the corridor from the organ room is an iron cage. Inside the cage, on a shelf is a very strange photograph. "What is this?" asks Aleda, looking at a black and white photograph of a smiling young woman in a long Victorian dress and hat, walking two men on a double leash. The men are on all fours and wearing studded dog collars.

"The guy on the right is definitely Piatt Andrew," I say.

"Don't know who the other guy is or the woman. Looks like it was taken right around here on the rocks near the water."

"Wow! Look at this!" says Eric. It's a photo of a man being beheaded. Nobody recognizes anybody in that picture.

The end of the corridor opens up into a large and lovely library, floor to ceiling with shelves of books and a wheeled ladder on a rail to reach them.

"And up there," says Arrow pointing above the doorway, is a sleeping alcove with a small viewing hole in the floor to check out the goings on in the room below it."

"Errol Flynn had the same thing in his house," says Aleda. "What is it with men?"

I whisper into her ear, "We like to watch." And then louder, so everyone can hear, "But no paintings."

"Well, I know of another secret room upstairs," says Arrow.

Back we go, up through the seat by the fireplace and into the foyer. From here, Arrow leads us to a second floor bathroom where a false wall behind the tub opens to a small bedroom.

"The story is that the President negotiated the end of World War I in Red Roof, and that a Very Important Person, not from the United States, stayed here, in this room," says Arrow.

"No art," I say, looking around.

As fast as we can, we go through every other room in the house, finally ending up where we began, in the foyer.

Nothing. No Rembrandts, no Vermeer, no Degas.

"Those are all the secret rooms I know about," says Arrow. "Sorry."

"Hey," says Aleda, going over and putting an arm around her. "Don't worry about it. Those were plenty. I've never seen so many secret rooms in my life. At least not in the same house."

I lean up against the wall and rub my face.

"I was so sure this time. So *sure.*"

Eric comes running into the foyer with Abby on his heels. "I think you should know," he coughs, "I just saw some people walking across the front yard."

"Follow me," says Aleda.

"What're we gonna do?" I ask.

"Just follow me! Quick!"

Aleda directs everyone through the closet door that had brought us into the foyer from the cellar. I'm about to follow Aleda and go last, when I notice Abby's turquoise bracelet on the floor in front of the fireplace. I hurry across the room and grab it, then race back to the closet door. Grasping the knob, it comes off in my hand.

The front door is being unlocked and opened. I close the closet door with my foot and drop the doorknob into my jacket pocket just as Madeira and Hurling charge into the room, Madeira wielding a pistol.

"Who else is here? Where's Aleda?"

"I don't know," I say.

He hands the gun to Hurling. "Wait here," he says, and runs upstairs.

"I probably won't be writing that sequel now," I say.

"Probably not," says Hurling.

Madeira returns and disappears into the kitchen. When he comes back, he takes the gun from Hurling and looks at me intently.

Suddenly, the front door opens. It's Aleda and the kids and Arrow.

"Hello, Chester...Royal." Aleda speaks with utter coolness. "What the hell are you doing?"

"The hell is this, Aleda," says Madeira: "Your misguided friend here is still convinced that I robbed the Gardner Museum and that the art is in this house."

"Well—did you? Is it?" asks Aleda. Abby and Eric stand next to Aleda like little statues.

Madeira addresses Arrow: "I am going to ask you to take the children upstairs. There is a bedroom at the far end of the hall. Please go in there and shut the door and turn on the television."

"Woyt?" asks Abby, and she looks at Aleda.

"Go ahead," says Aleda. "Do as he says. It will be fine, sweetheart."

Holding hands, the three of them climb the staircase. Not another word is spoken until we hear the door on the second floor close.

"Chester," says Madeira, "why not get the *Garrafeira* in the dining room, and some glasses. "I am going to tell our friends a fascinating story."

"Royal," says Aleda, "wouldn't it be a good idea to put away that gun?"

I remember the pistol Aleda keeps in her purse, and I have no doubt she knows how to use it.

"Trust has been broken, Aleda. I am not the one who's invaded someone else's house. This Di Chiera fellow—I am beginning to think he might be insane. I may have to turn him over to the authorities. He's probably a flight risk."

"Oh, for God's sake, Royal," huffs Aleda.

"He's a troubled soul, Aleda. Believe me, I recognize troubled souls."

Hurling returns with a bottle and glasses. Wine poured all around, Madeira unfolds the following tale:

"When I was a child, I fell in love with this house. More than anything in the world, I wanted to live here. I memorized the names of all the people who came here. They became celebrities to me. I wanted to be a part of them, but I could only pretend. You see, I was only allowed into the house because my grandmother and grandfather worked here. They cooked, cleaned, did laundry...chauffeured. They brought me up, really. My father was your basic sperm donor, and my mother ran off with some other jackwipe when I was only four. My grandparents raised me. I never saw either of my parents after my mother left.

"But that was OK. My grandparents good, kind souls and I spent many happy hours here while they worked. Sometimes, I'd help my grandmother peel potatoes or strip beds. Sometimes I played with the children of the owners. After Piatt Andrew died, ownership of the house passed into the hands of several of his relatives who had children of their own.

"I was never fully accepted because, after all, I was only related to the *help*. And I didn't have money.

"I won a scholarship to Boston University. It was in Boston that I met Chester, and later, at The Museum School, your friends Ray and Julie, and Julie's sister, Susan."

"You looked lovely back then, as a girl," says Aleda.

"Ah," says Madeira, surprised. "You found a picture. Audrey Hepburn. It was always, 'You look just like Audrey Hepburn....' I brought Chester to Gloucester and showed him Red Roof and told him of its wonderful history, of Piatt Andrew and Henry Sleeper and Isabella Stewart Gardner.

Later, when the shiftless heirs squandered their inheritances and were desperate for money, Chester drove right out here and bought it for me. Of course, the family was scandalized that someone *off the street,* so to speak, would have the audacity to propose such a thing. But as Chester kept jacking up his offer, their loyalty, their love—if they'd ever felt such a thing!—dissolved, and it was Chester's, and he promptly signed it over to me for my birthday. Can you imagine!

"Now comes the good part, Di Chiera; the part that unsophisticated sentimentalists such as yourself can never see, because you are so consumed with reviewing your own life. During the time I was a student at the Museum School, Ray and Julie and Susan, and sometimes even this old Philistine, Chester, made innumerable visits to the Gardner Museum. We learned all we could about Isabella and her looting of European art with her protégé-crook, Berenson.

"It was during one of our visits that Ray and I realized that we could walk away with half the stuff in the place because the security was so lame. Chester chimed in and said that his father's electrical company had installed the alarm system and he could get the details on it. As for guards, we knew the museum only employed some doddering old fool and few kids from Berklee Music School. And because Julie was working there as a conservator, we could obtain all the schedules of who was working when."

I'm dumbfounded.

"You're saying that it was you and *Ray* who robbed the Gardner?"

Madeira shot a look at Hurling and then took a sip of his port.

"It was the perfect heist, Di Chiera. All the necessary inside information about the guards, the one alarm button to summon outside help....Making it look like brutes stormed in, smashing the glass that held the Degas drawings—after they'd been removed, of course. Leaving the Rembrandt self-portrait on the floor after making it look like the thieves tried to cut it out of the frame before realizing it was painted on wood. By cutting the canvas of the big Rembrandts and Vermeer and Manet out of their frames. The truth is, nothing is really lost when you do that."

"Taking the eagle finial and Ku," I say. "Souvenirs. Something to toast the victory, an eagle to hold high."

"Exactly," exalts Madeira. "Just animals! Your typical museum smash and grab. Brilliant! Well. The day after the heist, so perfectly pulled off in those fuddle brained hours after St. Patrick's Day, your friend Ray calls me and says, 'Somebody beat us to the punch.'

"You should see your face, Di Chiera. What's that old expression: 'If only we could see ourselves as others do.' Di Chiera, it gets much more interesting. After the details of the theft came out, we were thrilled, really thrilled that what we had thought could be so easily done had in fact been done. We'd been right!

"Years passed. Years! I became a man, my life found a career, I eventually ended up at RISD. Happy, actually, felt quite satisfied. I kept in touch with Ray and Julie, even contacted him when Chester was getting rid of the Pandora.

"And then one afternoon, Ray and Julie invited us down to Newport and out to Rose Island for a Sunday brunch. Ray was acting a little funny; not his usual laid back self. I knew he'd been busy out there, isolated, and I thought maybe he was nervous about showing us some of his new work.

"After lunch, he takes us outside and leads us into one of those bunkers on the island. Apparently they'd been used to store explosives during World War II. Very tight. Very climate controlled. He has a lock on the thing the size of a baseball. He unlocks it and we go inside. There are a couple of wooden boxes in there. Guess what's inside of them, Di Chiera?"

For the second time in my life, I am speechless.

"That's right. And everything in pristine condition. Julie, being a conservator, knew how to store everything properly. Ray apologized for the many years of silence, for pulling the job, duping us...everything. Gleefully, he told us how he and his 'accomplice'—how cute—had talked their way inside and pulled it off. Now, the poor boy was feeling remorseful. His plan was to return the art. Somehow. Anonymously. He hadn't figured that part out yet. Wondered what we thought, about how to do it. Obviously, he also wanted to prove to us that he'd pulled it off.

"Chester and I had the same reaction without even saying it to each other: What an *Asshole!* We plan this thing together to have some major league fun, then he goes and does it on his own, never tells us the truth, and now fourteen years later, his conscience has finally caught up with him and he wants to return the art and he wants us to help him?

"*Vaffanculo!* So we hatch a little plan of our own, Chester and I do—a plan you've probably already figured out, Di Chiera."

"You get rid of Ray and Julie and go back to Rose Island and grab the art."

"Very good, Di Chiera, very good! However—"

"Let me finish the story," I say. "Time passes and you decide to add to your collection by lifting the Degas' from RISD. Piece of cake, even easier than the Gardner. The problem is, Susan starts putting it together and suspects that you robbed the Gardner and now boosted the Degas from the biggest show RISD's ever had, and she's gonna nail you. She confronts you with this and you get rid of her."

Madeira relaxes and chuckles. "Oh, Swanson....You still need to listen more and talk less. Don't be so eager. Don't *try* so hard. You have a couple of things correct, but if you would only *listen* and let me finish—"

Beams of light suddenly flash into the room, roaming the walls and ceiling. Hurling peers out one of the narrow windows alongside the front door. "Cops," he says flatly.

"You called the police," says Madeira in disbelief. Looking back and forth between Aleda and me, he declares: "They will never understand any of this!"

His mirror eyes go black. He turns to Hurling.

"Chester—I will never forgive you for selling *Red Sweater* to finance a mere movie."

He then shoots Hurling directly in the heart. Shoots him like he's a stranger, like some poor slob who just happens to be in the wrong place at the wrong time. Hurling falls forward to the floor like a toy soldier. Aleda slips her hand into her purse. Madeira steadies himself in front of the massive fireplace. He tosses back what's left of the port in his glass, then flings it smashing into the fireplace.

"Di Chiera: I want you to find that goddamn Gardner art! *C'est mon plaisir.*" Shoving the gun barrel upward into his mouth, he fires one fatal shot, blood and brains splattering up against the portrait of himself and Hurling as he falls back into the fireplace.

"Jaysus!" Aleda and I scream in one crazed voice.

After the bodies have been removed and the police finish with their questions and depart, Arrow and Eric go into the kitchen. In the refrigerator they find a pot of *coq au vin* and go about heating it up.

I glare at Aleda. "Why did you come back here with the children?"

"Because, Swanson—After I called the police, I started to call Tiny to come and get them, but they wouldn't leave you. And Arrow wouldn't leave them."

Abby comes out of the dining room, carefully bearing two snifters of cognac, three fingers each.

I phone Tiny and tell him to come back. "Park the car and come up to the house for something to eat."

"Is everything OK?" he asks.

"Now there's a question."

"Well—how are we gonna figure out where the art is now?" asks Aleda. "Do you still think it's here?"

"I don't know. I'm confused. I have no idea what he meant by that *Red Sweater* reference. We figured they took *Storm on the Sea of Galilee* to Italy."

I watch the kids running around. Were they never too tired to badger each other?

"I've got you now," says Eric, and he backs Abby into the enormous fireplace until she disappears. Suddenly, she pops out between his legs and runs toward me. I lift her up and begin walking toward the fireplace, remembering the day we placed Susan's ashes on the mantle, and how Abby had said she loved to sit in front of a fire and "...see the pictures."

I put her down. The fireplace is tall enough for me to stand inside. I run my hands over the back wall, as though reading Braille until my fingers find a purchase, a cleft similar to the one in the rock that had secretly let us into the house. I pull on it, but nothing happens.

Understanding what I'm up to, Aleda urges me, "Push, don't pull."

I push and push, but nothing.

"Oh well," I say, backing out. "It was just a thought."

"And a good one, too," says Aleda. Walking into the fireplace she says, "Let me try."

"What difference is it gonna make?" I grumble.

"I'm a little taller than you."

"You are not!"

"Oh, Swanson...don't be silly."

"I'm not being silly," I protest. "It's simply not true that you are taller. We're the same height."

"So then, I'm taller on tip-toe. I've got long toes."

"That's possible," I sigh.

Aleda runs her hands over the stones. With both hands above her head, she probes the cleft and grabs something with her fingertips. She pulls on it, and as she does, pushes against the stones with her free hand and they begin moving.

"Swanson! Swanson!" she shrieks.

The stone wall at the back of the fireplace swings inward to create an almost full-sized doorway. As we step forward into darkness, lights come up.

"Oh my," whispers Aleda, raising both hands to her throat.

"It's like a museum in here," says Eric.

It takes a minute to comprehend—there is so much art on the walls. Right away, we see Degas' *Six Friends at Dieppe* and some of the other pastels stolen from RISD. Then I start recognizing other stolen paintings—oils and watercolors—that I'd come across in my research about art theft.

"Any Rembrandts?" asks Aleda.

"I don't think so," I say. "But now I know what *Red Sweater* means. *Boy in a Red Sweater,* by Cezanne. It was stolen in the mid-nineties from the Collins Museum in New Bedford, Massachusetts. And there's Van Gogh's *The Potato Gleaners,* stolen in 2000 from the Adirondack Museum."

"But no Gardner art," says Aleda.

"No Gardner art," I say.

There's a library table in the center of the room and I sit down. Abby brings me my snifter of cognac. I take a big gulp and rest my elbows on the table and place my palms together. I rest my chin on top of my thumbs.

"I just figured it out," I say.

"What, Swanson? You know where it is?"

"No. But I now know what happened." I polish off the cognac in one, big gulp. "Those idiots killed the one person who knew where the Gardner art is."

"Susan?" asks Aleda. "Why would they kill Susan?"

"Because she knew about all this," I say, looking around the room. "My hunch is they brought her out here at some point soon after killing Ray and Julie, to shake her down about the Gardner art. Suspecting she has it, they show her this stuff."

"To say, 'See—we're all art thieves together. No secrets here,'" says Aleda.

"Exactly. Only she doesn't break. She leads them to believe she knows nothing. And it's while she's out here that she does the sketches I found in her portfolio."

"So, why doesn't she blow the whistle on them?"

"Because, she knows that they know the truth—or at least

part of it—that Ray was one of the thieves in the Gardner heist. So, if she blows the whistle on their art theft activity, what's to stop them from blowing the whistle on Ray? Then, the kids would forever have to live with the stigma of having a father who pulled the biggest art theft in history. Or, it might eventually lead to her."

"But the RISD theft pushed her over the top?" conjectures Aleda.

"That's what I'm guessing. 'A disturbance on the grounds.' The modus operandi is so similar to the Gardner she immediately suspects those she knows most familiar with it, besides herself. Hurling and Madeira. She confronts them, probably when I had the kids at my place right after the theft. She demands the RISD Degas back, or she'll go to the cops."

"But wouldn't she still be worried about them spilling the beans about the kids' father robbing the Gardner?"

"Here's where she plays a very tricky card. Because they're unsure what she knows or doesn't about the Gardner theft, she tells them that she'll tell the cops they robbed both RISD and the Gardner. She'll certainly tell the cops about all this," I say, gesturing around the room.

"And it gets her killed!" exclaims Aleda.

"Yep. Hurling and Madeira buy that she doesn't know anything about the Gardner, so they don't need her to find the Gardner art, and they're not gonna part with the fresh Degas from RISD. So, they get rid of her. As the saying goes, she just knows too much."

"So then, Ray and Susan robbed the Gardner," says Aleda.

"Yep. It was Ray and Susan disguised as police officers. And right after Ray and Julie died—probably that very night—

she went over to be with the kids and grabbed the art out of the magazine on Rose Island and took it...somewhere else."

"But why didn't she return it? Madeira said your friend planned to return it, he just didn't know how."

"It's a good question. I don't know why she didn't return it."

"If something didn't happen to it...if she stashed it someplace, she must've left a clue, Swanson. She must've known that if something happened to her, the art would be lost forever."

"One would think." I rest my head down on the table and close my eyes. Aleda's fingers begin massaging my scalp. It feels so good.

"She would leave the clue for you," murmurs Aleda.

Footsteps come into the room and stop. Abby's voice:

"Are you two gonna get married now?"

Acknowledgments

I must thank Jim (James Cass) Rogers for reading the drafts of this book and offering much helpful advice. Larry Di Fiori made many strategic suggestions and spent countless hours listening.

Mark K. Kauffman has remained my friend through it all.

Steve Longley's affection, expertise, and generosity has always been there when I've needed it, and at times that have astonished me.

At St. George's School, Geoff Spranger taught me the exquisite pleasure to be had in reading critically. He, Norris Hoyt, Bill Prescott and Roy Penny taught me that novels, poems and plays are important.

Richard Grosvenor gave me an early appreciation for art: that which had come before me, and my own.

Along the way there has been generosity and influence from Larry and Hallie Dixon. Leon and Charlotte Michell. Marcia Haufrecht, Francesca De Sapio and Charles Gordone. Court Miller and Bob Rosen. Arnie Warwick and David Rieff. Anne Goursaud. Sarah Cressy. Nomi Hurwitz.

Also, Mike Tardiff. John Keeler. Paula Frankel. John Rallis. Eve Ziegler Marx. James Lapine. Cybill Shepherd. Bill Lewis. Gary Kolligian. Robert Whitcomb. Bill Lewis. Nancy Hart and Sandor Bodo. Ed McIlvane. Dagmar Frinta.

Larry Baxter and Dan Rosenthal.

Beth Nation. Alex and Hannah Soifer.

Betsy Burr was there and so was Beth Whitney.

Christine Scholes showed me perfect sorrow and perfect bliss.

Caroline Unruh rode, and often frothed, the stormy seas.

Hal Hamilton and Tamara Bolotow have helped keep the engine chugging. So too, Judith Reilly.

Your lives have made this book, and hopefully its author, immeasurably better.

My brothers, John and David are always there, even when they aren't. My grandparents, Maria and Manuel Ponte and Granny Twele always gave me love.

Many others, here and gone, are indelibly stamped upon these pages: Steve Somerall, Andy Lashley, Grantley Michell....

Thank you to Rosalie Siegel for understanding that politically incorrect is so much more fun and meaningful than the alternative and for being so enthusiastic in bringing the book to editors.

Finally, Daubenton Press brought me back to a childhood awareness of, and admiration for the courage and unshackled intellect of the French. Just as without French help there would be no United States, so too was this American overjoyed to see friendly sails from a distant shore. My editor, Catherine Bonnard, and her redoubtable assistant, Louise Ducroz are without peer; absolutely irreplaceable. My deepest thanks also to Mathieu Ligonnet, Florent Ollier, Agnès Arnaud, and all who worked on the book at Daubenton.

ABOUT THE AUTHOR

Charles Pinning was born in Newport, Rhode Island and graduated from Johns Hopkins University. His writing and photographs appear regularly on the pages of *The Providence Journal,* and in various other publications. He also teaches in the Department of Writing & Rhetoric at the University of Rhode Island.

Visit his official website at: www.charlespinning.com.